STRANDED

STRANDED
NATHAN HUFFAKER

BONNEVILLE BOOKS
AN IMPRINT OF CEDAR FORT, INC.
SPRINGVILLE, UTAH

This is a work of fiction. The characters, names, incidents, places, and dialogue are products of the author's imagination and are not to be construed as real. The opinions and views expressed herein belong solely to the author and do not necessarily represent the opinions or views of Cedar Fort, Inc. Permission for the use of sources, graphics, and photos is also solely the responsibility of the author.

ISBN 13: 978-1-4621-1619-5

Published by Bonneville Books, an imprint of Cedar Fort, Inc.
2373 W. 700 S., Springville, UT 84663
Distributed by Cedar Fort, Inc., www.cedarfort.com

LIBRARY OF CONGRESS CATALOGING-IN-PUBLICATION DATA

Huffaker, Nathan, 1974-
  Stranded / Nathan Huffaker.
    pages cm
  ISBN 978-1-4621-1619-5 (perfect : alk. paper)
  1. Mormons--Fiction. 2. Church of Jesus Christ of Latter-Day Saints--Missions--Fiction. I. Title.
  PS3608.U34985S86 2015
  813'.6--dc23
                        2014038714

Cover design by Michelle May
Cover design © 2015 by Lyle Mortimer
Edited and typeset by Melissa J. Caldwell

Printed in the United States of America

10 9 8 7 6 5 4 3 2 1

Printed on acid-free paper

To my wife and kids.
Thank you for letting me pursue my dreams.

PROLOGUE

The ringing phone shattered the silence and startled President Russell awake. President Howard Russell was used to phone calls at all hours of the night. Usually it was a missionary flying in that had gotten lost and missed his connection. He had been president of the Kazakhstan Astana Mission for almost two and a half years now. His heart beat rapidly as he climbed out of bed and headed for the phone.

There were no elders due in for another week. Something was wrong. Hopefully it was nothing too serious. Missionaries frequently called him at odd times with concerns that could probably have waited until morning. This didn't feel like one of those.

"Hello," he answered in Russian. "This is President Russell." Although he was an American, most of the people he talked to on the phone spoke Russian. His Russian was excellent. He had taught at Kiev Polytechnic Institute in Ukraine for many years. He had left a good teaching job to become mission president—a decision he never once regretted. He loved missionary work.

The voice on the phone spoke quickly and softly. He closed his eyes as Sister Russell turned on the lights and sat up in bed.

"Yes, I understand," President Russell answered in English. "Thank you. I will."

"What is it?" Sister Russell asked.

He hung up the phone but didn't answer her. He wasn't sure how to answer her.

"What's happened?" she asked.

President Russell walked from the nightstand and sat softly next to her on the bed.

"That was the prophet." He shook his head in disbelief. "We need to get the missionaries out of the country immediately."

"What?" Sister Russell said.

"The prophet said we are in great danger and need to get all the missionaries out of the country."

"Oh my!" Sister Russell gasped, putting her hand to her mouth. She started to tremble.

"Will you please call the assistants for me? I need to call Yevgenie."

"What am I supposed to tell them?"

"Just get them on the phone. I'll talk to them." His voice was surprisingly calm. He patted his wife's back and walked toward his office to call Yevgenie. Yevgenie Vashuk was a local member who worked for the mission. He was instrumental in obtaining visas, train tickets, and just about anything else the mission president might need. His methods were not always straightforward—sometimes they were just barely legal—but he always got the job done, and now President Russell needed a big favor. To obtain that many tickets on the same day was going to be a feat, but he was confident that if it could be done, Yevgenie was the man to do it.

ONE

One day earlier

Up and at 'em, Elder," Elder Johnson called as he turned on the light and shook Elder Schofield's shoulder. "Today is going to be a good day." He walked quickly out of the room to get started on breakfast.

Elder Johnson was an enthusiastic elder. To him, every day was a new day, and a day in which he believed they would have great success. If they went with no obvious success, then they had just planted a lot of seeds that would someday grow. It was hard to get him down, annoyingly hard.

Elder Schofield dragged himself out of bed, at least enough to get to his knees so he could pray. He was coming up on the end of his mission and had run out of steam. He still played by the rules; he had just lost some of his enthusiasm.

"*Dobroye utro,*" Schofield said as he walked into the kitchen and began setting the table.

Elder Schofield was a master of the Russian language and insisted on speaking Russian most of the time. He had been promised that if he put forth the effort he would learn the language well enough to touch the lives of all those he came in contact with. He put forth the effort and studied, and as a result, he spoke masterfully.

"*Dobroye utro,*" Elder Johnson responded as he washed potatoes in the sink.

"Hey, that was pretty good," Elder Schofield said. "I could almost tell you weren't from Texas."

Elder Johnson flicked some water off a wet potato at him.

"Today we are going to meet some great people, some people who are going to change the world."

"Whatever you say, Elder," Elder Schofield replied, shaking his head as he pulled the juice out of the fridge.

The elders left their apartment shortly before 9:30. The cool autumn breeze blew between apartment buildings. They were serving in Almaty, a beautiful city set at the foot of the Tian Shan Mountains. Their apartment building sat atop a little hill that had a perfect view of the snow-covered mountains in the distance.

Elder Johnson took a deep breath as he left the building.

"What a magnificent morning!" he exclaimed, admiring the view for a brief moment before pulling a map of the city out of his backpack. Missionaries had only been in Almaty for few months and so the city was wide open. Johnson had been here just two weeks.

Elder Johnson stared at the map for a moment, seemingly waiting for inspiration even though they had planned the day in advance.

"To the *voksal*," Johnson declared in a mix of English and Russian. He stood pointing in the distance.

"To the train station," Elder Schofield repeated in Russian, shaking his head. They headed down the tree-lined street to catch the bus. The cars racing by seemed to match Johnson's excitement. Schofield trudged along behind, moving just fast enough to keep up.

It was an hour bus ride to the train station. Elder Johnson thought that it would be a good idea to tract at the train station. There would be a lot of people coming and going, and they had had good success there before.

"Good morning," Elder Johnson said to a young couple on the bus in his big Texas accent. His Russian was mostly understandable, but his accent marked him American immediately. Schofield tried not to wince as Johnson talked.

"Please share a minute with me," he continued.

"Please," the man responded with a smile.

The bus swayed back and forth as it slowly made its way to the station, the smell of the exhaust seeping up from the back.

Elder Johnson went into his standard message about Jesus Christ and how families can be together forever.

Elder Schofield stood by for support, but his mind quickly wandered. He listened to the conversation, but the chatter on the bus distracted him. Tomorrow was preparation day, the one day a week when they got to relax a little bit. Usually it was still pretty busy, but they still found some time for relaxing. They had been invited by some investigators to attend a soccer game. Elder Schofield was a huge soccer fan and was excited to watch the match.

As they got off the bus at the train station, they wished the young couple a good day and parted ways. Johnson was excited he had gotten their phone number. It was a fake number, but he didn't know that. Most of the morning was unproductive. They talked to a lot of people, but most were too busy to hear their message. They had lunch at a gyro stand and decided by midafternoon it was time to go tract a little closer to home.

The line for the bus was massive. Several trains had recently arrived at the station and the bus was late. As the bus pulled in, the crowd got a little excited and began pushing and shoving, trying to get onto it. The elders weren't in a big rush, so they just stood back to wait for the next bus. The people were in such a hurry to get on the bus that they weren't letting people get off the bus. One young man struggled with a large duffel bag. He squeezed out as the others were squeezing in. Finally he forced his way off the bus. He looked at his duffel bag and then walked right in front of the elders on his way to the station.

A man running to catch the bus pushed Elder Johnson from behind. Elder Johnson crashed into the young man with the duffel bag, who fell over and dropped his bag. It landed with a loud thud. The young man cringed as it hit the ground.

Elder Johnson quickly jumped to his feet and apologized vehemently to the young man.

"I'm so sorry about that. Let me help you up."

The young man took his hand and pulled himself up, never taking his eyes off the bag.

Elder Schofield reached down to pick up the bag.

"Don't touch," the man said.

Schofield jerked his hand back.

The young man eyed the bag for a brief moment and then slowly picked up the bag by the handles and walked away.

"He's a little touchy," Schofield commented, turning again to the bus stop.

"I'd say," Johnson agreed.

* * *

Ivan quickly carried his bag to the main terminal of the train station where Taras was waiting.

"Everything okay?" Taras asked.

"There was almost an accident," Ivan replied.

"An accident?"

"Yes. Some stupid American knocked me over and I dropped the bag."

"That could have been bad."

"Yes, very."

Ivan and Taras walked to the ticket booth and bought two tickets for tomorrow's 8:00 a.m. express to Astana.

* * *

The only meeting the elders had was a follow-up with some recent converts.

The elders gave several copies of the Book of Mormon away on the way to their appointment. Elder Johnson, ever the optimist, believed everyone he talked to would become a member of the Church.

He had even tried to convert a Russian Orthodox priest they had met on the street. It had been their first day together, Johnson and Schofield. Two weeks ago.

"Excuse me, sir," Elder Johnson started.

"Yes," the Russian Orthodox priest said, his smile creeping wider as he recognized the accent and the name tag. He stood in his gray and black robes that covered his feet and hands, his long beard and hair both streaked with gray.

"Can you share a moment with me?" Johnson asked, leading with the traditional introduction he had been taught by his trainer.

"Of course." The priest pulled out his Bible, opening it before him.

Schofield wasn't sure if Johnson knew whom he was talking to or not. He doubted it. Johnson was in trouble. Schofield thought for a moment about pulling him away but decided to see how it went. He had heard of elders having amazing gospel discussions with Russian Orthodox priests, but he had had enough conversations to tell that this wasn't going to be one of them.

"Jesus Christ." Elder Johnson opened the Book of Mormon and held it up.

"You know nothing." The priest knocked the book out of Johnson's hand. "Don't talk to me of this Mormon. There is no Mormon in the Bible."

"No," Johnson started. "But they talk about him."

Schofield stood and watched as Johnson and the priest traded verses trying to prove points of doctrine. He thought on several occasions about interrupting, but decided it would be a good way for Johnson to learn that this was not how to teach people.

Finally, as tempers flared and voices rose, both in half English and half Russian, neither one truly communicating, Schofield interrupted.

"Excuse us, sir." He offered his hand to the priest. "Perhaps we can continue this discussion another time," he said and then led Elder Johnson away.

They walked in silence for just a moment before they rounded a corner. Schofield stopped, turned to Johnson, and asked, "Do you know what you did wrong there?"

"What do you mean?" Johnson had held up his hands like he didn't know something had gone wrong.

"That went horribly wrong," Schofield said, "because you were trying to convince him he was wrong rather than let the Spirit convert him. We don't convert people, Elder. That is not our job. We are here to help the Spirit convert people. No amount of arguing is going to convert anyone. It will just drive the Spirit away."

"I had him," Johnson said. "I proved him wrong with his own Bible four times."

"Were you even listening?" Elder Schofield asked.

"Yes, but you're wrong. I had him. I proved him wrong, and he knows it," Johnson argued.

"Elder, you didn't prove anything. You can't prove anything."

"But I did."

Schofield shook his head and walked away.

TWO

The elders arrived at the Kolchuks just before seven. The Turovskis lived in the same apartment building.

"The Turovskis are running a little bit late," Valeri Kolchuk explained as he invited the elders in. "But Vadim is bringing a friend that he wants you to meet."

"That's great," Elder Johnson said as he slipped off his shoes and slipped into a pair of slippers provided for him. This was a common practice in most Slavic countries. They would not wear their shoes around the house, but instead would wear house slippers. When guests came over, the hosts would provide them slippers. This practice allowed them to keep the snow and mud from the streets out of the house while keeping everyone cozy inside. Schofield slipped into his slippers and followed Johnson inside.

They sat down on a green couch, and Sister Kolchuk brought them some herbal tea and crackers while they waited. The Kolchuks always brought out the nicest china they had for the elders every time they came over. Elder Schofield sipped his tea. It had taken him a long time to get used to drinking hot drinks, especially in the summer. He had been at the Kolchuks many times and each time was amazed at the decor. They lived in a wealthy part of town, and Elena Kolchuk had the apartment furnished nicely. Fine tapestries hung on every wall. Expensive paintings adorned the halls. All together it was way too much, but if you took time to admire each piece individually, they were each exquisite pieces of art.

Finally the Turovskis and their guest arrived.

"Good evening," Elder Johnson introduced himself. "Very nice to meet you."

They stood and shook hands. The guest was introduced as Michael Ivanov. He was not an old man, but he looked weathered. His skin was wrinkled and splotchy from years of smoking. His hair was thinning and gray, but he still had a firm handshake. The elders could tell a lot from a man by his handshake.

He wore what was once a nice suit, but was, like him, looking a little worn around the edges.

"What is it you do for a living, Michael?" Elder Schofield asked, expecting the typical answers of "I work in a factory, at the store, drive a taxi." Michael's answer caught him off guard.

"I am the chief detective of the antiterrorism task force."

The antiterrorism task force was well known for capturing several notorious terrorists with ruthless vigor.

"I'll bet that keeps you busy," Johnson said.

Elder Schofield was certain Elder Johnson had no idea what Michael Ivanov had just said. He suspected Michael Ivanov was not really here to learn about the Church.

"Yes, it certainly does." Michael Ivanov looked carefully at the elders.

* * *

Michael Ivanov was not interested in Jesus Christ. He wanted to learn more about these two Americans. In his line of work, he could trust no one. He was suspicious of everyone until he found enough evidence to put his mind at ease. His country had lately been plagued by civil unrest and terrorist acts. They had done a great job to keep the media attention to a minimum. They had been quick to apprehend most of the perpetrators quietly, but he was certain the violence could easily escalate into a civil war.

"So tell me about yourselves," Michael said to the elders as he sipped his tea.

Elder Johnson enthusiastically began talking. "I'm from a small town in Texas. I was raised on a farm. I have six sisters and three brothers. I came on a mission to share the gospel of Jesus Christ and help people come unto Him." Johnson smiled at Michael.

Johnson was tall with short, bright-red hair, and his face was covered with freckles. Not really someone you would send on a covert mission. Too obvious. Then again, sometimes that is the point. Make it obvious, so nobody suspects it.

Sounds like he practiced that, Michael said silently to himself as Johnson finished up. *He can barely string three words together in Russian without pausing to think. That could be part of a ploy, but I doubt it.*

"What about you, Elder Schofield?" Michael turned his attention to the other American. This one was not immediately recognizable as American. He was shorter with short, black hair and a slightly darker complexion.

"I was born in California and moved to Utah when I was a child. My parents are converts to the Church. The Church changed their lives. Having the gospel of Jesus Christ come into your house changes things for the better. It is a wonderful thing. It brings great joy to our lives. I saw firsthand how the gospel of Jesus Christ changes people's lives. I came to share that joy. There are people here who need the gospel in their lives. They need the Church. They need to feel God's love so that they might have joy with Him forever."

Michael was silent afterward; he had completely forgotten he was speaking with an American. Elder Schofield's mastery of the Russian language was indeed impressive.

"We should start with a prayer," Elena suggested, interrupting the silence.

"Yes," everyone agreed.

"Yes, of course," Michael added, thinking he could find out more about the Americans as the lesson went on.

Elder Johnson offered a prayer and Valeri began his lesson. It was a lesson about many of the basic principles of the gospel. Michael was quiet, just listening to the others talk and share their feelings. He sat and listened most of the meeting. Just listening and studying the two Americans. He had ruled out Johnson as a threat almost immediately. That didn't mean he wasn't a potential threat; it just meant he wasn't high enough on his list to warrant his personal attention. But the more he listened to Schofield speak Russian, the more he was concerned about him. He was a young man barely twenty years old who spoke Russian like he was born in Ukraine. Michael was certain if he talked to him on the phone and not in person he wouldn't be able to tell the difference.

The meeting itself yielded no helpful information about their cult. He would need to dig deeper into that to determine if it was a threat, but the meeting was overall a success.

As they were all preparing to depart, Elder Johnson asked if they could come to Michael's house and meet with him again.

"Yes, of course," he agreed. He thought Johnson was harmless enough, but the mastery of Schofield's Russian unnerved him. He had to find out more about him.

"Great. How about tomorrow?" Johnson asked.

"Let me give you my number." He handed the elders a business card. "Call me tomorrow evening. I will try to free up some time to meet with you."

"Great!" Johnson quickly snatched the card from Michael's hand almost as if the missionary feared Michael would change his mind. He looked at the card and quickly tucked it into his planner.

"Until tomorrow then," Michael said as he turned and left.

"Wait!" Elder Johnson called and ran after him. "Please take this." He handed him a copy of the Book of Mormon in Russian. "If you have time, you can read this."

"Thank you," Michael said as he took the book. He was curious about the Book of Mormon. A large number of cults that turned to violence could trace that violence to the propaganda that their leaders fed them. He was interested in reading what it had to say. He thought back to the religious mass suicide in Ukraine, 1994. He had been in the military then, not the police. Some cult had put some lady up as the returned Savior, and everyone was following her. Some got it in their heads that they were all supposed to die for her. Hundreds died. Of course, suicides nowadays take innocent people with them with the use of guns and bombs. A little more violent in this century. *That's why we can't take any chances. Sometimes we have to shoot first and ask questions later.*

He shook hands with Elder Johnson and walked into the elevator.

"*Do zavtra.*" He waved from the elevator.

* * *

After waiting for the elevator to close, Johnson returned to the apartment. Elder Schofield was already saying his good-byes. Elder Johnson traded the slippers on his feet for his shoes and met Elder Schofield at the elevator.

"That went really well." Johnson was excited.

"Which part?" Schofield asked.

"The whole thing. Valeri's lesson and talking with Michael."

"I don't think Michael is interested in the Church."

"Why do you say that?" Johnson asked, confused.

"He's doing his job. He's checking up on us. He thinks we might be terrorists, and he needs to find out for sure."

"Why did he take the Book of Mormon and give us his number?"

"So we'll call him and so he can see if the Book of Mormon advocates terrorism."

"That's absurd," Johnson said.

"That's the truth," Schofield stated flatly.

"I'll tell you what I think," Johnson began excitedly. "I think he's going to read the Book of Mormon I gave him and he'll believe it. It will change his life, and someday he's going to be baptized."

"Believe what you want, Elder," Schofield stated coldly as he walked out of the apartment building and headed home.

He stopped and looked back at Elder Johnson, who hadn't moved.

"Look, I admire your enthusiasm," Schofield finished. "You handled this discussion a lot better than you have others. You did great, in fact, but not everyone you meet is going to become a member."

* * *

Michael Ivanov walked into his apartment and set the Book of Mormon on a nightstand next to a stack of religious material from several different religious organizations.

Immediately his phone began to ring. He walked into the kitchen to answer it.

"Hello?"

"Where have you been? I've been trying to get a hold of you for hours."

It was Sasha, his lead detective and second in command on the task force.

Michael pulled his cell phone off his belt and looked at it. Strange, it was off.

"Apparently my phone is not working. What's happened?"

"Nothing yet, but all indications point to a big event tomorrow. We have nothing solid, and Yuri was supposed to get back to me, but I've not been able to get a hold of him either. Something big is happening tomorrow, but we still have no idea what or where."

"Keep at it." Michael sighed deeply. "Let me know as soon as you hear anything. Just in case, let's get everyone out tomorrow morning and hope we get lucky."

"Yes, sir."

Michael hung up the phone and collapsed onto his bed. It had been a busy week, and he could tell it was just getting started.

* * *

The elders knelt together in prayer. Johnson prayed for the branch members, for those they met that day, and for those they were teaching. He prayed for those they would meet soon, and then he asked a special blessing for Michael Ivanov, that he would read the Book of Mormon and be touched by its message of peace and love. Johnson felt immediately that his prayer would be answered. He often shared his feelings with Elder Schofield, who was always quick to point out that if you pray about enough stuff, some of it is bound to happen like you want it to. Johnson decided to keep this particular confirmation to himself.

"Do you know what I think, Elder?" Elder Johnson asked as he climbed into his bed.

"What's that?" Schofield asked from the doorway.

Johnson jumped out of his bed and threw a Nerf ball at Schofield.

"Tag, you're it!" Schofield deftly knocked the ball aside and threw his own ball at Johnson, pegging him in the chest and knocking him back to his bed.

"Nope, you're still it."

"Ahhhh." Johnson rolled around on his bed in mock agony.

"Good night, Elder," Schofield said softly as he climbed into bed.

Johnson prayed for several more minutes before climbing into bed.

"Are you awake, Elder?" Johnson asked just loud enough for Schofield to hear if he was awake, but not loud enough to wake him.

"Elder, are you awake?" he repeated slightly louder.

No answer. He rolled over and went to sleep.

Schofield was awake; he just didn't want to talk to Elder Johnson at the moment. He had felt it when Elder Johnson had prayed about Michael Ivanov. There was something about him, but he didn't know for sure what it was, so he kept quiet. He wanted to say something to Elder Johnson about it, but Johnson had questioned him so many times, Schofield couldn't bring himself to do it. So he just waited, knowing Johnson wouldn't wake him if he thought he was asleep.

THREE

Hello," Elder Apple groggily answered. It was 3:07 a.m.

"Good morning, Elder," Sister Russell responded as cheerful as ever. "Just a minute. The president wants to speak with you."

"Okay," Elder Apple said calmly. He had been an assistant to the president for four months. He assumed they needed to pick someone up at the train station or something, although he didn't remember hearing about anyone coming in.

"Good morning," President Russell said as he came onto the phone.

"Good morning, President," Elder Apple responded, looking at Elder Jones, who was now sitting up in his bed.

"We have a situation," President Russell stated. "We need to get everyone out of the country as soon as possible. Yevgenie is working on getting tickets. Call all the zone leaders and have them tell their zones that we need to leave immediately. Have them pack their things and await another call. As soon as I have the information about the tickets, I'll let you know."

"What is this about?" Elder Apple asked, confused.

"The prophet called and told me we had to leave. That is all I know right now. Get your people up and ready to go, and I'll call you when I know more."

Elder Apple hung up the phone. He closed his eyes and counted to seven. He really wanted to curse and counting was the only way for him to resist the urge.

"We need to get everyone awake and ready. We're leaving the country immediately."

Elder Jones stared at him. "Yeah. Whatever." He rolled over to go back to sleep.

"That's what the president said. He said the prophet called and we need to leave the country."

"You're full of it. You got Elder Dennis to call as a gag. It's too early to deal with your pranks, Elder," Jones replied.

"I'm serious," Elder Apple pleaded. He now regretted having Elder Stini call last week and play music over the phone in the middle of the night.

The phone rang again. Elder Jones rushed for the phone.

"Hello?"

"Elder Jones," the president started, "stop arguing with Elder Apple and get everyone up and ready to go. I'll call you as soon as I have more information."

Jones hung up the phone, a look of bewilderment on his face.

"What's going on?" Elder Jones said quietly to himself.

"I don't know, but if the prophet tells me to get out of the country, I'm getting out of the country," Elder Apple said.

Elder Jones began calling all the missionaries, while Elder Apple packed his stuff.

* * *

Elder Schofield finally dragged himself out of bed to answer the phone. They kept the phone in the other room and the volume wasn't very loud. He wondered how long it had been ringing.

"Hello," Elder Schofield answered.

"Good morning, Elder. This is Elder Jones. We got a call from President Russell, and we need to get out of the country immediately. I don't know all the details, but I do know that we're supposed to get our things packed and wait for a call from the president. He's going to call as soon as he has ticket information."

"Okay," Elder Schofield said quietly.

"I'll call you soon."

"Okay. Bye." Elder Schofield went and climbed back into bed. He was awakened twenty minutes later when Elder Jones called him back.

"Elder Schofield, your train leaves the main train station at 8:00 a.m. You need to be on that train. Your tickets will be at will-call. Just show them your passport and they will give you your tickets."

"President Russell will wait for you in Astana. Your train will arrive in Astana at 7:00 p.m. this evening. The president's train leaves at 8:00. Make sure you are on that train. The elders from Aralsk, Orsk, and Sevney will all meet you there on the way to Moscow."

"Why are we leaving?" Schofield asked.

"The prophet called the president in the middle of the night and told him to get the missionaries out of the country. That's all I know."

"Oh," was all Schofield could say.

"Remember, 8:00 a.m. from Almaty to Astana. Don't miss it."

"Okay." Schofield hung up the phone, his mind racing through all the possibilities. *Why would the prophet tell us to leave the country? We must be in grave danger.*

"Elder!" he yelled as he walked into the bedroom.

They quickly and quietly packed all of their things into their suitcases. They were ready to go at 5:00 a.m.

"We have two hours before we have to leave," Johnson commented. "Do you want a quick power nap?"

"That's tempting, but I don't want to miss the train. Let's make something to eat, and then we'll go catch a cab. We can sleep on the train."

They fried some potatoes with *sala* and anything else they could find in the fridge. No point in letting it go to waste.

As they stood in the doorway ready to leave, Johnson looked at the empty apartment. "Do you think we'll come back?" he asked Schofield.

"I don't know," Schofield replied.

They had been told by the prophet of God to leave the country and that was what they were going to do.

* * *

President and Sister Russell had far too many things to take it all with them. They got what was important to them— the scrapbooks, photos, some souvenirs—and loaded it all into the mission van. The driver drove them quickly to the train station where they would wait for the rest of the missionaries. They were leaving Astana at 7:00 p.m. heading for Moscow. Twenty-four elders, six sisters, and two older couples would be leaving for Moscow this morning, and fourteen more elders in the evening when they arrived from the other cities. President Russell was planning on sending Sister Russell with the group in the morning and waiting for the elders in the evening.

"What do you suppose is the problem, dear?" Sister Russell asked.

"I don't know, but the prophet would not just send us running for no reason."

They arrived at the train station and were promptly greeted by Yevgenie with a stack of tickets. It had taken a lot of effort for Yevgenie to obtain all of the tickets.

"Good morning, President."

"Good morning, Yevgenie. Thank you so much." He took the tickets and shook Yevgenie's hand. "I really appreciate this."

"It was nothing," Yevgenie replied, wiping the sweat from his brow onto the sleeve of his shirt. "I have secured a small room where you can wait for the others. There are some already there.

Please come this way." Yevgenie guided President and Sister Russell to a small conference room inside the train station.

The driver, Sergei, followed closely with President and Sister Russell's luggage.

There were six companionships already waiting in the little room when President Russell walked in. They all swarmed around him wanting to know what was going on.

"Let's wait until everyone gets here, and I'll tell you everything I know."

At 6:15, all the missionaries from the city of Astana sat in the small conference room waiting for President Russell to speak. The atmosphere was jovial despite the nervous mood of those there. People speculated all sorts of scenarios as to why they were leaving. He stood for a moment and watched them. He then closed his eyes and whispered a silent prayer for all there and the many more that were still coming.

At last President Russell began to speak.

"Elders and sisters, early this morning I got a call from the prophet. He said it was urgent that we all get out of the country. I don't know why we need to leave; I can only imagine that we must be in some sort of danger. Yevgenie has arranged for these tickets to Moscow. You'll all be leaving on the 7:00 a.m. train heading to Moscow. Sister Russell will be joining you. Elders Apple and Jones are in charge. Please listen to them. The mission president in Moscow will be waiting for you when you arrive. I will stay here and wait for the elders from the other cities, who should arrive this afternoon. We'll take the 8:00 p.m. train this evening and meet you in Moscow. Make sure you have your passports. Come get your tickets and get on the train. We have a little over half an hour."

President Russell handed the tickets to the missionaries and wished them good luck as he sent them on their way. Sister Russell did not look very excited about leaving her husband, but she reluctantly agreed, knowing it would be best if she went with the first group.

She gave him a huge hug and held him tightly for a moment before she put her hands on his cheeks and kissed him carefully on the lips. Tears streamed down her cheeks.

"You hurry along now and be safe," she ordered, wiping away the tears.

President Russell watched as all the missionaries boarded the train. Slowly, the train pulled away from the train station. President Russell headed back to the mission home to collect a few more things before he left the country.

* * *

The taxi driver grunted as the car slammed to a stop. Another car slammed into the back of them pushing the taxi forward into the car in front sandwiching them in between. "What's happened?" Elder Schofield asked.

"That idiot!" the driver cursed, and he hopped out of the car.

Another car slid up alongside of them and bumped into the side, smashing into the door next to where Johnson was sitting, narrowly missing the taxi driver.

"Are you okay?" Schofield asked Johnson.

Johnson looked down at himself and nodded. "I'm fine."

Schofield tried to get out his door and found he too was boxed in.

"Are you okay?" the driver asked when he saw Schofield had rolled down the window.

"We're fine, but it's very important that we get to the train station. Our train leaves at eight."

"We're not going anywhere right now. But you've got plenty of time. It's only 6:30."

* * *

Director Michael Ivanov awoke early and headed out the door to his office. He called ahead to see if anything had changed.

"Any news?" he asked.

"Nothing yet, sir. I have extra people at the train station and all the subway stops. If something is going to happen, those would be the probable locations. Hopefully we get word or get lucky," Sasha said.

"Good work. I'll be there soon. Keep me posted."

* * *

Elder Johnson and Elder Schofield wanted to get out and find another way, but they were truly stuck. They sat in the back of the taxi, realizing that no one would move the other cars to let them out until the police arrived to sort things out. It was fortunate they weren't injured.

The large clock at the train station struck 7:30 a.m. as the taxi pulled into the parking lot. The elders tossed the driver his payment, grabbed their things, and rushed to the will-call desk.

"Good morning," Elder Schofield said to the woman at the desk. He handed her his passport. "I believe you have tickets waiting for us."

She took his passport and checked it. She compared the ticket with the passport, verifying they were the same person.

"Here you go." She handed Elder Schofield his ticket and passport. He tucked them quickly in his suit jacket pocket and stepped aside so Johnson could get his ticket. Johnson handed the girl his passport.

She checked it against the ticket.

"I'm sorry, sir, but the spelling doesn't match. I'll have to get my supervisor to approve this. Just a minute, please."

She set the passport on the desk and walked away with the ticket.

"What's going on?" Johnson asked nervously, more to himself than to Schofield.

"I don't know. It sounds like Yevgenie misspelled your name on the ticket."

"Is that going to be a problem?"

"I don't think so."

The young woman returned with his ticket several minutes later.

"He said it's okay. Just make sure you get the spelling right next time. You'd better hurry. Your train leaves from track four in ten minutes."

She handed Johnson the ticket, and the elders raced to the train. Fortunately track four was close to the main terminal.

They boarded the train and quickly found their compartment. It wasn't a room; it was smaller than a regular room on a train, but better than just sitting on a bench for several hours. The put their luggage away quickly and Schofield crashed on the bottom bunk.

"I need a nap."

"Oh no," Johnson said in a panic as he patted all his pockets.

"What?" Schofield sat up on the bed.

"My passport!" Johnson exclaimed. "I left it at the will-call desk."

"You did not!" Schofield said, wishing he were wrong.

"It's not here," Johnson said, now rummaging through his backpack. It's at the will-call desk. She never gave it back."

"We'd better run," Schofield said, jumping to his feet and checking his watch. "I hope the train is late leaving." His watch read 7:59 a.m. Johnson threw his pack on as they ran out of the train back toward the main terminal. The girl was waiting for them when they returned. She handed the passport to him apologizing profusely.

They ran back to the train, but as they reached track four, they could see the train pulling away.

"Wait!" yelled Johnson.

"Wait!"

They climbed onto the platform and chased the train, hoping to catch it. But it was too late. The train was gone.

Johnson put his hands on his head.

"No!"

"It's okay," Elder Schofield said between breaths as he watched the train pulling out. "We'll catch the next one."

"I'm sorry," Johnson said, almost in tears.

"We'll call the president and have him get us new tickets and have someone pick up our luggage. It's okay."

He put his hand on Johnson's shoulder as they watched the train leave the station.

Then the train exploded.

It turned into a massive fireball as the explosion shook the train station, shattering the windows with the concussion. They covered their ears to block the noise, but it did no good. The roar of the explosion ripped through the station. Elder Schofield stood in shocked disbelief, watching the billowing flames race skyward, chased by thick black smoke. Orange, yellow, and red projectiles rocketed through the air. Shrapnel from the train, large burning pieces of twisted steel, came crashing to the ground around them, shaking him into action.

"Run!" he yelled.

Chaos erupted on the platform. Screams and cries of horror were followed by wailing sirens. The elders ran for the cover of the terminal, forcing the doors open. The surging masses of people racing from the oncoming blaze squeezed through the doors behind them. They raced across the terminal, trying to get to the exit on the other side. The terminal quickly filled up with people.

Flaming pieces of the train crashed through the roof, scattering burning debris across the inside of the terminal. The people fled, and Schofield pulled Johnson aside to avoid the collapsing ceiling.

"Let's get out of here!" Schofield yelled through the chaos. They ran through the train station, trying to avoid the fire and the panic-stricken crowd that trampled everything in its path. They ran from the train station.

FOUR

Let's stop by the mission home," President Russell said to Sergei, his driver. "I'd like to pick up a few more things."

"The eight bags you sent with Sister Russell are not enough?" Sergei joked.

President Russell laughed heartily. Oh, it felt good to laugh. He remembered when he had first met Sergei, a recent convert. He had retired from the military to join the Church, a decision he said he had to make. He was so stern all the time, with his permanent scowl. President Russell had felt inspired to offer him the job as the mission van driver. But still, it was only after several months that Sergei had finally loosened up. Now Sergei was almost a constant jokester.

They drove in silence for several minutes before Sergei began talking.

"President Russell, why do you think the prophet is asking you to leave?"

"I don't know, Sergei."

"Do you think it will be permanent?"

"I don't think so. The work of the Lord must go forward."

"What will happen with the rest of us?"

"What do you mean?"

"Without you here to guide us, do you think the Church can survive?"

"The Church will be fine, Sergei. The Lord knows what He is doing. There are very righteous men here leading the Church."

"What about us as a people? If you are leaving, that probably means there will be a war or something."

"We don't know that, Sergei. Besides, you served in the military. I'm sure you'll be fine."

"That's a time I do not like to remember, and one I do not want to relive, but it's not me I'm worried about. It's my wife and kids. I worry about them."

"You're a strong member of the Church, Sergei. Use your priesthood to protect your family. Listen to the guidance of the Holy Ghost, and you'll be fine no matter what happens here."

"Thank you." Sergei wiped tears from his eyes, obviously trying not to let President Russell see.

President Russell watched him hide his tears. Sergei had changed so much. The Spirit had truly touched his heart and changed him.

"Here we are," Sergei announced as he pulled into the parking spot behind the apartment building.

"I'll only be a minute," President Russell said as he walked into the mission home.

"I'll wait," Sergei replied and began drumming softly on the steering wheel.

President Russell went in to gather more of his personal effects, particularly a souvenir he had purchased for his wife. It was to be an anniversary present. He didn't dare pack it earlier for fear she might see it. He spent only five minutes in the house and was on his way back out to Sergei when he felt the need to stop. He stopped, looked around, and listened. There wasn't anything. He thought through everything else. He hadn't forgotten anything. Why had he stopped? He shrugged and headed back out to Sergei.

He handed Sergei a key.

"Will you look after the place while we're gone?"

"Of course." Sergei took the key.

President Russell could see that Sergei was honored to watch the mission home while he was gone.

They drove away slowly. President Russell looked back at the mission home. He couldn't escape the feeling that he had just made a massive mistake, but he had no idea what that might be.

"To the train station?" Sergei asked.

"Yes, to the train station."

* * *

The crowd stampeded away from the burning train station. Large chunks of burning shrapnel littered the square. A young man tripped and fell. Johnson stopped and offered him a hand. The young man turned and looked at Johnson. It was the same man that he had knocked over the day before. The young man's eyes went wide as he recognized Elder Johnson.

"You," he said and reached for his waist, instead of reaching for Johnson's outreached hand. The crowd surged and washed Johnson away from the young man.

"We need to call the president," Schofield gasped between breaths. They now stood several blocks from the train station. The blast had destroyed the train, the train the elders were supposed to be on. It had still been in the train yard when it exploded, so the explosion had also destroyed the trains on either side of it, sending burning shrapnel into the station, which now belched black smoke into the air. The beautiful stained glass windows had shattered in the initial concussion of the blast.

Sirens wailed over the screaming masses as the emergency vehicles got closer to the fire that now raged in the train station.

The elders hunched over, gasping for breath, coughing, and wheezing. "I'll call," Johnson said holding out his hand to Schofield.

Schofield paused for a moment, patting his pockets, and then shook his head.

"The phone," he said, panting. "It was in my backpack." He pointed to the plume of black smoke pouring into the sky from the remnants of the train.

They both paused for a moment.

"That's okay," Johnson said, finally catching his breath. "We can use a pay phone. They still have pay phones here."

"Do you know his number?" Schofield asked, following Johnson to the nearest pay phone.

"No, but I have the number to the mission home in here somewhere." He pulled off his backpack and found the number to the mission home on his planner.

Johnson picked up the phone to call President Russell.

"No dial tone," he said and hung it up.

"It doesn't look like there is power at all." Schofield pointed to the shops that were dark. No trains were leaving Almaty today. "Let's go home."

They slowly headed in the direction of their apartment. Schofield put his arm around Johnson's neck and pulled him close.

"Thank you for forgetting your passport."

* * *

As soon as he recognized Elder Johnson, Ivan had reached for his gun. But before he could pull it out, the crowd had jostled them away from each other, and the missionaries were lost in the mass.

"We have a problem," Ivan informed Taras as he walked into the apartment that had been designated as their rendezvous point.

"What is it?" Taras asked.

"The American that knocked me over yesterday. He was there today. He saw me. He can place me on the scene."

"Is he CIA?"

"No, he's a missionary. He wore one of those badges on his chest." Ivan pointed to his chest.

"Then what's the problem?"

"He can tie me to the bombing. I was there yesterday with one of the bombs in hand. He saw me today running from the wreckage. What if he starts talking?"

"I think you're overreacting."

"Okay, what if he is CIA?" Ivan suggested. "If he knew I was responsible, he would tie me to you. They could get us both, then where would we be?"

"I think you took a bump on the head. But you're right, if they are CIA posing as missionaries, we cannot take any chances. Even if they're just stupid Americans, we cannot take the chance of them reporting us. Take care of it quickly and, preferably, quietly."

"Yes, sir."

FIVE

It took the elders some time to reach their apartment. All the taxis were full and no one wanted to pick up the Americans. Schofield could pass for a Russian or a Kazakh, but Johnson was distinctly American.

They were exhausted when they entered the apartment. Johnson went to the phone to call President Russell at the mission home. He dialed the number and waited patiently for it to ring. It rang but nobody answered. Johnson tried to call again, but still no answer.

"Nobody's home. What a day."

Johnson walked into the kitchen where Schofield stood quietly.

He opened his mouth to speak.

Schofield quickly quieted him, putting his fingertips to his lips.

"Did you lock the front door?" Schofield whispered.

"Yes, I always lock the door."

"Someone is trying to come in."

"What?"

"Listen."

They listened intently. Someone was trying to open the door. They never had anyone over. Very few people knew where they lived. *Someone is trying to rob us*, Schofield thought.

"Hand me the broom." Schofield held out his arm.

Johnson handed him the broom and followed him quietly into the entryway.

The door slowly swung open. A young man crept into the apartment with a gun drawn in front of him.

Schofield raised the broom high and swung it down on the man's wrists, knocking the gun to the ground. It discharged into the wall, the bang echoing loudly through the apartment. The young man turned to Schofield, who slapped him across the face with the broom, knocking him backward into the hallway.

"Run!" Johnson yelled. "It's him."

Schofield hesitated for a brief moment, knowing they had the upper hand, but decided to listen to Johnson for once. He dropped the broom, and the elders ran past him out of the apartment, down two flights of stairs, and into the street.

"Well, he picked the wrong place to rob." Schofield laughed as they came to a stop in the market several blocks away.

"He wasn't trying to rob us. He was there to kill us."

"Whatever," Schofield said.

"I'm serious. He was the guy at the bus stop yesterday that I knocked over. I saw him at the train station today. He was surprised to see me. Scared even."

"What? Do you think he holds serious grudges? You knock him down and he comes to your apartment and kills you?"

"I don't know, but that was him yesterday and this morning."

"Whatever the case is, let's not stick around here."

They made their way to a pay phone on the other side of the bazaar and tried to call the president. There was still no answer.

"We need to get a hold of President Russell. Where is he? I wish I knew his cell number."

"You and me both, Johnson. Is that the only number you have in there?" Schofield pointed to Johnson's backpack that was still on his back.

"That and the mission office, and nobody is answering there

either. All the other numbers were on the phone. I never needed to write them down."

* * *

Michael Ivanov had been interviewing people at the train station for several hours and hadn't gotten one lead that he thought was decent.

"Michael," a detective called and waved him over. "You might want to hear this one."

"What is it?" Michael asked as he approached. He was trying not to get frustrated. Most of the people couldn't even remember what train it was that had exploded, yet they knew for sure who blew it up. He had developed patience with people who were honestly trying to help but just didn't have a clue. He had learned through years of experience to tell when someone had something that was of potential value.

"Tell him what you told me," the detective directed a young man.

"I was hauling luggage for people to the trains, and I saw two guys in suits. I think they were American by the way they were talking. They got off the train two minutes before it left and ran away as fast as they could. People usually run toward trains, not away from them."

"Could you describe them for me?"

"Sure. They were wearing dark suits and had these badges on their chest. One wore a backpack. One had short black hair, and the other was tall with red hair and his face was covered in freckles."

"Thank you. You have been very helpful." Michael dismissed the man to leave.

"Do you know them?" the detective asked.

"Yes. I met them yesterday, and one caused me some concern." Michael reached for his phone. "Let's go pay them a visit." The Kolchuks would know the Americans' address.

SIX

President Russell had Sergei drive him around the city for a while
before taking him back to the train station. He needed to
make sure everything was taken care of. He trusted the local
leaders, but he wanted to meet with them one last time before
he left. As Sergei drove him around the city to meet with them,
it also gave him a chance to see some of his favorite places again
before leaving tonight. It was a second home to him. He had lived
all over the world, but he had really fallen in love with Astana in
the time he had been there. They arrived back at the train station
just as two elders from a nearby city arrived. He escorted them
to the conference room that they had rented for the day. Yevgenie sat in a chair staring at the TV. On the TV were scenes of
an explosion and a massive fire at the Almaty train station. His
face was pale as a sheet.

"What is it, Yevgenie?"

He pointed to the TV that was replaying video from a security camera that had caught the explosion on tape.

"That is the train Elder Schofield and Elder Johnson were
on. A terrorist blew it to pieces this morning. There were no
survivors."

President Russell collapsed in a chair, put his head in his
hands, and wept.

* * *

Elders Johnson and Schofield had tried to go to the Kolchuks, but nobody was home. They didn't know where else to go, so they tried to stay in heavily populated areas for most of the day. They thought of going to other members' houses, but most of the small branch membership was spread throughout the city, and they didn't have addresses or phone numbers. All those had been lost with the phone. They attempted to call President Russell several times, but he never answered.

"Has he left already? I thought he was waiting to go on the train with us this evening."

"He probably thinks we're dead," Schofield pointed out. "Our train did explode this morning."

* * *

Michael Ivanov got to the elders' apartment and found the front door wide open. He entered cautiously. He saw the broom on the ground in the entryway and cautiously stepped over it, peering both ways as he stepped into the apartment. It was quiet. He stepped to the left into the kitchen and noticed a bullet lodged in the plaster wall. The fridge had been overturned, and the cupboards' contents emptied onto the floor. He turned and walked into the other room, finding the beds overturned and books scattered about the room. He stepped cautiously through the room to the balcony and looked out. Then he focused on the room again and found a small pile of religious pamphlets dumped in a pile. He used his pen to rummage through them, making sure nothing else was there before grabbing a couple and tucking them in his pocket.

"Someone was looking for something," Michael said quietly to himself. It only added to his suspicions of the elders. He would have his people fully search the place and make sure they didn't miss anything.

* * *

"Have you verified that they were on the train?" President Russell asked Yevgenie.

"They picked up their tickets," Yevgenie answered solemnly. "That I could verify. The only record of who was actually on the train was destroyed with the train. It will be sometime before they will begin to identify the bodies. I tried calling their phone too, but it went straight to voice mail."

"This is something I hoped I would never have to do. I need to call their families." President Russell slumped in his seat. "Sergei, we need to go back to the mission home and get their parents' phone numbers. You elders wait here for the rest of the elders. Sergei and I will return shortly."

President Russell's heart ached. If only he could have gotten them out sooner. *Why did the prophet tell us to leave? If he hadn't told us to leave, the elders would still be alive.* The sweat began to bead on his forehead as he thought about it, anger swelling. He tried not to think about that; he didn't know all the answers. The prophet told him to leave when he did and now they were leaving, all but two of them. He wanted to be mad. *If they had all stayed home this morning, they would all be safe. Why? Why did they have to die?*

Painfully he practiced in his head what he would say to the parents.

* * *

President Russell sat solemnly at his desk. He still wasn't sure how to tell the parents of Elder Schofield and Elder Johnson that their sons had been killed in a horrific act of violence. He, of course, would point out that they died serving the Lord and would probably continue to serve Him on the other side, but that couldn't take away the loss of a loved one. He thumbed through his list of phone numbers. He had a collection of cards that had all the contact information for all the missionaries as well as some other information in helping him when he needed to talk to missionaries' families. He took a deep breath and reached for the phone.

The phone rang. President Russell jumped, startled at the noise shattering the gloomy silence. He quickly calmed himself and picked up the phone.

"Hello, this is President Russell."

"Finally," the voice said. He took a deep breath. "President Russell, this is—"

A loud explosion shook the mission home, and the phone went dead.

President Russell dropped the phone and grabbed the desk.

"What was that?" he asked, picking up the phone, hoping the person would still be on the other end, but he was gone.

"President Russell!" Sergei yelled as he rushed into the building. "We need to get out of here. A building up the street just exploded. The whole street is on fire."

President Russell grabbed the elders' files and rushed out of his office into the street. Two blocks away, a raging fire had spread to three neighboring buildings and was spreading quickly. The streets filled with chaos as people ran out of their buildings away from the raging inferno. Black smoke billowed from the wreckage, enveloping the street.

President Russell stopped for a brief moment and looked at the scene. This was why the prophet had told him to get his missionaries out of the country. The country *was* falling into a civil war. He regretted doubting the prophet earlier. It had been a tense political situation for months. He had talked to Sergei and Yevgenie about it. They both thought it would blow over, but not anymore. Now he needed to get the rest of his missionaries and get to Moscow before he lost any more.

"Let's go!" he called as he climbed into the mission van with Sergei.

President Russell watched, tears pouring down his cheeks,

as the people fled their burning homes. Sergei carefully drove the van through the mass of people until he could turn off the side street and onto a major thoroughfare.

President Russell walked into the conference room at the Astana train station, relieved to see the elders waiting for him. Some elders stood to greet him, but others just sat and watched the television, the fire raging near the mission home.

The train station was swarming with police and dogs, making sure the incident in Almaty wasn't repeated.

* * *

"I had him, but the line went dead," Johnson told Schofield as he hung up the pay phone.

"We need to pray," Schofield announced.

"I've been praying since we woke up this morning."

"There's a park on Aralsk Boulevard. Let's go there."

They found a nice secluded place in the park and knelt together to pray. Schofield, who lately had been hesitant to offer the companionship prayers, offered up a heartfelt prayer asking for guidance and protection.

"Our Father in Heaven," he began. "We thank Thee for this wonderful opportunity to serve the people of Kazakhstan and share the gospel with them, and we pray that we will be able to continue to do so."

As Schofield prayed, Johnson felt a strong outpouring of the Spirit that he was not done sharing the gospel here. He wasn't sure what that meant, but he knew that in the time he had left, he had to continue sharing the gospel.

"And please guide us in this confusing time. Help lead us to safety."

In that moment, Johnson felt the Spirit as strong as he ever had.

"Please help those that must stay here. Bless them and protect them."

As Schofield concluded the prayer, he looked at Johnson. He could tell they both had felt the Spirit strongly during their prayer; he loved moments like this when the Spirit of the Lord would guide them.

"We need to get to Astana," Schofield stated.

"Okay," Johnson said softly. He had felt the Spirit. And if Schofield had received revelation that they needed to go to Astana, then they would go to Astana.

"How much money do you have?"

"What?" Schofield asked, obviously confused.

"How much money do you have? We need to know how much money we have so we can figure out a way to get to Astana."

Between the two of them, they had about two hundred and fifty US dollars, most of which was hidden in Johnson's belt or in his shoe. They also had nearly twelve thousand Kazakhstan tenge. Astana was nearly five hundred miles away in a straight line, but Lake Balkhash blocked the way. It would be much farther by road.

The Spirit had revealed to them that they needed to get to Astana, but they would have to find their own way there.

"I'm thinking we go by bus," Johnson suggested. "We could be there by this time tomorrow."

"Let's go then."

Johnson took off his backpack, the only thing either of them had besides the clothes on their backs. He pulled a map of Almaty out of it and looked for the bus depot. The depot was located on almost the exact opposite side of Almaty from where they were. "It will probably take an hour or two to get to the depot by bus. Do you want to take a cab?"

"No, we had better save our money," Schofield replied. "We don't know how much we are going to need."

They left the peaceful park and headed for the bus stop that would provide a ride to the bus depot where they could hopefully catch a bus to Astana.

* * *

Schofield and Johnson arrived at the bus depot a little after 5:00 p.m. Schofield stopped on the hill that overlooked the bus depot and looked at the chaotic mess. Thousands of people were trying to catch a bus to somewhere. It reminded him of an anthill that had been disturbed. The train station was closed; no trains would be leaving for a long time. For those without cars, which was most of the population, the only way out of the city was the bus or an airplane. And most people couldn't afford the airfare, so they chose the bus.

The elders fought their way through the swarming masses to the ticket booth, where they were told it would be two days before they could get on a bus to Astana. And more than a day before they could get on any bus at all.

Johnson screamed in frustration as they exited the crowded depot. They couldn't wait two days to leave Almaty. A big empty blue bus pulled up outside the depot. A sign in the window read, "Astana—5,000 Tenge."

"Elder, what about that?" Johnson pointed at the bus.

"I don't know," Schofield said. It was not uncommon for a bus owner to hire out his bus like a taxi; it happened a lot at sporting events and other times when a huge crowd of people needed to go from one place to another. It wasn't that expensive for the passengers and the driver usually made a killing, so everyone was happy. The price of this bus was on the expensive side, but it could mean the difference between getting to Astana tomorrow or in three days.

"C'mon, let's go." Elder Johnson pulled Schofield's arm, dragging him toward the bus.

Elder Schofield reluctantly agreed to take the bus. There was already a crowd of people piling onto the bus, within minutes the driver had collected his payment and was getting ready to go. The elders had seats halfway back on the driver's side, with Schofield against the window and Johnson next to him.

With a bang and a clatter, the bus took off on its way to Astana.

* * *

Michael Ivanov left the briefing room at 6:00 p.m. His men were following up on some leads. He had a lead he wanted to follow up on himself. He walked into his apartment and put away his work things. He picked up the Book of Mormon off the end table as he slipped off his shoes and put on some slippers. He walked into his big front room and set the Book of Mormon on a table next to a large orange chair. The chair was absolutely hideous, but it was the most comfortable chair he had ever sat in, and he wasn't about to get rid of it.

He wolfed down a sandwich from his refrigerator and returned to his chair with a cup of tea and some crackers. He sat in the chair and pulled over the ottoman to rest his feet on. He opened the book. Just inside the front cover was the phone number and address for the mission office in Astana. He made a mental note to call there tomorrow and check it out. Across from the address was a handwritten message from Elder Johnson. The Russian wasn't perfect, but the message was clear.

Dear friend,

I testify to you that this book is from God. His prophets wrote the words in it. The book has a promise that you too may know of its truth. In Moroni chapter 10 verses 4 and 5, the prophet promises you that if you read this book and ask God if it is true you will know of its truth and it will bless your life. Please read the book and ask God if it is true.

I promise you that if you do this, He will testify unto you, by the power of the Holy Ghost, that it is true. I testify this to you in the name of Jesus Christ, amen.

Sincerely, Elder Johnson

"Interesting," Michael said to himself.

Elder Johnson's words were powerful. It was clear he was confident that whoever read this book would know that it is true. He turned the page and read two more testimonies and an introduction. It piqued his interest, so he read on.

* * *

"It's time to go, elders," President Russell announced. They had been watching the chaos unfold all day and now it was time to escape it. He had sat with Elder Jackson and Elder Pitcher for a while, discussing the future of the Church in Kazakhstan. While nobody could really know what would happen in the coming days or months, they all hoped the escalating violence would subside quickly and the missionaries would be able to return and continue their work. President Russell had found himself confiding his doubts from earlier to the elders. Not as a confession but as an encouragement to trust in the Lord. *The Lord does lead the Church and knows what is best for it.*

"I don't know if we will return here when things have settled, but at least we have established a foundation upon which can be built a mighty stake of Zion. One day there will be a temple here where worthy Kazakh members can fulfill the glorious plan of redemption that has been established for all God's children. I hope to live to see the day when the Kazakh people receive their own temple," President Russell said. "Let us pray for the people of Kazakhstan."

President Russell offered up a sincere prayer blessing the people of Kazakhstan. After his prayer, President Russell led the others to their train, where they would depart, not knowing if they would ever return.

As he led the elders to the train, he remembered the phone call from before. "Did any of you call me earlier today at the mission home?"

None of the elders here had called him. And none of the elders on the earlier train could have called him. *Which elder was it then?*

SEVEN

Johnson wasted no time at all before striking up a conversation with the gentleman next to him on the bus. Soon they were engaged in a discussion about the Bible. The gentleman was an avid Bible reader and thought himself a bit of a scholar on the matter.

Schofield sat quietly looking out the window as they left the great city behind. He had only been in Almaty for a couple months, but he absolutely loved it. He loved the atmosphere of the city, the majestic mountains just to the south of the city. He had hoped to take a trip into the Tian Shan Mountains, but it appeared that wasn't going to happen. He was leaving a city he loved, and he prayed that he would be able to return. A tear rolled down his cheek, falling softly onto his hand. He lifted up his hand and looked at the tear sitting there. He smiled and wiped the tears from his eyes.

* * *

President Russell had hoped to call the parents of Elder Schofield and Elder Johnson before he left the country, but he just wouldn't have time. And now it would be at least twenty hours before he could call. They would not get to Moscow until late tomorrow afternoon.

President Russell sat in his cabin on the train and opened his scriptures for some guidance. He had a great love of knowledge. He loved to read. He loved to read the Bible long before he had met the missionaries who had introduced him to the Book of Mormon. He had quickly developed a great understanding of the scriptures and how they applied to everyday life. He learned to read for guidance. The scriptures always had a way of telling him which way he should go and what he should do. If ever he needed guidance, it was now.

He read from the Book of Mormon about Abinadi before flipping ahead a few pages. President Russell was the leader of a mission that was being abandoned. He had lost two of his missionaries. He needed something that would strengthen him. He read about Alma the Younger and the sons of Mosiah. Tears streamed down his cheeks as he flipped back and forth, searching the scriptures for the answer to the question he didn't know. The more he read, the more he began to think he had made a mistake in leaving.

* * *

Elder Schofield tried to get some sleep. He dozed off periodically, only to be awoken by haunting memories of the explosion that morning. He'd stood watching the train drive away as it erupted into a massive ball of fire. The chaos that ensued was unnerving—the crying children, the smell of burning steel. People covered in blood and ash, running by, screaming. Heat from the flames melting the hair on his arms as he ran from the burning train station. He didn't stop to help those injured, those that were lost. He just ran. He had the opportunity to do good, to help those in need, and he just ran. He tried to justify his actions. He was saving himself first, but he still felt anguish that he might have helped another. He had heard that more than a thousand people lost their lives at the train station. He could have helped just one of them, but he didn't. He just ran.

He heard bits and pieces of Johnson's conversation with the man next to him. It seemed Elder Johnson was going to explain the whole plan of salvation in one sitting. Currently Johnson was on the subject of Christ's Resurrection, and Schofield knew he would move on to the Apostasy and Restoration of the Church. Schofield thought about adding to the conversation, but Johnson seemed to have it under control.

Every time Schofield woke up, Elder Johnson and the gentleman were talking about a different subject. They talked for what seemed like hours, Johnson never losing his enthusiasm for sharing the gospel. He met every challenge the man threw at him with grace and dignity. He didn't bash or try to prove wrong. He testified and expounded on the scriptures. It was a sight to behold and feel as Johnson helped open this man's heart and helped the Spirit testify to him that all he had heard was true.

Schofield only added a comment when Johnson's Russian failed him, which had been surprisingly little for the length of the discussion.

The bus came to an abrupt stop.

Schofield sat up in his seat. Only a single light shone outside, that of a flashlight from a man standing near the front of the bus. The people on the bus stirred uncomfortably in their seats. The hair on the back of Schofield's neck stood on end.

He could sense something wasn't right. They were in great danger. "This is bad," Schofield whispered. He needed to silence Johnson's outgoing personality.

He turned to Johnson and put one finger to his lips. "Not one word. Not one word until I tell you so."

"What?" Johnson asked.

"Not one word!" Schofield ordered. "If anyone asks you something, point to your throat and act like you can't talk. Act like you have a sore throat."

"Why?"

"Just do it!"

A gunshot shattered the nervous silence on the bus. Women screamed, and a baby cried. Three men in masks with machine guns stormed onto the bus. The first one grabbed the driver and threw him out of the bus. The second man stood at the front of the bus and fired another shot into the ceiling.

"Quiet!" the man yelled.

"You!" He pointed his gun at the man sitting directly behind the driver seat. "Stand up."

The man promptly stood up, holding his arms up near his head.

"Give him your valuables." He pointed to the third man, who was now holding a large canvas bag.

The man pulled out his money clip and tossed it in the bag.

"What is this?" One of the men noticed his watch, which was a nice knockoff. He grabbed the watch and threw the man outside. He stumbled on the steps of the bus and collapsed to the ground at the feet of three more men. One offered him a hand and helped him to his feet. As soon as the man was on his feet, they began punching and kicking him. The next person on the bus followed the same routine. She stood and emptied her valuables into the canvas bag, only to be grabbed and thrown out of the bus, where the three thugs greeted her. They tossed their previous punching bag aside and began on the next victim.

She screamed as they took her.

The bus was emptied that way. They stood up and put all their valuables in the bag, were verbally abused, and shoved off the bus, where they were beaten until the next person came out.

Elder Johnson's turn came. The man pointed his gun at him. Johnson threw his local money in the bag as well as his watch. Schofield hoped they didn't check Johnson's shoe or his belt, where most of their American money was hidden.

"What's this?" The man pointed to Johnson's backpack. Johnson opened his mouth to speak, but Schofield interrupted.

"Our religious supplies," Schofield said in his best Ukrainian accent. He had studied the Ukrainian accent carefully from a companion who was from Kiev, Ukraine. He had gotten very good at imitating him.

"Was I talking to you?" the man yelled at Schofield.

Schofield stood up.

"Excuse me, sir. My friend is very sick. I must get him home so that—"

Schofield took the butt of the gun in the forehead, knocking him backward into his seat.

The man threw Johnson out the door and dumped the backpack out on the floor by Schofield.

"So it is." The man looked at the copies of the Book of Mormon and the pamphlets that strewn across the floor. Schofield picked up one Book of Mormon. The man kicked him in the face.

Still holding the Book of Mormon in one hand, Schofield reached up with his other hand to touch his bloody lip. He had never wanted to hurt someone so bad. It took all his strength to restrain himself.

"May we please take our things?"

"No!" the man yelled, punching Schofield in the face. He grabbed his arm, pulled him to his feet, and shoved him toward the front of the bus. Schofield tucked the Book of Mormon under his arm before being thrown from the bus toward the welcoming committee that was thoroughly enjoying the extra time it had with Johnson.

After a quick beating, Schofield landed on the ground next to Johnson, who was holding his bloodied and bruised face. When the last of the people were off the bus, all six men climbed onto the bus and drove away, leaving a hundred beaten people in the middle of nowhere. Beaten, bloody, and trapped with nothing but the clothes on their backs and the Book of Mormon in Schofield's hand.

* * *

Michael Ivanov couldn't put the book down. It had piqued his interest after just a few pages, and he just read and read. He had learned to read exceptionally fast while at school. He could briefly glance at a file and know and remember all the important details, a skill that made him very good at profiling criminals quickly. Based on what he had read so far, there was no indication that the two Americans were religious fanatics. And there was that different feeling while he read.

* * *

Some of the people who managed to keep matches after they were robbed started several campfires. The people hunched around the fires to keep warm; the cool autumn air blew in from the north with an extra chill this night. The night was going to get colder and most people were not dressed for warmth. They didn't have proper supplies for a cold night and no shelter. It was only grassland for what seemed like an eternity in the dark. The elders huddled silently around a fire trying to keep warm. The bus driver came over and sat next to them.

"My name is Yuri." He held out his hand.

Johnson shook it but didn't say anything.

Yuri leaned in close.

"You owe me your life," he said boldly to Johnson.

"Excuse me?" Elder Schofield said, confused.

"They weren't just robbing the bus. They were also looking for two Americans." He looked Schofield in the eye. "I told them there were no Americans on the bus, although I know for sure you are American." He looked at Johnson. "And you are guilty by association." He looked back to Schofield.

"Why would they want us?"

"I heard them talking . . . they are looking for two Americans. If they find them, they are to take them back to Almaty."

"Thank you," Schofield said. He checked the inside pocket of his suit coat to make sure his passport was still there. That could have been disastrous. He realized they had thrown him off the bus without taking his wallet. "I still don't know why they would want us."

"I'll bet it was that guy who broke into our apartment," Elder Johnson suggested.

"Why would he send people after us?" Schofield asked. Johnson paused, running some ideas through his head.

"He blew up the train," he blurted out excitedly.

"Shhh!" both the bus driver and Elder Schofield said.

Johnson lowered his voice. "I can put him at the train station the day before the explosion, when he planted the bomb, and on the day when he went to the train station to blow it up. I saw him running from the train station. He was scared. I could see it in his eyes. And then he shows up at our apartment. That has to be it."

"Wait. You saw the bomber?" Yuri asked.

"I think so," Johnson said.

"I don't really believe that," Schofield said, "but that would explain why he has tried to kill us twice now."

"It doesn't matter," Yuri stated. "In the morning, there will be many cars coming. People will learn what happened. You will not get sympathy from the others. Word will spread that the masked men were after the Americans. They will blame you and may try to capture you or kill you themselves. We must leave now."

"Now?"

"Yes, we'll slip away in the dark. I have a house on the shores of Lake Balkhash. It is not far from where we are now. You'll be safe there. If we leave now, we'll be there by tomorrow midday."

"Why are you helping us?" Johnson asked cynically.

"I know who you are. I recognized you when you got on the

bus. My sister belongs to your church in Samara. I know you are good men."

"Thank you."

"Let's go."

The three of them crept away silently into the night.

"My name is Yuri," the bus driver said again as soon as they were well clear of the makeshift camp of refugees.

"Elder Johnson."

"Elder Schofield."

"Interesting," Yuri said.

EIGHT

At 2:00 a.m. Michael Ivanov finally decided he needed to put the book down and get some sleep. He had to get up early, but the book fascinated him. Several times he set the Book of Mormon down only to pick it up again and read a few more pages. He no longer suspected Johnson and Schofield had anything to do with the bombing. He hoped to contact them soon to learn more about their church and this book. He had a little notebook filled with several questions that he wanted to ask the elders.

* * *

The elders and Yuri followed a road in the dark for several hours. Once the sun began to lighten the horizon, the elders, exhausted and sore from the beating on the bus and hiking through the night, trudged on. Schofield could see that Johnson nursed a blister on his foot.

The lake loomed large before them, a pool of deep blue surrounded by a sea of green trees, the early morning light reflecting majestically off the water. They stopped to take a break shortly after sunrise. Their legs ached from walking through most of the night. Yuri estimated they had three or four kilometers left to go before they would reach his cabin on the shores of Lake Balkhash. The cabin was on the south end of the lake in a small community.

Most of the walk had been spent in near silence, and the elders were somber from the beating they had taken earlier in the night. The rising sun lightened the mood, and as they started walking again, Elder Johnson started to ask Yuri about his sister in Samara and her involvement in the Church. Yuri told Elder Johnson all that he knew about his sister and their church, which wasn't much. She was taught by two American men, and they wore name badges like these two did. The name on the badge was the same—they too were both named "Elder."

Johnson smiled at the misconception and was happy to explain that "Elder" was not actually a name but a title. Yuri asked them for their names.

"Just call us by Elder Schofield and Elder Johnson," Schofield interjected.

"Almost there." Yuri pointed to a small cluster of houses that lined the lake. Most of them were just little houses. Yuri said that most of the big vacation homes were on the other end of the lake.

When they arrived at the cabin, Yuri opened the door and let them in. He showed the elders to a room upstairs that had two beds. Johnson collapsed onto one of the beds and stretched out. He looked over at Schofield, who was stretched out on the other and had almost immediately fallen asleep. The bed was not the softest bed that Johnson had slept on, but at that moment all the bruises and blisters faded into nothingness as he let the chaos of the last day slip away into peaceful slumber.

* * *

A groggy Michael Ivanov awoke to his ringing cell phone. It was his office.

"Hello?" he mumbled

"Michael, where are you?" his assistant asked.

"I must have overslept."

"I'd say."

"Go ahead and start the briefing without me." Michael knew

they were having a briefing this morning to go over all the legitimate leads and determine where they stood.

"We already did. We're finished. It's nearly nine o'clock."

"Wow," Michael said, looking at his clock and wondering how he had slept so much. "What did I miss?"

"I've already farmed out most of the work. I've got a couple of guys following a lead on your two Americans. It seems they were on a bus that was hijacked up by the lake. The hijackers were actually looking for the Americans. Somehow they escaped detection. I've got guys up at the site asking about them. I'll let you know what we find out."

"Why would some thugs be after the Americans?" Michael wondered out loud.

"I don't know, but they probably won't survive if they are caught."

"Thanks," Michael replied. "I'll be in the office in an hour or so. Keep me posted."

* * *

Elder Schofield awoke early in the afternoon to the smell of potatoes and bacon. He stood up and stretched. His body ached from the beating, and he could feel the tightness on his face where he was swollen, but fortunately he hadn't suffered any cuts. His ribs ached and his legs were sore from walking all night, but he would survive. He walked slowly down the stairs to the kitchen and stopped in the doorway.

A beautiful young woman stood at the stove frying potatoes and bacon in a skillet. She heard Schofield, turned, and smiled. Her long black hair was in a ponytail, and she wore a red-and-white flowered apron.

"Good afternoon."

"Good afternoon," Schofield replied, unsure what to do. He just woke up in a strange house with a beautiful young woman making breakfast. He knew he shouldn't go into the room with a young women by himself, especially one his age.

"I hope you slept well."

"Yes, thank you." Schofield still stood in the doorway, not daring to enter, but not wanting to be rude.

"Come in and have a seat." She motioned to the table that was set for four. "Lunch is almost ready."

"Where is Yuri?" He looked around the kitchen, hoping to see an escape from a missionary's worst nightmare.

"He went out for a bit. Are you going to wake your friend or let him sleep?"

"Wake him, of course," Schofield said and bolted to the bedroom to wake Johnson. He looked like Schofield felt. His left cheek was swollen and he had a black eye, but there were no cuts. He looked like he had been rolling in the dirt. He grabbed his side as he stood up but quickly let go.

Johnson quickly climbed out of bed at the first indication there would be food.

He washed his hands and sat down at the table. He looked up at the young woman bringing food to the table.

"Oh, hello," he said casually.

"Hi," she replied, smiling at him.

"Elder Johnson." He stood and offered her his hand.

She set the skillet on the table, wiped her hands on her apron, and shook his hand.

"I'm Ludmilla."

"Nice to meet you. I'm Elder Johnson."

"Yes, you said that." She smiled at him.

The kitchen door opened and Yuri walked in with a handful of fish.

"Hello," he said as he put the fish in the sink. "I see you've met my daughter."

Schofield breathed a sigh of relief. Waking up in a strange

house with a strange woman cooking him lunch made him feel uncomfortable. He wished he could be a little more like Johnson, who didn't seem to have any problem with the situation.

Yuri sat at the table and took a sip of the brown drink in his cup. "The bus hijacking made national news. You boys must be really something!"

"What do you mean?"

"Buses are hijacked all the time, and none of them ever make the news. This one is all over the news, among all the bombings of the last two days."

"And you think that has something to do with us?"

"I think it could. I don't know why else it would make the national news. Especially since there have been dozens of bombings since yesterday's train bombing. It is a good thing you guys left Almaty when you did. The military is rounding up all the foreigners for detainment. It is getting pretty ugly all over the country. The police and military are locking the country down."

"The different factions are fighting with each other and with the government. It looks like a nationwide riot. It is good you are here. Nothing ever happens here. We are a boring little fishing town off the lake. Just hang out here for a few days until things cool off, and then we'll get you to the embassy in Astana."

"Is there a phone we can use?" Schofield asked. "We need to get a hold of our mission president."

"Is the phone in the hall working?" Yuri asked his daughter.

"Yes, it is," she answered.

"Okay, after lunch you can make some phone calls, but now you need to eat, keep your energy up. Eat." Yuri pointed to the elders' food and made an eating motion.

"So, Ludmilla, tell us about yourself," Elder Johnson said.

"Call me Mila," she said enthusiastically. "I go to school in Dostyk. I'm studying biology and ecology. I'm hoping to be able to save this wonderful lake."

"What's wrong with the lake?" Schofield inquired.

"The fish population is slowly declining. The lake is endorheic. That means it doesn't drain anywhere. Several rivers and streams feed the lake, but the water just sits there. It is a magnificent lake. Half of the lake is saltwater and half of the lake is freshwater."

"How does that work?" Johnson asked.

"There is a sand bar that runs down the middle that keeps most of the salt water on the east side."

"No way!" Johnson said in disbelief.

"It's true. if you would like I will take you out there."

"Okay," Elder Johnson said.

"If you will excuse me," Schofield said, standing up from the table. "I'm going to try and call the mission president."

"Please, the phone is in the hall by the front room." Yuri pointed in the general direction.

"Elder Johnson," Schofield said, "do you have the number?"

"Yes, it's in my jacket pocket on the chair next to the bed," Johnson replied as he finished his meal. "I'll grab it for you."

* * *

Elder Schofield tried to call the president three times but never got an answer.

He only got a message about the number being out of service. After the third attempt, he slammed the phone down, wishing they had some other way to get a hold of the president. He had a cell phone, usually. President Russell was pretty good at breaking them. There had to be another way to contact him.

"No luck?" Johnson asked.

Schofield shook his head.

He set Elder Johnson's planner on the end table by the phone and went back to the kitchen.

He asked Yuri, "Is there a shower I could use?"

"Yes, of course," Yuri answered. "Mila, will you get him a towel?"

"Sure," Mila said, standing up from the table. "I think we have some clothes around that should fit you. I'll try and find them too."

"Thank you," Schofield said.

"If you need anything else, let me know," Yuri said.

Schofield waited as Mila cleaned off the table. He looked around, anxiously wondering where Johnson had wandered off to, and then followed her into the hall.

* * *

While Schofield was talking to Yuri and Mila, Johnson picked up his planner and saw Michael Ivanov's card. He was supposed to call him yesterday and set up a meeting.

I should call him and apologize for not calling him. He found the number and called. There was no answer, but the voice mail picked up. "Hello, please leave a message."

"Hello, Michael. This is Elder Johnson. We met with you the other day and we were going to call you last night and come visit you, but something has come up and we had to leave, but I just wanted to check in with you and see if you had a chance to read some of the Book of Mormon. I could answer some questions for you, and I—"

The beep cut him off and his message was done.

At least he'll know we are thinking of him, Johnson thought.

* * *

Schofield and Johnson walked behind Mila to the back door where she pulled towels from a linen closet.

"Follow me." She headed out the back door and down a stone path. Seven houses shared a community backyard. In the center was a cement building.

"The men's shower is on the other side." She pointed to the door nearest them. "This is the women's shower. I'll go get you some clean clothes and place them at the entrance." She handed Schofield the towels.

"Thank you. That would be very nice."

The elders walked slowly around the building to the entrance on the far side. Schofield was a little leery about using a community shower, but he figured since it was early afternoon they would probably not have any company. Johnson waited outside.

Schofield stood in the shower for a long time, just letting the hot water pour over his aching body. He was scared. In the last two days, the train they should have been on exploded, their apartment was broken into while they were in it, their bus was hijacked, they were beaten, and they had to walk miles to a little house on a lake that couldn't decide if it was saltwater or freshwater.

He missed the day-to-day routine of missionary work: teaching people, helping people feel the Spirit, and helping people recognize what the Spirit was. He missed seeing the joy on their faces when they accepted the gospel and were baptized.

Tears poured down his cheeks, mixing with the shower water and flowing down the drain.

He silently began to pray. If ever in his life he needed guidance, the time was now. He had turned to the Lord on many occasions and always received help. It wasn't always what he wanted or expected, but always what he needed.

He poured his soul out to the Lord. There had only been a couple of times when he prayed with such earnest. But he had the faith that the Lord would provide the guidance he needed.

A soothing calm washed over him, and he knew everything was going to be okay. It seemed to follow the water from the shower, beginning with a tingle in his hair that flowed down his back and meeting warmth that emanated from his chest. His whole body relaxed and for a few moments he couldn't feel the bruises and cuts. The hair on his arms no longer felt singed. The calm washed his worries down the drain. The Lord would soon provide him the guidance he needed.

Schofield finished his shower. Mila had left him some brown pants and a T-shirt on a small bench next to Johnson. He got dressed in the new clothes and folded his filthy suit to be washed. He traded Johnson places and sat as sentinel for Johnson as he showered.

Yuri informed them that some friends on the lake had invited them all to dinner that evening.

"Mila and I have some things we need to attend to. We will come for you around six."

That left two and a half hours. Schofield hoped to get some scripture study in. He was saddened by the realization that he had lost his scriptures on the train.

He found a Bible in the bedroom he had slept in and proceeded to read. He usually read his scriptures in English to allow for greater understanding, but he enjoyed the opportunity to study the Bible in Russian. They still had the Book of Mormon too, but Johnson was reading that. It was significantly easier to read in Russian than the Bible.

They studied together for thirty minutes.

"Would you like me to wash your suit while I wash mine?" Johnson asked Schofield.

"Thank you." He had forgotten he was planning on washing his suit.

* * *

Johnson went down to the kitchen and filled the sink with soapy water and plunged both suits in the water. He let them soak for a few minutes. They were quite filthy and were covered in ash, dirt, and blood. Johnson went to the phone and tried to call President Russell again and again, but a message kept saying the line was no longer in service.

He tried Michael Ivanov again and got is answering machine again. He decided maybe Michael was at his office. He remembered the business card had both a home phone number and an office number on it. He decided it would probably be okay to call him at work.

* * *

"Hello," Sasha said.

"Is this Michael Ivanov?"

"No. Michael is out of the office right now. I'm his assistant. Can I help you?"

"No, that's okay."

Sasha recognized the voice as American and was anxious to find out who it was.

"Please let me take a message for him," Sasha said.

"Okay."

"Just one minute." Sasha scrambled to make sure the phone-tracking device was working properly and tracing the call. He had a feeling this was one of the Americans they were looking for.

"Okay, go ahead with the message."

"This is Elder Johnson. We met him a couple days ago and were supposed to talk yesterday, but we had to leave town. I just wanted to call him and ask him a couple questions."

"Is there a number he can reach you at?" The trace was nearly complete.

"I don't know the number here. I'll just call him back later. Just tell him I called."

"Wait one minute! Got it." The trace was complete. The call was coming from a house on the shores of Lake Balkhash.

The phone line went dead.

NINE

Presient Russell felt impressed to check in with Yevgenie. At a twenty-minute stop in Russia, he got off the train to find a pay phone. He got no cell phone service between stops out here, and it was draining his battery.

"Hello?" Yevgenie answered.

"Yevgenie, this is President Russell."

"President, I'm so glad you called. I just got confirmation that Elder Johnson and Elder Schofield were not on the train."

"What?" President Russell's heart leaped into his throat. Johnson. *It was Elder Johnson who had called me.*

"There is surveillance video of them leaving after the train exploded."

President Russell breathed a huge sigh of relief. "That is great news."

"Not exactly." Yevgenie's voice was somber.

"What do you mean?"

"The video was released because the police think they may have had something to do with the bombing."

"They what?"

"They got off the train minutes before it exploded, leaving their luggage on the train. The terrorism task force thinks the bombing was performed by foreign nationals, and those two fit the profile."

"That's terrible," President Russell said. He slumped against the pay phone.

"Yes. More than you think."

"What do you mean?"

"The terrorism task force is notorious for shooting first and asking questions later. If they find them, it could come out badly."

"But I'm sure they had nothing to do with that bombing," President Russell said.

"I know that and you know that, but they don't know that. Fortunately, the police seem to have no leads as to where they are."

"Where are they?" President Russell asked, mostly to himself.

"I called their apartment and only talked to the police. They tried to find out who I was. I told them I had questions about the Church. Hopefully, the elders are smart enough to stay out of the way until the police catch the people responsible."

"Thank you, Yevgenie. I'll call you when I get back to Astana."

"You are coming back?"

"Yes. I have to find my missionaries."

"You can't come back here. The city is in disarray. There is talk of a coup."

"I'm coming now. I'll call you when I get there."

President Russell hung up the phone and left to find Elder Jackson. He had to leave him in charge of the missionaries. They would be fine, and Sister Russell would meet them in Moscow. And the Moscow mission president will get them settled.

"Elder Jackson," he said as he walked into his cabin. "I'm going back to Astana. Yevgenie said Elder Johnson and Elder Schofield are alive. They weren't on the train when it exploded."

"That's great!" Elder Jackson exclaimed, jumping out of his seat.

"I need you to let the other elders know. You're in charge

until you get to Moscow. I'll call the Moscow mission as soon as I know more."

"When are you leaving?"

"Now." President Russell turned and walked off the train to buy a ticket back to Kazakhstan on the first available train.

* * *

Michael Ivanov returned to his office from a late lunch.

"Sasha, do I have any messages?" he asked his assistant.

"No, sir," Sasha replied.

"Thanks," Michael said and headed into his office.

Michael sat down at his desk. Where had those two Americans gone? He had a lot of questions he wanted answered. He wanted to ask them. Of course, there were the important questions about the bombing yesterday, but strangely those were not the most important questions to him right now. He had always put work first. Work was his life. He worked at the expense of everything else.

Now something had crept in that was more important to him. The book he had been reading. He had so many questions about the Book of Mormon. He needed answers and he needed to find the missionaries before his colleagues did. They wouldn't show restraint and the elders could end up dead. He didn't think the elders were involved in the bombing. He was certain they had nothing to do with the bombing except being in the wrong place at the wrong time.

He had a lot of questions about the Book of Mormon and the funny feeling he got every time he read the book. It wasn't really funny; it was new, different. He liked it—a lot. He was positive it had something to do with the Book of Mormon, but he needed confirmation.

Many times in his career he had acted on a hunch or a feeling and usually he was right. That is how he got where he was, knowing he could follow his feelings. Now he had a feeling that was good, he wanted to act on that feeling, but he didn't know what to do.

He had to find those missionaries. He closed the blinds to his office, locked the door, and sat at his desk. He pulled the Book of Mormon out of his briefcase and opened to Alma chapter 32.

* * *

Sasha had lied when he said Michael didn't have any messages. He'd decided that the trace of the phone call from Elder Johnson, the suspected terrorist, would help him better if he kept it to himself. It was time for him to move up in the world.

Sasha walked slowly to a pay phone three blocks from his office. As soon as he had gotten off the phone with Elder Johnson, Michael had walked in and Sasha left for lunch.

Sasha did not enjoy the work he had. He used to when he first started, but along the way it wasn't enough. It was never enough. He was good at his job, but he didn't like it. His job paid him well, but he wanted more. The government paid well, but the Mafia paid better. It was never enough. He always wanted more. And now he had a chance to get more. In the seven years he had been in the police force, he had had many contacts with the Almaty underworld and had been paid nicely for his services. Now something possibly very large had fallen into his lap. For some reason a certain member of the underworld wanted these two American missionaries more than the antiterrorist task force he worked for and now he had them. He knew their exact location, thanks to Elder Johnson.

Sasha picked up the phone and dialed the number.

"Hello," the person on the other end said.

"This is Sasha. I may have something for you."

"What's that?"

"I know where those two Americans are."

"Really?" The voice was excited. "Where are they?"

"That depends on what you are willing to pay for it."

"If it is true, you will be taken care of."

"I want to retire," Sasha stated.

"Very well."

"I intercepted a phone call from an Elder Johnson. He called from a house on the shores of Lake Balkhash." Sasha gave him the address and added, "In three hours, I'm going to tell my people the location, so you need to act quickly."

"Thank you, Sasha. You will enjoy an early retirement."

"Remember—three hours head start is all I can give you."

The line went dead and Sasha walked slowly to the restaurant. His hand that held the receiver shook nervously.

* * *

Johnson and Schofield sat on the porch of Yuri's house waiting for him to arrive at 6:00 p.m. He soon appeared with Mila, her smile beaming. The four of them walked down a dirt road to the northwest. They walked for several miles along a trail that wound its way along the edge of the lake over a number of wooden bridges, crossing small streams that fed into Lake Balkhash, before coming to another small cluster of houses. Most talk along the way was about the lake and life in America.

"Is this it?" Schofield asked, pointing to the houses.

"Yes. It is the house of my friend I haven't seen in a while. I ran into him earlier today and he invited me for dinner. I told him I had guests, and he insisted I bring you along. He loves to have visitors."

Yuri knocked on the front door. A massive man opened the door. He was much taller than Elder Johnson and had bushy hair and a big beard. He was very intimidating until he smiled.

"Welcome," he said, holding out his arms. His eyes lit up,

and his beard parted, revealing his smiling mouth. "My friend!" He threw his arms around Yuri and gave him huge hug.

"Who is this?" he asked, motioning to the elders.

"This is Elder Johnson, and this is Elder Schofield."

"You share a name? How interesting." He stepped out of the house and shook their hands heartily. "Welcome, welcome. Please come in, and I will show you my family."

He turned and walked into the house. Schofield turned to Yuri.

"What is his name?" Schofield whispered.

"Call him Dima."

They followed him into a large room where many people were gathered.

"Attention, attention!" He waved his arms above his head. "We have some guests. This is Elder and this is Elder. They will be joining in our celebration this evening. Please make them feel welcome." Yuri quickly introduced everyone in the room to the elders and they immediately began fielding questions: "Where are you from? What are you doing here?"

Johnson was more than happy to answer all their questions. Schofield seemed to evade the questions, only answering questions when he couldn't avoid it. Johnson wondered why but was quickly distracted by another question and forgot it.

The dinner was fantastic: several species of fish prepared a variety of different ways. The mood was jovial with immense laughter filling every corner of the house.

* * *

The setting sun reflecting off the calm lake made for a picturesque setting. Schofield stood on a dock behind the house. The sound of the water lapping against the support calmed his troubled mind. Johnson stood just inside the house entertaining others with stories of his youth.

Mila walked up beside Schofield and stopped.

"You are missing the party."

Schofield startled, turned, and looked at her. The setting sun turned her long black hair a deep shade of red. Her smile shone like a thousand sparkling stars.

Schofield looked nervously back at the house. He could see Johnson through the window and hear his jovial retelling of a camping mishap of his younger years—he was technically following mission rules. All the same, Schofield was intensely uncomfortable standing on the dock by himself with this beautiful young woman.

"I just needed a moment to myself," he answered.

"I didn't mean to interrupt. I'll leave you alone."

"No, you can stay," he said, not sure why but knowing he needed to talk to her.

"Are you sure?"

"Yes, please."

"It is a beautiful view, isn't it?" Mila leaned up against the railing next to Schofield and looked at the lake.

"Yes, it's a fantastic view."

"Do you miss your family?"

"Yes, I do," Schofield sighed.

He did miss his family. He had thought about them a lot lately. He had a brother who was leaving on a mission soon, before Schofield would get home. It would be nearly four years until he saw him again. Four years is a long time. He missed his whole family: his mom, his brother, and his sisters.

"Why don't you go home to them if you miss them so much?"

"I will soon enough. I still have work to do." The statement struck him like a ball to the stomach. He hadn't even thought about it as he was saying it, but now that the words were out, he knew it was true. He still had work to do in Kazakhstan. He may have forgotten that for the last several weeks, but that didn't make it any less true. "For a while I had forgotten that. I have a lot of important work to do here still," he said. "And then, when my work is done, I will go home."

"How long have you been gone from home?"

"Nearly two years," he said.

"That is a long time to be without your family."

"I know, but being here is important. I need to share the gospel with people here." He paused and looked at her. He wanted to invite her to learn of the gospel, but he was leaving. They were all leaving. But she needed to know, and he was still a missionary. "Let us teach you about Jesus Christ and His atoning sacrifice."

"I would love to learn more about your church. My aunt writes me all the time telling me how wonderful the Mormon church is. I always told her someday I would learn about it. She prays for me; she tells me so. She says she prays every day that I will agree to meet with the missionaries and learn of the Church. I met them once in Astana, two women missionaries, but it didn't work out to see them anymore, but I guess now I have no excuse. You are here, and I have nowhere to go."

Elder Schofield knew this was why he had come to the dock, to talk to Mila.

"Will you and Elder Johnson teach us, me and my father, about the church? We need something more in our lives. It has been so hard since my mom passed. There has been an empty hole in my heart."

"We can teach you how to fill that hole," Schofield started.

* * *

President Russell sat nervously at the train station waiting for his train. Four hours ago he had sent his missionaries off to Moscow in the nervous hands of Elder Jackson. He sat, waiting for his train to Astana, a train that was almost an hour late. He needed to get back to Astana as soon as he could. His elders were alive and probably trying to get a hold of him, but he wasn't there. They must be terrified, stuck in a country at war with itself, feeling like everyone abandoned them.

He felt guilty for leaving them, but there was nothing he could have done. He had thought they were dead. He'd had other missionaries he had to think of. But worst of all, he felt guilty for ignoring the promptings telling him they were still alive.

He wanted to be positive, but he was worried about them. There was so much that could go wrong.

Finally his train rolled into the station. He waited for people to exit before he got on the train, but no one got off. He stood up and walked onto the train. It was nearly empty. The man taking tickets told him they had closed the borders and no one was getting into or out of Kazakhstan. The train was going as far as the border. If they let them continue, they would go on through to Astana. The conductor was anxious to get home. If they were stopped at the border, they would ride the train back to Chelyabinsk.

* * *

Michael Ivanov sat at his desk reading the Book of Mormon.

A loud knock at his door awoke him from his reverie. Only then did he realize that the knocking had been going on for some time and he hadn't realized it.

"Michael, Michael."

Michael put the book down on his desk.

"Just a minute." He took a deep breath, stood, and then walked to the door. He opened it quickly.

"Are you okay, Michael?" Sasha asked.

"Yes, I'm fine."

"They say you've been locked in your office all afternoon."

"Yes, I'm fine. I had something to take care of."

"We have a lead on those two Americans," Sasha said.

"Really?" Michael was surprised.

"Yes, they were spotted in a little fishing village on the shores of Lake Balkhash. I dispatched a team to investigate. They should be there in a couple of hours."

"What about our other leads?"

"Nothing substantial yet, sir. This is the only lead that looks promising so far."

"Sasha, I think we are chasing the wrong men."

"That may be so, but they were there on the day of the explosion, they were on the train that exploded, and they were seen running from the train minutes before it exploded. If they are not responsible, then I would bet they know something. In any case, we have to bring them in. If you want, I will put out the capture at all costs command."

"Yes, let's catch them. I would like to talk to them." Michael turned away from Sasha and added, "Keep me posted."

Michael was uncertain that this lead was any more reliable than the other two dozen sighting reports they had received. He wasn't sure why Sasha even told him about this one. He hadn't mentioned any of the others except in passing and they all proved to be false.

* * *

Sasha was concerned. Michael was not himself.

I wonder if he knows what I did, he thought.

Sasha wondered if he had let something slip, some hint that might have given away his connection to the whole mess that was going on right now. No, he was certain that his tracks were covered well. What could it be then?

For years, Sasha had been doing random odd jobs for the Mafia. He was always careful to cover his tracks. This had led to some unfortunate accidents, but there was nothing recent that should have Michael acting so preoccupied.

Sasha vowed to find out. He couldn't have Michael discovering any of his past activities. Especially not his connection to the bombing. Not now when he was so close to retirement.

TEN

Two black SUVs without headlights on pulled slowly up to the front of Yuri's house. Eight shadowy figures slipped out of the vehicles and crept into the house. They quickly and quietly searched the house by flashlight. They talked softly with each other on radio headsets.

One called to the others from the back of the house. Two others emerged from the back door. Hanging on a clothesline behind the house were the suits the two Americans were wearing.

"They were here," one said to the other two.

"The house is clear," a call came over the radio. "They've moved on."

Ivan cursed. His suspicions of the Americans seemed to be true. He didn't know what they were, but they escaped every attempt to capture them.

One man grabbed the damp suits off the line and carried them to the SUV. Ivan gave a command on his radio, and he and three men left as quickly as they arrived, leaving four men in the house to finish their business.

* * *

Elder Schofield and Mila stood on the dock looking at the lake. Mila was explaining how she hoped to save the lake but didn't know if she would be able to when they heard a noise. A bright ball of fire climbed quickly into the sky from across the lake followed by a roaring thunder. It looked like a house burst into a giant ball of flames.

Mila gasped and threw one hand over her mouth. She gripped Schofield's shoulder with the other to keep from collapsing. He looked at her hand on his shoulder and back at the fireball, not sure which one shocked him more.

Everyone inside the house raced out the back door to see what happened. They looked across the edge of the lake to the giant mushroom of fire that rose slowly and faded into the night sky, leaving a red and orange burning mass on the ground.

"What is that?" Johnson asked as he reached the dock.

"That was my house," Yuri replied softly.

"Are you certain?" Dima asked. His normally soft expression had faded to a stern stare.

"Yes. I know the location of my house from here. It is my house, possibly my whole neighborhood."

"Vasya," Dima commanded. "Grab the boat. We'll go check it out."

Vasya, an older-looking man with thin blond hair and wrinkled skin from years of smoking, ran inside and grabbed the keys to a boat that was parked on the nearby shore. He was spry for someone who looked so old.

Yuri, Dima, and Vasya climbed onto the fishing boat and were about to leave when Dima turned to the elders.

"You two." His friendly voice had turned gruff, almost angry. "Come with us."

The elders climbed into the boat. Mila followed right behind.

They sped across the lake at an impressive speed for a fishing boat.

* * *

Schofield gasped as they slowly approached the burning wreckage of the small cluster of houses. All the houses had burned to the ground. Several people stood nearby watching the fires burn. There was no point in fighting the fires. Everything was gone. Dima, Vasya, and Yuri got out of the boat and approached some of the people watching the fire. Schofield, Johnson, and Mila also climbed out of the boat but waited near the shore.

"What happened?" Dima demanded.

A young boy looked nervously up at his mom. She nodded her head, allowing him to answer.

"I saw two big black cars pull up and some men went inside." He pointed to where Yuri's house once stood. "They came out with two suits. One of the cars left and then the other one left, and then the house blew up as they drove away."

"Thank you," Dima said. He turned to Yuri and Vasya. "Black SUV means either government or Mafia. Either way, our American friends are in a heap of trouble, and we need to find out why."

Vasya and Dima climbed back into the boat.

* * *

Yuri stood staring at the smoldering heap that was once his house, the house he and his wife had built with their own hands. A house where they could vacation in the summer at the lake. He had spent many summers here with his wife before she died.

Yuri bit his lip to hold back the tears, but they came anyway. His once beautiful house. His broken heart. *Why did she have to die? Why?* It was pointless. One day she was here and the next day she was gone. It caught him off guard. Not that it would have made things any easier if he had known it was coming.

Oh, how he missed her.

Dima called to him from the boat.

Yuri held up one finger asking for one more minute.

He wiped the tears from his eyes, watching the last remnant of his house burn. The house he had built with his wife was destroyed. Why? All because he had helped two Americans. He helped them and they had brought him nothing but trouble. He wiped the last tear from his eye and stormed toward the boat, his anger at the Americans swelling within him. His hands shook. They had destroyed his house and his happiness. They needed to pay.

* * *

President Russell tried to get some sleep on the train. It would be after midnight before the train reached the border, and he wanted to be ready for what was to come. The guilt of ignoring promptings still gnawed at him. He tossed and turned for hours before finally deciding to get up and go for a walk. Walking always cleared his head. It relaxed him. Oftentimes he would take a break from school when he was teaching and walk to the botanical gardens to enjoy the beauty of nature.

He walked slowly down the aisles on the train until he found a gentleman to talk to. He introduced himself as President Russell of the Kazakhstan Astana Mission. Maybe a little missionary work would get his mind off his worries.

"Ruslan," the man said, shaking hands with President Russell.

"Have you heard of Jesus Christ?" President Russell asked, pulling out his Book of Mormon to show to the man.

"Of course," Ruslan answered and pulled a necklace out from his shirt. It had an ornate silver cross on the end of it. He smiled. "My grandmother gave this to me when I was a child." He spoke with reverence.

"Let me share with you something special that was shared with me," President Russell began, holding out the Book of Mormon so Ruslan could take it.

Ruslan took it and turned it over in his hands, looking it over and reading the title before opening it. "Is this another Bible?"

"This is like the Bible, in that it testifies of Jesus Christ."

"We could use more people thinking about Jesus Christ right now," Ruslan stated. The man set the book in his lap and looked at President Russell.

"Why are you going into Kazakhstan now?" he asked.

"I accidentally left two missionaries there. I have to go back for them."

"Into a war zone?"

President Russell slowly nodded his head. "They are my responsibility. I need to make sure they are okay."

Ruslan didn't say anything. He just looked at President Russell for a moment.

"What about you, Ruslan? Why are you going to Kazakhstan?"

"Fortunately I am only going as far as Chelyabinsk, which is still a little too close for comfort, but better than where you are going."

"I hope to enter, get my missionaries, and get out before it gets much worse, but I'm not even sure where they are. They seem to have lost their phone. I can't get ahold of them at all." He pulled his cell phone out and looked at it, wondering why they hadn't tried calling him. He still had some battery power left. He realized he was pouring his problems onto a complete stranger and decided to change the subject back to the gospel. "But I have faith that the Lord will guide me to them. Just like He guided me to this book." He pointed to the book in Ruslan's lap. At that moment he realized that he did believe the Lord would guide him to the elders. Somehow he would find them. He just hoped it wouldn't be too late.

* * *

Without a word, Yuri punched Schofield in the face. Schofield withstood the blow. He stood in stunned silence, thoughts racing through his mind. *Why did he hit me? Should I hit him back?* Schofield clenched his fist and flexed his arm and shoulder but resisted the urge to fight back. Instead they stood silently staring at each other.

Yuri screamed at Elder Schofield and punched him again. The smoldering house behind him cast dark shadows on Yuri's face. Schofield turned his face the other way. He smiled and nodded to Yuri after accepting the blow. His jaw ached—he thought it might be broken. He wished he could rub it, but he didn't want anyone to think he was going to retaliate, so he stood with his hands at his side.

"Papa, stop!" Mila yelled as she rushed in between them.

Dima rushed to the pair and put a hand on Yuri's shoulder. "Are you okay?" he asked. Yuri nodded, rubbing the knuckles on his right fist. Dima turned to Schofield. "Are you okay?"

"Yes," Schofield answered, finally rubbing his jaw.

"Everybody on the boat," Dima ordered.

Schofield watched as Yuri, Mila, and Johnson got on the boat before he did. Dima was the last to get on the boat; he whispered in Vasya's ear. Vasya drove considerably slower back toward Dima's house.

"You two have a lot of explaining to do," Dima started as soon as they were clear of the shore.

"What?" Schofield asked, confused.

"I know that you are wanted by the police for questioning about the train bombing in Almaty. I've seen your picture in the news. I don't think you did the bombing. I have connections that tell me so. But now the Mafia blew up Yuri's house and took your suits with them. The Mafia is after you and the government is after you. I need to know why."

"I don't know," Schofield replied.

Dima looked him in the eyes.

Does he really think I had something to do with the bombing?

"I have a theory," Johnson started.

Dima turned toward him to listen.

"The day before the bombing at the train station, I was pushed into a young man and knocked him over. He was quite nervous that he had dropped his big duffel bag. Schofield tried to help him with his bag, but he wouldn't let him. The next day after the train blew up, we were running from the chaos and I saw the same man again. He was surprised to see me, upset almost. Then later that day he broke into our apartment and tried to kill us, but Schofield clobbered him with a broom and we ran away."

"What does this have to do with anything?" Dima interrupted.

"Just hear me out," Johnson said.

Schofield rolled his eyes. He didn't believe the theory, but he didn't have a better one about why the police would think they had blown up the train.

"I think that guy planted a bomb and was upset because I could put him at the train station on the day the bomb was planted and the day of the explosion. That's why they want us dead, because I can place him at the scene of the crime."

"Very interesting." Dima rubbed his chin. Dima pulled out his cell phone to make a call.

ELEVEN

A frantic knock on the door pulled Michael back from Christ's visit to the Americas.

"What is it?" he called.

"Something has happened," Sasha answered.

"One moment." Michael closed his Book of Mormon and went to the door. "What is it?" he asked as he opened the door.

"Come and see."

Michael followed Sasha to the surveillance room. "We were following a lead we had on the two Americans. We zoomed a satellite camera on their suspected location and discovered this."

Michael looked at the screen. What were once seven houses and a bath were now just burning piles of rubble.

"This is the house they were staying in." Sasha pointed to the screen. "That's where the fire started. It wasn't just any fire; it was an explosion. A bomb like the one on the train. We have men on the scene now searching the wreckage. We have confirmation the two Americans were there today but had left late afternoon. It seems they are leaving a path of destruction in their wake."

"Do we have footage of the explosion happening?"

"No. Our satellite feed picks up shortly after the fire started."

Michael was confused. He was certain that the elders had nothing to do with the explosion on the train, but this second explosion . . . they were spotted at that house earlier that day. Something was amiss. He needed to find these two, but

Michael had no idea where they were. They probably wouldn't get far from that house. The military was seizing control of the country and shutting it down in hopes of stopping the escalating violence.

"I need to go to Lake Balkhash," Michael stated. "We need to find these two before any more damage is done."

Michael grabbed some things from his office, including his copy of the Book of Mormon, and headed to his car.

"Shall I accompany you?" Sasha asked.

"No, I need you to maintain the investigation from here. You are in charge for now. I'll check in and see how things are going. We need to find the people responsible for the bombing before the military has total control of the country, because they may not give it up once they take it. Do you understand me?"

"Not exactly," Sasha replied.

"I think the bombing was planned as the start of a military coup. They needed the civil unrest to roll out the troops and get them in position to seize power from the government. The bombing was not a random act. It was the first step in a greater plan. If the military seizes control of the government, there will be great changes, and certainly not for the better of Kazakhstan."

Michael was not certain where his theory came from, but he was certain it was at least mostly true. He had had strange hunches before and they always seemed to be true. He was also certain the Americans were in great danger if he didn't find them.

*　*　*

Sasha realized he may have played right into the Mafia's hands. Head Mafioso had connections in the military, and if they kept the madness going by not letting the police catch the men in charge, the military would be in control and that would be bad.

He needed to check out Michael's theory on the coup, because if it were true, he could be in big trouble.

Things were going so wrong so fast. He needed to find the Americans before Michael found them. Suddenly he felt like having a late dinner.

"I'm going out for a bite to eat," Sasha told the others in the office and headed for his usual pay phone to make some calls. He needed an update from his underworld contacts.

* * *

Schofield silently watched the smoldering houses fade in the distance as Vasya slowly drove the boat. Dima talked quietly on his phone in Kazakh. Schofield couldn't understand Kazakh and wasn't sure he wanted to. Mila and Yuri whispered silently in the back of the boat, and Johnson looked out onto the lake. Schofield wondered what Johnson was thinking about because he kept shaking his head back and forth. For some reason, they were in trouble. Schofield thought Johnson's theory was total rubbish, but like with everything else, Johnson was the optimist. He believed he had figured it all out. Schofield didn't have a better theory. He just thought it was coincidence that they happened to have left the train to get Johnson's passport, and the police, grasping for straws, are trying to blame it on them.

"Please forgive me," Yuri pleaded softly, looking at Schofield. "I was wrong was to hit you. I just lost my home, the home I built with my wife. She has been gone now for four years and that was all I had left of her. I blamed you. I realize now it was not your fault. I hit you and you didn't retaliate. You turned, for me, the other cheek. Like Jesus Christ would do. It made me so angry that you didn't hit back.

"I've never met a man capable of that. Mila told me how you two have talked. She said you are a man of God. She said you talked about her mom, how her death left a void. She said you could teach us how to fill that void."

He paused.

"How? How can you fill the void?" He held his hand to his heart.

Tears poured down his cheeks.

Schofield pulled him close, put both hands on his shoulders, and looked him in the eyes.

"I know you miss your wife. I know that was the hardest thing in the world for you to lose her and tonight losing your house, the house you built together, brought back all those painful memories."

"I lost my father when I was young. I understand what it is like to lose a loved one, but I also know that Jesus loves me. He made a way that I will see my father again. He made that possible."

Schofield looked up at Yuri to see if he was following him. He could see that Yuri understood and wanted to know more. His eyes pleaded for it.

"Jesus loves you. He took upon Himself all of your suffering. You don't have to go through this alone. He wants to help you. He loves you. He wants you to see your wife again. He wants you to be with her forever. And He made that possible."

Yuri looked at him with questioning eyes.

"Yes, Yuri, you can be with your wife again. This time forever. Never to part. All because Jesus loves you. He gave His life that we may live again after death. I can show you how to be with your wife again. Would you like that?"

"Yes." Yuri wiped the tears from his eyes. "Yes, I would."

"There is a lot to learn and a lot to do. Are you willing to do it?"

"Yes, I will do whatever it takes," Yuri sobbed.

"Good." Schofield gave Yuri a hug and wiped a tear from his own eye.

The Spirit was strong on the boat. Schofield knew Yuri felt it. He saw Yuri's anger at the him and Elder Johnson melt away like snow on a hot summer day.

Yuri broke the embrace and apologized again to Schofield. "I am sorry I hit you twice. I'm sorry I blamed you for my house being destroyed. I know it is not your fault."

"Actually, it was," Dima announced as hung up his phone. "Well, technically his." He pointed to Elder Johnson.

"Mine?" Johnson asked.

Everyone looked at Dima in shock and then to Johnson.

"It looks like your story checks out. I called some people who know some people. And the Mafia is after Elder Johnson. And also Schofield by association. I don't know the details, but your story sounds like a plausible explanation."

Schofield and Yuri looked at Johnson. Johnson looked back with what Schofield was sure was an I-told-you-so expression on his face.

"A bounty has been placed on your heads. A fairly large one at that." Dima stopped and looked at Johnson and then Schofield. "You two are wanted dead or alive."

"What?" sputtered Elder Johnson.

"It seems some important people want you dead. I don't know why, but I suspect if this man you saw at the train station is connected to the bombing, that could be very bad. I have people asking questions, but they must be discreet. Neither they nor I can be linked to you. That would be disastrous."

"Haven't you already been connected to us by us being here?" Schofield asked.

"No. No one here will tell anyone anything. They are very loyal people."

"How did they find us then?"

"That is a very good question. One I don't have an answer to. In any case, you both must leave."

"Where are we supposed to go?" Johnson asked frantically.

"Don't worry, my young friend." Dima chuckled. "I will not abandon you entirely."

"What do we do then?" Schofield asked.

"You need to go to your country's embassy in Astana."

"How do we get there?"

"You walk."

"It's, like, six hundred miles from here."

"Yes, I know, but all of the roads into Astana and out of the south will be blocked and checked. You are wanted men, remember? And the country is soon to be controlled by the military. They don't want you to get to Astana, but you will get to Astana and to your embassy. And they will protect you until this situation is resolved and the criminals responsible are brought to justice."

"Can't we just go to the police?" Johnson asked. "Won't they protect us?"

"I would like to think that they would," Dima said, smiling, "and honestly most officers probably would, but the reward on your head is huge. A very tempting thought for any man. And there are a lot of bad apples out there. Do you understand? You could turn yourself in and you might get a good cop who protects you and takes care of you, but then you are probably going to be in a jail somewhere where someone will go after the reward. Or you could get a bad cop who just kills you on the spot and takes the reward. I think going to the police would be a bad idea at this time.

"Don't worry," Dima continued. "You don't have to walk the whole way, but you do need to stay out of sight as much as possible. Travel inconspicuous. Maybe at night when people can't see you well. And you, Elder Johnson, don't speak. You are a dead giveaway American when you speak. Schofield could be from Ukraine, he speaks so well." Dima smiled and nodded to Schofield.

Schofield returned the smile, obviously enjoying the compliment. Schofield was always so smug about his superior Russian. Sometimes Johnson just wanted him to stumble and make some mistakes, but he never did.

"You can take my boat to Balkhash, but from there you are on your own."

"Aren't we at Lake Balkhash?"

"Yes, and on the other side of Lake Balkhash is a city called Balkhash. In Balkhash are my docks. Park the boat at the docks and get out of the city as soon as possible. People in Balkhash will probably not be looking for you, but don't take any chances."

"Oh boy." Johnson sighed softly as he considered the task ahead of them. They needed to go six hundred miles through the middle of Kazakhstan without drawing any attention to themselves. A task he would not have found hard a week ago, but now things had changed. People used to ignore him, the American with shiny red hair and the funny accent, but now every time he opened his mouth, people would know he was American, and they would want him. The train they were on had been destroyed. *I was minutes away from being blown to bits.* A man had broken into their apartment and tried to kill them and then had blown up a house they were staying in. From what he heard, his picture was frequently being shown on TV along with the announcement that there was a reward for his capture, and word on the street was the Mafia's reward was much larger than the police reward and the Mafia didn't care if he was alive or dead. *What have I gotten myself into?*

"When do we leave?" Schofield asked Dima.

"Vasya will get the boat ready. You will leave at first light. I don't expect you to navigate the lake in the dark. We will gather some supplies and have them ready for you to leave in the morning. For now you must get some rest. I will give you a room to rest in for the night."

"What do we do when we get to the embassy?" Johnson asked.

"Your embassy will protect you from the Mafia and hopefully clear you as suspects in the bombing." Dima paused. "I suggest you pray to your God for help, because you are certainly going to need it. When we get to the house, it's off to bed with you. Let us prepare your supplies for the journey."

Johnson couldn't sleep. He tried, but there was too much noise coming from downstairs. It seemed like arguing, but it was too muffled for him to understand what the argument was about. Eventually he faded off to sleep.

* * *

Michael drove until he was at the burnt wreckage where the Americans were last seen. It was dark. The fire had burned itself out. There were several local police officers still around. He wondered where the team was that had been dispatched to investigate. They were not around.

He decided not much could be done tonight anyway, so he pulled away from the scene and leaned back in his seat back to catch some sleep before he started another busy day.

* * *

A knock on President Russell's door awoke him from a restless sleep. It was the conductor. President Russell opened the door.

"Good morning," the conductor said with a smile.

"Good morning," President Russell responded.

"How important is it that you get into Kazakhstan?" the conductor asked.

"Very important."

"How much money do you have?"

"What?"

"Like I told you before, the borders are closed. They are going to allow this train to come in because I have several cars on the back with supplies, but all the people need to get off at Chelyabinsk. I am to drive the train in alone. I have a place where you can hide until we are in Astana, but it will cost you."

"I have roughly two hundred American dollars." President Russell pulled his money clip out of his wallet.

"That will do." The conductor snatched it away from him and put it in his pocket.

"Come with me." He turned to walk away.

President Russell followed him toward the conductor's cabin.

"We must move quickly. We are nearing the border. Everyone except me is to leave the train now. I am supposed to continue on alone to Astana. You must hide in my cabin until we have safely reached Astana."

"Isn't there some other way to get into Kazakhstan?"

"No, all the borders are closed. Nobody is going into Kazakhstan except a choice few. This really is the only way you are going to get into Kazakhstan anytime soon."

"Where will I hide?" President Russell asked.

"You'll see," the conductor commented and hurried his pace. "I am taking a great risk in getting you into Kazakhstan. If we're discovered, there could be grave consequences."

He opened the door to his cabin and walked in, closing the door behind President Russell. He turned to his bed, which sat atop a row of drawers. He opened all the doors as far as they would go and removed his mattress. Underneath the bed and the drawers was a small compartment. There wasn't much room except to lie down.

"In you go," the conductor ordered.

"Now?" President Russell protested.

"They will be searching the train for passengers soon. You

must hide now or they will find you and remove you from the train, or worse."

"How long until we reach Astana?" President Russell asked.

"Probably four or five hours. You'll be fine in there, I promise." He looked President Russell in the eyes.

President Russell reluctantly climbed under the bed and into the small compartment under the drawers. It wasn't much larger than a coffin. And it certainly felt like one.

"There is a switch on the side," the conductor said, pointing into the compartment. "It will turn on a light so you can see. I am sorry it will be uncomfortable for a while, but it really is the only way into the country." He paused for a moment and then asked, "Why is it you want to go back?"

"I have a responsibility. Two of my friends there need my help. I cannot abandon them."

"That is very noble of you. I will let you out as soon as I can."

"Thank you," President Russell said to the man as he covered the bed, and closed the drawers under the bed. President Russell turned on the light for a moment. It was a dim light, just enough to see around the small box. He checked his watch. 2:30 a.m. He turned off the light and closed his eyes, trying to get some sleep.

TWELVE

Elder Schofield woke from his restless sleep as the first morning light began to peek over the horizon.

Both elders quickly arose from their beds, stumbled out of the room, and down the stairs. The spacious house seemed empty without the crowd from the night before. Only a handful of people remained. In all the confusion, Schofield couldn't remember who exactly they were, but he suspected they were Dima's family. They fed the elders a hearty breakfast of potatoes and eggs. Both ate like they hadn't eaten in days, knowing that the next few days could be hunger filled.

They wished those in the house good-bye and good luck and headed for the dock. There Dima's very fast fishing boat was loaded with supplies. Yuri sat at the wheel and Mila in the seat next to him.

"What is this?" Schofield asked Dima, who was leading them to the boat.

"Against my wishes and better judgment, both Yuri and Ludmilla are going to accompany you to Astana."

"That's great!" Johnson exclaimed, climbing into the boat.

"No, it's not," Schofield stated. Turning to Mila and Yuri, he continued, "You are putting your lives in great danger by accompanying us. They have already tried to kill us twice. I don't think you should come."

"We could sit here and argue all day, but the fact is we are going to escort you to Astana and there is nothing you can say or do that is going to change that. So get in the boat and let's get going before the day is gone," Mila said.

Schofield could see he wouldn't win this argument so he turned to Dima. "Thank you," he said, shaking his hand. "I hope to meet you again under more favorable circumstances."

"And I you." Dima patted him on the back.

"All the way to Astana?" Elder Schofield asked Yuri and Mila as he climbed into the boat.

"All the way." Mila smiled.

"We could not abandon you. That would be the same as betraying you. We will help you until you are safely within the walls of your embassy," Yuri assured them.

"Thank you." Schofield was glad they were coming. It was a long way to Astana. It would be nice to have someone who knew the country better than he did.

"Shall we be on our way then?" Yuri asked.

"Thank you!" Schofield said to Dima and waved.

He sat down and watched as the dock slowly faded in the distance.

"Wait! Stop!" Schofield yelled frantically.

Everyone looked at him, and Yuri eased back on the throttle, slowing the boat to an idle.

"What is it?" Yuri asked.

"We need to pray," Schofield stated. "Every time I start a long journey, I begin it with a prayer that I might have a safe journey. We need to start this journey with a prayer."

"Yes," Johnson quickly agreed. "Would you like me to say it?"

"No, I will," Schofield answered. He looked at Yuri, who stopped the boat. He copied the elders by folding his arms and kneeling in the bottom of the boat.

"Heavenly Father, thank you for guiding us to these great people." Schofield was always uncomfortable praying about people when they could hear it. He did it anyways but it was a little embarrassing. "Please protect us as we embark on this journey. Help us to reach our destination." He remembered the inspiration that he had received to go to Astana, and now Dima had told him that would be the safest place in the country for them. "Please bless Yuri and Mila that they might feel Thy love for them and that they might have Thy blessings and joy." He asked again for guidance and protection before closing. Both Mila and Yuri turned to Schofield.

He simply nodded and pointed his arm to the north.

"Let's go."

Yuri pulled back on the throttle and soon they were cruising on the lake, heading north toward the city of Balkhash.

Schofield pulled out the only copy of the Book of Mormon they had managed to keep and began reading silently to himself.

* * *

The lake was huge and all they could see in front or behind was water. Off to the sides, Schofield could still see land in the distance. It was nearly a hundred miles from where they left to Balkhash, so they would be on the lake for several hours.

"So tell me about yourself," Mila asked Schofield. "What do you like to do?"

"Well . . . ," Schofield started slowly, setting the Book of Mormon on his lap. "My favorite thing to do is to play soccer. I've played since I was a little kid. I played in high school. I could have played in college. I was offered several scholarships, but I turned them down to do something more important."

"What's that?" Mila asked.

"This." He held his arms up high. "To come on a mission. The gospel is absolutely the most important thing in life, and I need to share it with everyone I can."

"So you gave up a lot to come here?"

"Yes and no. I gave up a lot, but I am getting so much more in return. It is well worth the trade."

"So how much does your church pay you to come here? If it's not a secret."

"They don't pay me." Schofield smiled. "I paid for most of it myself and my mom helps out."

"You pay to be a missionary?"

"Yes, I do." Schofield said.

"Do you enjoy being a missionary, Johnson?" Mila asked.

"Absolutely. It is the greatest experience of my life," Johnson answered.

"What is so good about it?"

"For one, I traveled halfway around the word to this wonderful country of Kazakhstan. The people here are great. I'm helping people change their lives for the better. There is no better cause than helping other people."

"How do you change people's lives for the better?" Yuri asked from the front of the boat.

"I share with them the gospel and help them to believe it is true, and the gospel changes their lives. It brings them joy," Schofield said.

"How can a belief in something bring you joy?" Mila asked.

"It gives them purpose in life. They know why they are here on this earth, why things happen the way they do," Johnson answered.

"Are you saying there is an actual purpose for us being here on earth and it's not just an existence?" Mila asked.

"Yes. Earth life is an important part of God's plan of happiness. Our life here has great meaning. It is a test to see if we are worthy to go back and live with our Father in Heaven," Schofield said.

"So this life is just a test?" Mila asked.

"Yes, but there is so much more to it," Schofield said.

"Are we supposed to be happy during this test? Because it seems to me most of the world is suffering and certainly not happy," Yuri said

"Most of the world doesn't have the gospel either. There are more than six billion people in the world and only fifteen million members of the Church. It is not enough. That is why I came on a mission for two full years. I share the gospel full time. That is all I do," Schofield said.

"When you are not running from the Mafia and the police," Mila joked, smiling at him.

"Yeah." Schofield smiled and realized he was far too comfortable joking with Mila.

* * *

Michael Ivanov awoke and climbed out of his car. He stretched his sore muscles. Sleeping in the car was certainly not the most comfortable thing in the world, but sleep in the car was better than no sleep at all.

He looked back at the place that used to be a group of houses. There was nothing left but smoldering ashes. There were several investigators at the scene gathering evidence and talking to people. He walked over and asked for the lead investigator.

"What do you have so far?" Michael showed his badge to them. He didn't recognize the investigators.

The lead investigator recognized him immediately and quickly explained what they had discovered so far.

"The houses were destroyed by the same type of incendiary device that was used to destroy the train in Almaty. We are not sure who did it; only a few people would have the access and finances for such a device. They must have wanted this area destroyed pretty bad to use such an expensive bomb."

"Or they are trying to send a message," Michael suggested.

"Perhaps."

"What have you gotten from the witnesses?"

"Two black SUVs pulled up and spent several minutes in the house. They came out with two suits, like dress suits. One SUV left and then two minutes later the other left and then the explosion."

"Were the SUVs government?"

"No, I've checked that. We suspect a Mafia connection, but we've got no connection to them or this house. I don't know why they would destroy this house . . . or these houses, rather. We are curious about the suits. That was the only thing removed from the house before it was destroyed."

"Thank you," Michael Ivanov said and shook the man's hand.

The elders wore black suits. Perhaps it was their suits. *If that's true, where are the Americans now?* They were not in the house. There were no fatalities in this explosion, amazingly.

He walked the perimeter of the blast zone, and then stepped carefully into the site, examining the ground. The house that had stood here was completely obliterated in the blast. Some of the other houses had retained bits of bricks and frames. It was a far larger bomb than would have been needed to destroy this house. *Why use such a large device?* He knelt and examined some of the residue. The lab would get him proper results soon enough, but that would just confirm what he already knew. It was a similar, but smaller incendiary device.

Michael walked back to his car to collect his thoughts and sort out his next move.

* * *

President Russell lay silently in the compartment under the conductor's bed. It had been several hours. His legs were beginning to cramp. His back ached. He really needed to get out soon. It had been an hour since he heard any movement in the conductor's cabin. He was tempted to try and climb out.

Footsteps softly approached and stopped. He saw the drawers above his head slowly slide out and then the bed lifted up. The conductor peered over the edge with one finger to his lips. He motioned for President Russell to follow him. President Russell slowly climbed out of the crypt he had been trapped in for what seemed like an eternity. His legs and back creaked with each labored movement. He stood by the bed and stretched.

The conductor closed up the secret compartment and gave President Russell a conductor's outfit to wear.

"My name is Lev," the conductor said as he handed President Russell the suit.

"President Russell."

"The train station is barren. They will question you in a suit. We will quickly leave the station. You follow me. If anyone stops us, let me do the talking. Do you understand?" he whispered softly.

"Yes," President Russell whispered, his throat parched, and nodded. He quickly slipped the conductors overalls on over his suit and put the hat on his head. The clothes weren't a perfect fit, but they would do. President Russell had to take off his tie and fold down his collar to hide it under his conductor suit.

He followed Lev out of the cabin, down some stairs, and out of the train onto the platform. The conductor carried a small duffel bag in his hand. They turned right and quickly walked toward a set of stairs and a walkway that led over the tracks and out of the train yard.

The conductor put his foot on the first step when a security guard yelled stop. President Russell turned to see not a security guard but a policeman standing on an adjacent platform, his AK-47 assault rifle in his hands. President Russell's heart skipped a beat and then raced away.

"We were just gathering some things from my cabin." The

conductor turned to the policeman holding up his bag so the guard could see it.

"Who gave you permission?" the police officer demanded.

"I brought the train in earlier and forgot some things. I had to come back for them."

"Throw me the bag," called the officer.

"It's just my personal effects."

"Throw me the bag." With one arm, he swung the rifle toward Lev and President Russell.

Lev tossed the bag across the tracks to the police officer.

The officer caught the bag. He slung his rifle over his shoulder and rummaged through the bag before zipping it back up. He tossed it back to the conductor, who caught it by the handle.

"Get out of here." He motioned with his rifle to the stairs and the walkway. "And don't come back until you have permission."

President Russell followed the conductor along the walkway, which went over the tracks until it came down on the other side of a fence outside the train station. They walked some way in silence.

"Thank you," President Russell told Lev.

The conductor stopped and looked at him.

"You are the most polite man I have ever met." He pulled the money he had taken from President Russell and handed it back to him. "Thank you."

"No, you keep it," President Russell said, gently pushing his hand away. "You have helped me immensely. Thank you."

"Where are you going?" Lev asked him.

"I have an apartment not far from here. I'll first go there."

"Do you need help with anything?"

"No, you have helped enough already."

"Good luck to you."

"Thank you."

The conductor turned to leave, paused, and then turned back.

"You should lose the outfit." He pointed to the conductor's overalls. "And lose the suit too. There won't be too many people out and about and even fewer wearing suits."

"Thanks for the advice."

President Russell slipped out of the conductor clothes and handed them to the conductor. He took them, shook them out, and stuffed them in his bag."

"Thank you." President Russell shook his hand, turned, and walked away toward downtown.

* * *

Michael Ivanov sat in his car, considering his options. The two Americans had been here, of that he was certain. He was also certain they had nothing to do with the train bombing, but this new bombing confused him. He could not figure out why it had happened. There were no casualties, little potential for casualties. Not like the train bombing or the many bus bombings that had happened across the country since the train bombing.

The elders were somehow connected to the train bombing and this bombing, but his instincts told him they were not responsible for either. His experience as a top detective would not let him exclude them, but he felt they were not to blame. The perpetrator was someone else. Someone he would let his team catch. He needed to find the Americans.

The questions now were what were they doing here at Lake Balkhash and where had they gone from here? He really didn't know. He had no gut feeling like he normally did. He could usually feel where the men he was chasing were going, he could guess ahead, but instead he was drawing a blank.

This wasn't at all like his normal investigations, where he

followed hunch after hunch until he captured them. He leaned his chair back and closed his eyes for a moment.

The only thing that came to his mind was to read the Book of Mormon. He sat for a while longer and the thought came back stronger. *Read the Book of Mormon.* He opened to the book of Ether and began reading.

THIRTEEN

After nearly three hours, the city of Balkhash loomed on the horizon. Smokestacks from the copper smelters dotted the horizon. The closer they got to the city, the more the lake took on an orange hue from the waste produced at the smelters. Docks lined the shore with all types of boats—some small, some large, some fishing, and some recreation. Most boats needed to go quite a ways from the city to catch any fish.

Johnson fidgeted nervously as Yuri pulled the boat up to the docks. Yuri said he had been in Balkhash several times before, usually for supplies.

Johnson noticed Schofield was looking a little scruffy. Neither had been able to shave in two days. They hoped this would help them go unrecognized.

"Are you ready?" Yuri asked nervously, looking back at the elders.

"Ready or not, here we are," Schofield stated.

Johnson was sweating, his nerves making him sick. He had never been in trouble like this.

"Are you okay?" Schofield asked.

"Not really." Johnson held his stomach and shook his head.

"Stomachache?"

"No, just nerves."

"I know how you feel," Schofield comforted him. "Every time before a soccer game, small or large, I would get really nauseated and my stomach would ache. Sometimes I thought I couldn't take it, but I just sucked it in and played. As soon as the game was on, the nerves went away and I was fine.

"As soon as we step off this boat, the game is on. I need you to keep your wits about you. It's going to be nerve wracking, thinking anyone and everyone could come after us, but if we stay calm and do what the Spirit tells us, we'll be fine." Schofield patted Johnson on the back. Okay?"

"Okay." Johnson's voice creaked.

"Here we go," Yuri said softly as he pulled up to the dock. Mila jumped out and tied the boat to the dock. She ran up to pay the docking fee as the others got their equipment together.

Yuri, Johnson, and Schofield put on backpacks of supplies that Dima had provided. Yuri held Mila's backpack in his hand and stepped out of the boat.

"Game on," Johnson whispered as he stepped onto the dock.

They quickly, but not quickly enough to draw attention to themselves, walked up to the tollbooth where Mila was just finishing paying for parking at the dock. Vasya would be by later to pick up the boat.

They headed off the dock into the crowded city. The area next to the dock was largely industrial, many factories and copper smelters. They saw a bus leaving the dock and heading downtown.

They had just missed it. Johnson picked up a rock and threw it at a sign on the side of the road, wanting to scream in frustration. They walked over to the bus stop to wait. They didn't know what they were going to do, but they knew they didn't want to be at the dock all day. It was a long ways from the dock to the main part of Balkhash and the only way there was to walk or take the bus.

Johnson looked around the bus stop at all the signs posted. There he saw a large poster with a picture of him and Schofield on it, obviously taken from the security footage at the Almaty train station. The picture was a little bit grainy, but it was clearly them. Johnson whimpered.

"What is it?" Schofield asked. Johnson nodded toward the board and the wanted poster.

They all came over and looked at the board.

Johnson knew he was wanted by the police for questioning and wanted dead by the Mafia and sometimes both were the same thing, but now that he saw his own wanted poster, the reality sunk in. His eyes wandered to the bottom where the reward offered was approximately ten thousand US dollars—a very, very large amount of money for most people in Kazakhstan.

The realization of how hard it was going to be to get to Astana unnoticed hit him like a fist in the face. He closed his eyes and took a deep breath. If there were wanted posters on this obscure bus stop, then they were all over the country, and everyone who saw him had the chance to identify him and turn him in for a massive reward.

His head began to swim, and he had to put his arm on the bus stop wall for support. He slowly shook his head back and forth.

"What are we going to do?" Johnson asked, turning to face the others.

"We are going to move fast," Schofield started. "Don't look anyone in the eyes. Don't draw any attention to yourself. Most people just go about their business and don't worry about anyone else. If we don't draw any attention to ourselves we'll be fine."

"That's easy for you to say. You could probably pass for a Kazakh. Look at me. I'm a redhead. I'm certainly not from around here. Even with this hat Dima gave me." He took the hat off and waved it around before placing it back on his head. "They're going to spot me for sure. My face is covered in freckles." He pointed at his face.

"Think positive," Mila interjected. "You'll be fine. You said you had work here to do still. You have to finish your mission."

"Let's go," Yuri ordered, motioning for them to follow him.

They walked away from the bus stop, away from the wanted sign that had caused Johnson so much grief. It was a long walk, but there was no telling how long the next bus was going to be. Johnson shook the sweat from his hands, trying to wipe from his mind the image of the wanted poster and thousands of people who wanted the reward chasing after him. He imagined a man with a gun at every intersection stepping out and ordering him to the ground.

They walked briskly along the road, which had little traffic for nearly an hour. Yuri made the right call. There had been no sign of a bus going in either direction.

The sun beat down on them as they trudged toward the city, center and hopefully a way to get to Astana.

A dark blue Eurovan pulled up beside them.

"Good morning," the driver called out. "Where are you heading?"

"To the city center," Yuri replied.

"Climb on in," the driver offered. "I'm going right past there. I'll drop you off."

"Thank you," Yuri replied, clearly deciding to take the ride.

He and Mila climbed in, followed by Johnson and Schofield, who sat in the back with their backpacks on their laps.

"How much is this going to cost us?" Johnson whispered to Schofield.

"Less than a taxi." Schofield chuckled. "And it beats walking."

"Where are you from?" the driver asked as he pulled out into the street.

"We live across the lake. We are traveling to Astana to see my grandmother," Mila answered. "She is very ill. She'll probably not live much longer."

"Well, good luck getting to Astana. Few trains are still

running and most of the bus drivers are afraid to drive. Too many bombings. There haven't been any here in Balkhash, and I don't think there will be, but people are scared."

"You said there are still trains going to Astana?"

"Yes, just cargo trains. But for the right price you might be able to buy yourself a spot on one."

"Who would we talk to arrange such passage?" Yuri asked. Everyone else remained entirely quiet.

"I could help you."

"You can help?"

"My brother is leaving tomorrow on a cargo train to Karaganda. For the right price I am sure he would allow you to ride along. It may not be the most comfortable ride, but at this point, it will be the fastest."

"This train leaves tomorrow?"

"Yes, tomorrow morning. The train will depart early, but you would need to be on the train even earlier to avoid detection. You wouldn't want to get caught stowing away on a cargo train. If you're interested, meet me at the Bazaar at 2:00 p.m. near the fish racks."

"Thank you," Yuri replied.

"Where do you want to be dropped off?" the driver asked as they approached city center.

"Anywhere here is good," Yuri said, pointing to the sidewalk. They were now in the busy part of town. Shops and kiosks lined the street. A couple blocks away, the bustling market teemed with life.

"Here you go." The driver pulled over to the side of the street. Everyone climbed out of the van.

"Hey!" the driver called out. "Remember, two o'clock!"

Yuri nodded his head in understanding and turned away. Johnson checked his watch. It was nearly 10:00 a.m.

The driver drove past the bazaar and continued on until out of sight.

"What now?" Johnson asked Schofield quietly. "What do you think of that guy?"

"What do you mean?"

"You think we can take a train? That seems like the easiest way there. Cars are stopped at roadblocks and buses aren't really running. A cargo train might not be a bad way to go."

"I'm not sure if I trust him," Schofield stated.

"Why not?" Johnson asked.

"Why would he help us like that?"

"He did say, 'for the right price.' It will probably be very expensive, not that I care at this point."

"Good point," Schofield conceded.

"What do you think, Yuri?" Johnson asked.

"I think it is probably safe. He and his brother probably do it all the time. I have heard of people doing this before. Charging people on the side and sneaking them in. It is not any more uncommon than me renting out my bus as a large taxi. They are likely going to charge extra under the circumstances, but we won't know until later. We can't know for certain."

"But is it safe?" Johnson asked again, mostly to himself.

"First things first," Yuri said. "We need to find out what is going on around the country."

* * *

Michael Ivanov finished the Book of Mormon. He turned to the inside of the back cover. There was a piece of paper glued into the seam. It was a picture of Elder Johnson and his testimony of the Book of Mormon. Following his testimony, he quoted the scriptures in Moroni and issued a challenge to take Moroni's advice to pray about the Book of Mormon and ask God if it was true.

"I promise you," Johnson began. "If you really want to know if this book is true, ask God. And He will testify to you by the power of the Holy Ghost that it is true."

Could it be that simple? Michael thought. *Just ask God, and He will answer?* He looked around as if someone were watching. He felt silly even entertaining the idea of kneeling down and praying to ask God if the book was true. How would God tell him the book was true? Did he even believe in God? He never really had before. Sure, he had gone to church when he was a youth, but did that mean he believed? Should he try praying? Did he even know how to pray? God doesn't speak to regular people. *Why would He speak to me? Johnson promised me He would. Do I believe Johnson? God will reveal it by the power of the Holy Ghost. How does the Holy Ghost reveal it?*

He needed to pray. He wasn't sure he knew how, but he knew he had to. He needed to know if the book was true. The country was collapsing into civil war and he should be helping to stop it, but he needed to know if this book was true.

He looked for a good place to pray. Off in the distance he could see a group of trees. A nice secluded place to kneel and ask God about the Book of Mormon.

He slowly pulled the car forward until he was near the trees. He opened the door, and with Book of Mormon in hand, he walked slowly toward the trees. He followed a dirt path for a few yards into a small clearing. He looked around. He was alone.

He knelt in the center of the clearing. He held the book in his hand. He had never prayed before. He didn't know what he was doing. He remembered from the elders' lesson that Joseph Smith had knelt to pray and gotten his answer. Michael hoped it wouldn't be as dramatic an answer as that. He wasn't sure he could handle a visitation from heavenly beings. Nervously looking around again to make sure he was still alone, he began to pour his soul out to the Lord.

"Father," he began, "I don't know if you can hear me, but I believe you can. I met some men and they gave me a book. The Book of Mormon. I read the book." The more he talked the more comfortable he became. "In the back of the book there is a promise.

A promise that if I ask you if the book is true, you will tell me it is true through the power of the Holy Ghost." He paused and waited for a moment, not sure what to expect. He felt in his heart the same feeling he had felt when he read the book. Warmth was the only way he could describe it. He decided to continue praying, although he wasn't sure what more he should pray about. He had asked his main question. He knew he needed to continue talking to God. He wanted that feeling to continue for a while, and so he thanked God for allowing him to meet the missionaries. And then the more he talked, the more came to his mind. There was so much he wanted to say. He felt as if he was talking to an old friend. It was different, yet very pleasant. He had so much to say and so many questions. He excitedly talked to the Lord. He knew the Lord was listening and would answer him. A feeling of incredible peace came over him, and Michael prayed more fervently.

He didn't know how long he had prayed. He prayed until his heart was full. He prayed until he knew with a certainty that the Book of Mormon was true. It was a work of God. He felt it in his heart, a feeling so strong, like he had never before felt. The Holy Ghost brought to his understanding that the Book of Mormon was true and he needed to follow its precepts. It was like he had sat in a dark room and now there was light from all sides. It was so clear now. He needed to be baptized into that church.

He knelt in the lush green clearing until his legs ached and cramped. He shifted position and sat a while longer until his back ached. Then he lay looking at the glorious blue sky, with the occasional white cloud drifting by. He imagined he could see images of the Book of Mormon depicted in the clouds. He wanted to stay there to enjoy that feeling forever. He had never felt so good. He realized it was the Holy Ghost, and he never wanted the feeling to leave.

FOURTEEN

Schofield stood next to Johnson outside an electronics shop, watching a TV news broadcast. They watched in stunned silence. "The US State Department has recommended the immediate evacuation of all American citizens. The embassy will be evacuating within three days," the newscaster announced.

"Good riddance," a passerby yelled at the TV, and Johnson winced, trying to hide his face.

"As violence and civil unrest continues to escalate, more and more violence is focusing on foreigners. The US State Department has determined it is no longer safe for Americans to be in the country. The embassy in Astana will be evacuated. All Americans are encouraged to leave the country. Those needing assistance can come to the embassy as long as the doors are open and get help evacuating, but they encourage a swift departure. The embassy will finish evacuating within three days."

"We need to get to Astana now," Johnson said softly. "Should we take the train in the morning?"

"I don't think we have much of a choice," Schofield said, wishing there was another way. "If we can get to the embassy, we can get out of the country safely. If we don't, we would have to ride this out, however long it took. Based on what I just saw, that is not something I want to do."

"Riots have broken out across the country," the reporter stated. "Hundreds of smaller bombings have occurred since the initial bombing in Almaty." The TV displayed images of rioting and the aftermath of bombs across the countryside. "The police are being overrun in numerous cities. General Shevchenko has enacted martial law to try to regain control of the country. A countrywide curfew was issued prohibiting everyone except military and law enforcement personnel from being outside their homes from dusk till dawn. No exceptions.

"I am confident," the reporter continued, "that General Shevchenko will have everything under control in just a few days, but hundreds of fires are still burning uncontrolled. And there are riots and looting and greater violence in Almaty, and especially Astana. It will take a little longer there. But I have great confidence in our armed forces to restore order." He said it like he believed it, but Schofield was not so sure he believed him.

They needed to go to the city where there was the greatest violence, the city where people were now rioting for the sake of rioting with no purpose at all except to cause mayhem. They needed to go to the center of the madness, to the one place in the country where they might find safety. And they had two days to get there before the embassy was evacuated. They were stuck in the middle of a violent civil war.

Chills ran up Schofield's back as he thought of the terrifying prospect of being trapped here. He was a foreigner in the middle of a civil war. A prime target and a wanted man by both sides of the law. Why? He didn't know, but he knew he would probably not live if he was caught by either side. He had to stay safe. He had to get to Astana and out of the country he had grown to love—a country that was quickly being overrun by madness.

"We need to get on that train," Schofield stated.

"Do you trust this man?" Yuri commented.

"Do we have a choice? If we're not in Astana by tomorrow or the next day, we may be stuck here. And I'm not a big fan of being stuck in a country where I'm wanted by the Mafia."

"Not to mention the police," Johnson added.

"I would hope I would be treated fairly by the police and exonerated, but right now that is not a risk I'm willing to take. They could turn us over to the Mafia for the reward, or they could kill us and blame the bombing on us to try and stop the chaos. Even if they were good cops, we would be in with criminals, criminals who would love to have a large reward waiting for them upon their release," Schofield said.

"We can't take a car or a bus. It's way too far to walk. The only real option we have is that train," Johnson said.

"Why would he just offer us a ride on his brother's train?" Schofield asked.

"For the money," Mila answered.

"It will probably cost us two hundred dollars. That's a lot of money here. That will keep food on his table for months. That's all the reason he needs. Hopefully he didn't recognize us. I'm going to have faith that he didn't and that God is providing us a way to safety," Schofield said.

"Whether we like the idea or not," Yuri started. "We don't have a lot of choice. We need to get there quickly and that seems like the only way."

"So it's settled then?" Mila asked.

"Yes," Yuri, Schofield, and Johnson said in unison.

They stood silently for a moment.

"Let's eat," Johnson suggested.

"Yes, let's," Schofield agreed. "I'm hungry and I may not be in Kazakhstan much longer. Let's have a good Kazakh meal before we go."

"I know a good place that's just down the street from here. We could get a private room and dine in peace," Yuri suggested.

"That sounds great," Schofield said.

They followed Yuri down several side streets and along several blocks before coming to a small restaurant called Obolon.

The restaurant was actually owned by a Ukrainian who now lived in Kazakhstan. He named the restaurant after his neighborhood in Kiev. Although the owner was Ukrainian, the menu was strictly Kazakh.

"Here we are," Yuri stated, pointing to the small building. The name, in large block letters, hung on the side of the white building. It looked run down, but Yuri assured them the food was some of the best around.

Yuri opened the large wooden door and held it open as the others walked into the restaurant. The smell of cooking meat washed over them as the air rushed out the open door. A large rotund woman with a filthy white apron approached.

"Four?" she asked.

"Yes, please," Yuri responded.

She turned and walked away assuming the others would follow her.

They were seated in a booth in the back corner of the restaurant. The waitress would not give them a private room. She claimed they were all reserved, although the restaurant was nearly empty.

* * *

They were soon enjoying some of the best food they had had in a very long time. The mood turned jovial for Mila, Yuri, and Schofield. Johnson was painfully quiet. He could only talk when the waitress was not around and then he needed to talk in a whisper. They didn't want any undue attention, and Johnson's accent would certainly mark him as a foreigner. There weren't many western foreigners in Balkhash.

Johnson wished to join in the laughter and joke telling, but his Russian was poor. He understood and spoke the language well enough, but his accent was very pronounced. He had tried to work on it, and it was actually better, but it was still painfully pronounced.

Johnson sat looking at his hands in his lap as Schofield ordered his food for him. After the waitress left, he looked back up and joined the conversation in a whisper, but still with the long Texas drawl. Mila spent most of the meal trying to coach him on pronunciation. She was trying to help, but it only served to make him feel worse.

He got frustrated when he had to repeat himself several times. He had gotten fairly comfortable with his language skills, and when his self-conscious attitude was gone, he spoke better when he didn't try so hard, but now he was back to square one. Everyone was so critical of his Russian and his accent. It hurt.

He knew it was for the best if nobody recognized them as foreigners, but it still hurt that he couldn't join in the conversation and enjoy a few minutes before they were on the run again.

They ate and talked for more than an hour. Yuri was right. The food was fantastic. The waitress was not the friendliest, but they weren't really concerned with service. They just wanted to eat and relax for a while. The road ahead would be a treacherous one.

* * *

"We should be going soon." Schofield pointed to the clock. "It's almost 1:30. We need to be at the bazaar by 2:00 if we're going to meet this guy."

"Yes, yes," Yuri agreed.

"What's our game plan?" Schofield asked.

"What is our game plan?" Yuri repeated, confused.

"Yes, our plan for this meeting."

"I don't know," Yuri stated. "I guess we'll figure it out as we go."

Yuri paid the bill, and they headed toward the large wooden double doors they had entered through.

A large bald man with a short black goatee sprinkled with

gray wearing a sports coat and sweatpants walked through the door. Behind him on either side were other men who weren't as large, but certainly just as menacing. One didn't have a neck—his head just seemed to sit on top of his broad shoulders—and the other wore his long brown hair in a ponytail that reached his shoulder blades.

"That's them, Igor!" the waitress called out. "I saw them on TV."

"That's good. You did good, Masha," Igor said as he walked forward. "You did real good." He looked at Schofield and Johnson.

"You two are going to make me rich."

"You must have us confused with someone else," Schofield said in perfect Russian.

Igor wrinkled his nose.

Schofield was doing his best Ukrainian accent. There was no way this guy should confuse him for an American.

"You two look too much like them. I'll let Vita decide. Let's go." He motioned to his two thugs.

They walked around Igor, punching their fists together as they slowly came toward the elders.

"We're not who you think we are," Schofield pleaded, holding his hands up as if that would hold them back.

"You speak Russian very well for an American," Igor stated.

"Why do you think I'm an American?" Schofield asked.

"You are wanted by the police. I've seen your picture on TV. They are offering a big reward."

"You must have us confused with someone else," Schofield repeated.

"I don't think so."

"You don't want us." Schofield's voice wavered. He was clearly trying to think of a plan B. Reasoning with them was not working.

The two thugs had stopped their advance while Schofield and Igor argued, but Igor was not persuaded.

"The police are offering a huge reward, but Vita tells me he'll give me twice what they are offering. And that's not something I'm going to give up. Get them!"

Johnson's mind was turning. If they got caught, they would surely be killed. He had no choice. It was fight or flee. Or both.

He looked around at the others. His forehead was sweating profusely. His hands were shaking uncontrollably. Mila looked around nervously. Yuri just stood there. Calm.

"Wait!" Schofield yelled.

Everyone stopped and looked at him. He was taking off his backpack.

"I can prove it. Hold on." He held his backpack out in front of him. "Hold on," he pleaded again as the two thugs inched closer.

He opened the backpack and tossed it high in the air toward Igor.

Igor looked up at the backpack as it flew toward him, his hands reaching up to catch it. Schofield charged forward, ramming his shoulder into Igor's stomach. Igor fell to the floor with a crash, Schofield right on top of him. Igor gasped audibly, and Schofield rolled to his feet, grabbing the backpack.

"Run!" he yelled, looking back at the rest of the group for a moment.

Mila kicked the nearest thug in the groin and ran after Schofield. Schofield turned and ran out the large wooden double doors, Mila trailing right behind.

* * *

Johnson watched as Schofield tackled Igor. He turned to run from one of the thugs that was coming for him, but saw Yuri step in the way and head-butt him.

Johnson ran through the kitchen, knocking over a cart with pans, which clattered to the ground. He sped out the back door. He heard screaming behind him, so he kept on running.

* * *

Schofield sprinted for an alley just to the right of the restaurant. He hoped to get into the alley and out of sight before the thugs left the building. He ducked behind the restaurant and waited. Mila followed right behind and squatted behind him. Yuri burst out the door and sprinted straight ahead. One thug followed Yuri into the street ahead. Yuri slowly put distance between him and the thug. Igor came out of the door and watched them run down the street. He turned and looked around.

Schofield and Mila ducked behind the edge of the building, hoping Igor didn't see them.

The back door of the restaurant burst open, and Johnson raced down the street. A thug came out behind him, tripped, and fell to the ground.

He rolled to his feet and saw Mila and Schofield crouching behind the building. He looked back at Johnson, who was quickly distancing himself. He turned and ran toward the pair.

Mila screamed and ran down the street, Schofield following right behind her.

A gunshot rang out. The bullet hit a brick wall and the shrapnel sprayed Schofield as he turned and ducked behind a building. Mila ran with him. They ducked again behind another building, raced into the marketplace, and melted into the crowd.

FIFTEEN

Johnson ran as hard as he could. He glanced over his shoulder, hoping not to see the thug. He ran and ran until he thought his lungs were going to burst. His heart beat violently against his ribs. He stopped, gasping for air. A gunshot rang out, and he didn't know what to think. He hoped the thugs were shooting at him and not his friends, because he knew they hadn't hit him. He quickly checked himself to make sure.

They knew he was here in the city. He had to get out of the city, but how? How was he going to find Schofield and the others? The market. They would be meeting with the guy from the van at two o'clock. If they escaped capture. He was sure they had.

He was alone. Where was his companion? He needed his companion. *Oh no. What am I going to do? I can't be alone.* He hadn't been alone since the start of his mission months ago. *I'll be fine. I just need to find him.*

I need to be at the market at two, Johnson thought to himself. *I need some new clothes. They'll recognize these ones.*

He saw a little clothes shop just ahead. He walked in, still breathing heavy from his escape. It wasn't a fancy clothes store— just what he wanted. He picked out a dark green jacket, a black beanie, and some black pants. He didn't want to take the time to try them on. He hoped they fit. Just in case, he grabbed a belt. He set it all on the counter, still taking deep breaths.

"Did you find everything?" the cashier asked politely.

Johnson just nodded and pulled out his wallet, careful not to reveal his American money. He paid the woman the money and put the wallet away. The woman put the clothes in a bag.

"Have a nice day." She smiled and handed Johnson the bag.

"Thank you," Johnson said, replying with his long Texas drawl.

The woman cast him a curious look as he rushed out of the store, beating himself up inside for being so polite all the time.

Why couldn't you just stay quiet for two minutes? You had to open your mouth and give yourself away, he berated himself silently.

He found a public restroom and changed his clothes, putting the extra clothes in his backpack. The pants fit great, so he put the belt in his jacket pocket.

He knew nothing about Balkhash or where his friends would go. But he did know that at two they should be talking to the driver of the van at the fish stand in the marketplace. He hoped the meeting was taking place so they could get out of here and so he could find his friends

Johnson walked out of the restroom and looked around. He had no idea where he was or which way he had come from.

* * *

Schofield looked around and realized they had not only lost their pursuers, but they had lost Johnson and Yuri. He had lost his companion, the one person he was supposed to be with at all times. And he had lost him. *I'll find him.*

"Where are Papa and Johnson?" Mila asked, looking around.

"We'll find them," Schofield said. "But first we need new clothes. They'll be looking for me in these clothes."

"Come. I saw a shop over here." She reached out her hand and grabbed his. His already racing heart went faster.

He jerked his hand away. She looked at him curiously.

"Sorry," he said, shrugging. "Let's go."

She led him to a little kiosk that was selling jackets and hats. He bought a black leather jacket and a Spartak Moscow baseball cap. It was something he always thought amusing—soccer team logos on baseball hats. He threw the jacket on and set the cap on his head.

"What about you?" he asked Mila.

"They're not looking for me," Mila responded.

"They are now. You were with us at the restaurant. They'll be looking for all of us now."

He could see the shock and realization settle onto her like a heavy weight. The Kazakh underworld was now hunting her too.

"I'll take that," she said, pointing to a brown leather jacket and also a Spartak baseball cap. Schofield paid, and Mila put the jacket on and donned the hat, pulling her hair through the hole in the back and tipping the brim low to cover her eyes.

They thanked the shop owner and turned to walk away.

"Do you want a watch, sir?" a young man called to Schofield. "I have lots to choose from." He held up a handful of really nice knockoffs.

Schofield looked at the time on the watches. It was two o'clock. He checked his own watch.

"The driver," Schofield gasped. "We need to meet the driver by the fish right now. Let's go!" He led Mila through the crowded marketplace toward the fish stand. It was nearly five minutes after two when they got to the other side of the bazaar and the fish rack. The driver was not there.

"I hope he's running late," Schofield whispered to Mila.

They stood at the designated place and looked around cautiously. They needed to be seen but only by him. They couldn't see him anywhere.

"Where are Johnson and Papa?" Mila asked again.

"I don't know. I hope they think to meet us here. If not, I don't know what to do." Schofield looked around frantically, trying to find a familiar face in the crowd.

"Do you think they were caught?" Mila asked, her voice quivering.

"No," Schofield replied, trying to remain optimistic. "Johnson got away clean. The one chasing him came after us and your dad. I'm sure he got away."

"I hope," Mila whispered, softly wiping a tear from her eye.

At that moment Schofield realized that not only had he lost his companion, which was a huge violation of the rules, but he was also alone with a girl. He looked around the bazaar anxiously, searching for Elder Johnson.

* * *

President Russell approached the mission home. The normally busy neighborhood stood surprisingly barren. There were only a few cars on the streets and only a handful of people walking, and those people all seemed sad and distraught. He rounded a corner and looked up the street toward the mission home.

President Russell stopped and gaped. Just beyond the mission home, where a row of apartments used to stand, was nothing but a pile of ashes and rubble. For nearly a block on the other side of the mission home, everything was destroyed. On the street in front of one of the buildings sat the burnt remnants of a bus. The frame of the bus bent outward and was missing altogether in places. Several charred cars dotted the street.

The building next to the mission home was half standing and half a pile of bricks and mortar.

Across the street, the fronts of buildings had collapsed, while the backs still stood like used wooden torches.

President Russell stared for several long moments. He had never seen such destruction in person. It looked like the bus had been loaded with explosives and detonated. Why? Why destroy a bus in this neighborhood? The destruction made no sense to him. Such wanton destruction. Such a loss of innocent lives. What had these people done to deserve this? They had done nothing. Looking around, he was certain that many had died and those that hadn't died lost everything. There was nothing left in those buildings but memories. President Russell thought for a moment about the suffering. He couldn't ease the people's burden. He couldn't take away their loss and suffering.

But maybe he could.

He could teach them the gospel of Jesus Christ. He could teach them of the sacrifice Christ made for them, that He took their suffering and sorrow upon Himself, that they could lay upon Him their burdens, and He would ease them. He longed to help them. What a receptive people. They had lost everything and been brought to the depths of humility by a wanton act of violence.

He noticed some people going through the rubble and thought about approaching them, but he couldn't. He had been commanded by the prophet of God to get his missionaries out of the country. That was his goal at the moment. President Russell took a moment to pray that he would be able to return and help the people. He closed his eyes for a moment in honor of the fallen.

He pulled his mind from the destruction to the task at hand. He needed to find Elder Schofield and Elder Johnson and get out of the country.

He cautiously opened the front door of the mission home. It wasn't locked. He pushed the door in and looked around, worried that someone might be in the house. He thought of calling out but decided against it.

At first glance, it appeared that looters had taken everything. There was very little left in the apartment. President Russell had left a lot of things he really liked and wanted. He had hoped to see them again. It didn't look like that would be the case. He wandered around the apartment. The farther he got in, he started seeing cardboard boxes, full of his things, packed meticulously to prevent breaking. He opened a box and looked inside and found Sister Russell's stacking dolls. His house wasn't being looted. Someone was packing his things. He went up the back stairs. Stacks of boxes lined the walls, each box labeled with a list of its contents. Some of his furniture had been dismantled and stacked ready for moving.

Voices echoed up from the front room—jovial voices and laughter. He couldn't tell what they were saying; they were too muffled. One was familiar though. That voice. He recognized that voice. It was soft, but he knew it.

Sergei! I asked him to watch the place, not to clean it out. President Russell was angry. He crept over to the stairs and down a few steps so he could see what was going on. Sergei and Yevgenie carried his couch out the front door.

"Careful, Sergei," Yevgenie ordered. "Sister Russell loves this couch; she would not want it damaged."

"Yes, I know. I've been told many times to keep my feet off this couch." Sergei snickered. Sister Russell had become like a surrogate mother to him.

"I still don't get why we are cleaning out the president's house," Sergei stated.

"President Russell!" Yevgenie said, nearly dropping the couch.

They set the couch down and greeted the president.

"What are you doing here? You're supposed to be on your way to Moscow!" Sergei said.

"I came back for Elder Johnson and Elder Schofield. I couldn't leave them here alone." He looked around the packed up house. "What are you doing?"

"We're moving your stuff," Sergei answered.

"It's unsafe here," Yevgenie elaborated. "Especially with the house unoccupied. That bomb destroyed most of the block and now there is no power and won't be for days. And where there is darkness, there is hooliganism. I'm surprised it hasn't all been stolen already."

"Well, the police have been up here more lately," Sergei added.

"Yes, but that won't last long. We need to get all of your things moved to a safer location."

A knot tightened in President Russell's stomach. He had immediately suspected that Sergei was stealing his things. But Sergei was looking after his house, making sure no one would steal his things. President Russell felt guilty for not trusting Sergei.

"President Russell, you should not have come back," Yevgenie said.

"But I had to. I have elders here."

"You don't understand," Yevgenie said. "They're wanted by the police, and also by the Mafia."

"What?" President Russell did not doubt Yevgenie's statement. He always seemed to know what was going on. "Why the Mafia?"

"I don't know," Yevgenie stated. "But the reward from either group is a small fortune."

"All the more reason to find them," President Russell said.

"No, you need to get out of the country. Wait!" A look of confusion spread across Yevgenie's face. "How did you get back into the country?"

"That's not important. Why do I need to get out of the country?"

"The US Embassy has ordered all the Americans to evacuate the country. We're on the brink of civil war. Violence has escalated out of control since the bombing in Almaty. There have been hundreds of bombings since then. And rioting and looting. The military has been called up to restore peace. Soon the city will be crawling with tanks and soldiers. We have to get you to the embassy. It's the only place you'll be safe."

"What do you mean?" President Russell asked.

"Some of the media is blaming the bombing and the civil unrest on the United States."

"What?" President Russell was confused.

"They have video of Johnson and Schofield leaving the train station after the bombing. They were on the train itself right before the bombing. The police named them as persons of interest or suspects, and the media is running with it. Now they're saying that the Americans blew up the train to start a war so they can gain control of the country."

"That's crazy."

"I know it is crazy, but that is what people think. And so now all foreigners, particularly western foreigners, are targets of violence. If we don't get you to the embassy, you could be killed."

"Whoa." President Russell had no idea that all of this was happening. He didn't realize what a risk he had taken in returning to the country. He saw that he had no choice but to go to the embassy. Maybe he could help them from there.

"Do you understand?" Yevgenie asked.

"Yes. Can you drive me to the embassy?" President Russell asked.

"Yes, of course," Sergei answered.

"Okay." President Russell collapsed in a chair, resting his head in his hands.

* * *

Michael Ivanov awoke in the meadow. He didn't know how long he had lain there, but he didn't care. He now knew what he had to do. He needed to go to Astana, to the US embassy and wait for Elder Schofield and Elder Johnson. His instincts as a detective told him that was where they would go. It was the only safe place in the country. There they were assured safety and a fair trial. The US government took care of its people. The ambassador would make sure they were treated fairly.

His heart knew they would go there, but he feared that they might not make it. It was a long way to go. It was nearly five hundred miles from here to Astana, a long way to go for two men who were wanted by the police and the Mafia. He hoped they would make it, but he knew their chances were slim. He feared he had finally found something and he would lose it. If he didn't find the elders, it could be lost forever. *If they left, would I be able to join their church? I know a few people who are members of the Church, but I know so little about how it works. If I don't find them, I might never be able to join the church of God and have that joy the Book of Mormon promised.* The road to Astana could be treacherous. Based on newscasts, bandits and hooligans were causing trouble everywhere. He was certain he would be okay. After all, he was an officer of the law, but the Americans were a different story.

Even without his help, his anti-terror organization was the best at tracking and apprehending terrorists and criminals. Michael planned to keep getting updates from his office, but he had no intention of sharing any information he might find with them. He hoped to find the elders first. He had to find them first.

He checked in with his office to see if they had any new developments. There was nothing about the Americans.

"Thank you. Keep me posted." Michael closed his cell phone and started the long drive around Lake Balkhash toward Astana.

* * *

Sasha watched from the office as the tracking device in Michael's phone indicated that he was driving around Lake Balkhash to the north. He had mentioned nothing of that sort. All indications were that he was going to investigate the bombing by Lake Balkhash and then return to the office and guide the team from here. Yet now he was heading north. Did he know something they didn't? He was trying to keep all the glory for himself again.

"Not this time!" Sasha slammed his fist down on a table.

He called his younger brother, Andrei, who was one of the investigators at the scene and gave him the assignment of following Michael.

"Be careful not to be seen. I don't want him knowing we're following him. I think he knows something and is not sharing it with us. He wants to make the capture himself."

"Not a problem," Andrei said. He climbed into his car and turned on the navigation system. Immediately it began downloading Michael's information. And there on the map was a little flashing light indicating the location of Michael's phone.

* * *

Elder Johnson's heart beat rapidly. He was in a strange city and separated from his companion. For months he had always had someone with him and now he was utterly alone. To make matters worse, a thug had chased him, wanting to kill him. Now Elder Johnson was lost. He could be two or three miles from the market where he hoped Schofield and the others should be. They would still have to get to Astana from there, but at least they would be closer. At least they would be if he knew how to get to the market. But he couldn't even ask for directions. His accent would give him away for sure. He needed to stay discreet. After all, pretty much everyone in the country was looking for him.

He didn't know what to do. He had to get to the market, but all the streets looked the same. When he was running, he didn't have time to notice anything that might help him find his way. He looked around, desperately trying to recognize anything. Nothing looked familiar. He was lost and alone.

He closed his eyes and quietly asked God for help.

SIXTEEN

It was nearly 2:15 p.m. when the driver came out of his hiding place and approached Elder Schofield and Mila. He looked around nervously and then motioned them to follow him back into the little tent he had come out of. The tent was for the storage of fish and wasn't really big enough to hold them comfortably.

Schofield and Mila looked at each other. Both shrugged and slowly followed the driver past the stinking fish into the tent.

The man spoke softly. He didn't want to be heard.

"You've changed your appearance. I didn't recognize you."

"Sorry," Schofield apologized.

"It is okay. If I were in your position, I would change my appearance too."

"What do you mean?" Schofield asked.

"Will it just be the two of you?" the driver asked, ignoring Schofield's question.

"No," Schofield answered. "What do you mean if you were in our position?"

"If I was a fugitive, I would change my appearance too."

Schofield gasped as he realized the driver knew who he was.

"I have no love for the government," the driver continued. "I have no reason to turn you in. My family is poor and we could use the money, but I am a man of principles and I will not accuse and turn in an innocent man. And I believe you are innocent. Are you?" He stared at Schofield. "Can you look me in the eye and tell me you had nothing to do with the bombing?"

Schofield looked the man in the eyes. "I had nothing to do with the bombing."

The man held Schofield's gaze for a moment, took a deep breath, and said calmly, "I believe you. I have no more concerns for you, and you should not for me."

Schofield did believe him. He did not entirely understand him or his reasoning, but he did believe him.

"Just the two of you?" he asked again.

"No, all four of us," Schofield answered, feeling optimistic they would find Yuri and Elder Johnson.

"You need to be at the train station tonight at 2:00 a.m. The train leaves at 6:00, but the guards at the station change shifts at 2:00 and they usually talk a lot, which leaves at least a twenty-minute gap in security. Find train number 497. The third cargo hold from the rear will be open. Go in quietly. There will be a large crate. On the top is a hatch. Open it and climb in the crate. Wait there. My brother will check on you once the train is long out of Balkhash."

Mila and Schofield listened intently, trying to remember every detail.

"Where is the train station?" Schofield asked.

"You don't know where the train station is?"

"I've never been to Balkhash."

"Find a map. Enter from the north. There is a gap in the fence and the train is close by. Do not be late."

The man turned and quickly walked away with a handful of small fish.

Schofield thought it was odd that the driver had not asked for money. He turned to look at Mila. The whole encounter seemed strange, surreal almost. They were hunted in a strange town with a huge reward being offered for their capture, and a stranger offers to help them with nothing more than Schofield's word that he was innocent.

"Do you trust him?" Mila asked.

"I do. I don't know why, but I do trust him."

"So we will take the train then?"

"Yes. First we need to find Yuri and Elder Johnson, but I have no idea where to look."

"We should wait here," Mila suggested. "They both know that we were going to meet with the driver. Hopefully they will both think to meet us here."

"Okay," Schofield agreed. He looked around for a place to sit down. There was a bench nearby that would keep the meeting place in sight. They walked over and sat down on the bench. It was quite small and had just enough room for the two of them, but it did provide a great view of the fish market so they could watch for Johnson and Yuri.

Yuri showed up at the fish market just a few minutes later. Schofield waited on the bench as Mila ran up to greet him.

"Where is Johnson?" Yuri asked when they returned to the bench. Yuri too had changed his appearance.

"We don't know. We're hoping he'll come back here. This was the only place we all knew we were coming to. I hope he realizes he needs to come here," Schofield said.

"Yes, let's hope," Yuri agreed.

He sat on the bench next to Schofield and quietly retold his tale of the last hour and then listened to theirs. Schofield told him about the meeting with the driver.

They sat in silence on the bench, watching the crowd, hoping to spot Johnson. But there was no sign of him.

"What will they do if they catch him?" Mila wondered out loud.

"Stop," Yuri ordered. "We will not think that way."

"Look," Schofield said, pointing.

They saw the three thugs from the restaurant walk through the market.

"We need to go," Yuri ordered. He stood up and led them into the street behind the market.

* * *

Johnson probed his memory, trying to remember the way he had come and where he was going. Nothing. He looked around frantically, hoping to recognize something. It all looked the same. *Where am I? I'm lost. I am so lost.* He started walking. He hoped to find a bus stop with a map that could show him where the market was.

He didn't want to walk too fast and draw attention to himself, but wherever he was going he needed to do it quickly. Up ahead he saw a bus cross on a side street. His heart skipped a beat. Just what he was looking for. He jogged two blocks to the street he saw the bus on. There was a crowded bus stop just to his right. He walked over and looked for a map. Nothing.

A little old lady approached the bus stop with a huge bag of potatoes. *Is she going to the market or coming from the market?* A large man with massive shoulders carried a large sack of beets over his shoulder. A young woman had several fish on a string. *They might be going to the market. It is a little late, but better late than never.* A bus pulled up. They all climbed on the bus. Johnson took a gamble and got on with them. They were all carrying just one item as if they were going to sell rather than coming home with all their various goods.

The door closed behind him and they were off. The bus was packed with standing room only. He had been on worse. Some buses were so packed it was hard to breathe. This one was full, but he still had room to move. He stayed close to the door so he could get out easily and to look out the windows to see the city.

* * *

Mila followed Yuri and Schofield for several blocks before stopping to talk.

"We need to get back to the market," Schofield stated. "I'm positive that is where Johnson will go. If he goes there and we're not there, I don't know what he'll do. I don't know what I would do."

"I'll go back," Mila suggested. "I can hide there and watch for him."

"No," Yuri immediately said.

"I'm the least likely to be noticed." She looked at Yuri. "You and Schofield find a place to rest, and I'll go get Johnson and meet you as soon as I get him. Then we can all happily be on our way out of the city on the train in the morning." They all knew that it was the best option and that Yuri would hate it.

"Where will we wait for you?" he asked.

"There." Mila pointed to a small hotel behind him. Hotel Boris. "Papa, you go and get a room there, and I'll wait here with Schofield. Then you come and get him, and you two will wait in the room out of sight while I get Johnson."

Yuri went and got a room with two twin beds. It was the cheapest room available. He got the key, came back for Schofield, gave Mila the room number, and then led Schofield to the room.

Mila headed back to the market. She was worried she had missed Johnson.

* * *

President Russell hurried out of the mission home and climbed into the back of the mission van. Sergei and Yevgenie followed close behind. President Russell looked up at the driver seat and saw someone else sitting there.

"Hello," the man said as he finished hot-wiring the van and started the engine.

"Hey!" Sergei yelled from outside the van. President Russell turned to look through the open van door and saw three young men piling into the van with him. One of them knocked him over onto his back. The backseats had been removed to carry furniture, and now President Russell lay prostrate on floor with a young man on top of him holding his arms down. The doors slammed shut. Sergei and Yevgenie pounded futilely on the back door, but it was locked.

The van sped out onto the road, and the young men laughed loudly. President Russell began to protest. The man on top of him slapped him across the face. "Quiet!"

The man in the front passenger seat looked back and smiled. "What have we here?"

President Russell knew at that moment that he was in serious trouble.

* * *

Mila wandered slowly around the market before settling on the same bench near the fish stand where she and Schofield had waited earlier. She bought a newspaper and pretended to read. There on the front page of the paper was a picture of Johnson and Schofield from the surveillance camera at the train station. She looked closely at the picture. In the background of the picture was the explosion. They looked guilty. She didn't know if that was creative manipulation by the newspaper or not. It wouldn't surprise her.

She stopped and looked around. She didn't know why she was helping them. She was almost killed by helping them. She should just turn them in and let the police figure it out. With the reward money, she might be able to do something about the fish population in her beloved Lake Balkhash. The money could go a long way toward saving the fish, a dream she'd had for years. She grew up spending summers at the lake. All her fondest memories were at the lake. And now the opportunity to do something about the lake stood right before her. All she had to do was make one phone call and the police would have Schofield and she could have the reward. Or she could find the Mafia—they were paying more.

No. She wouldn't do that. It wasn't right. The Mafia would kill him; the police wouldn't kill him unless he deserved it.

She wondered how she had even gotten involved in this whole mess. She remembered the first meeting when Schofield nervously greeted her in the kitchen. There was something about him, something special about him. She couldn't put her finger on it, but something was definitely there.

Their conversation on the dock came to mind. There was a presence about him that night, something he carried with him on the boat. She knew he was good. He couldn't have done these things. He was a man of God. She knew that. She always did. It was always with him, that feeling. She couldn't turn him in. She had to help him.

She set the paper down and continued her search for Johnson.

* * *

Johnson stood patiently on the bus, looking out the window for some sign of the market. Nothing. He wiped the sweat from his brow and cautiously eyed the other passengers, worrying they might recognize him. No one seemed to pay him any attention. He continued looking out the window.

After twenty minutes on the hot, crowded bus, those with produce began making their way to the exits. Johnson made sure he was in a position to exit at a moment's notice. The bus rolled to a stop as the market came into view. Johnson had never been so excited to see a crowded market. Crowds of people spread out, each trying to sell their goods, others cautiously deciding how to spend their hard earned money. Johnson exited the bus and walked slowly toward the market. The market bustled with life—cheering, yelling, and laughter.

"Would you like a watch?" a young man asked, tapping Johnson on the shoulder.

Johnson simply shook his head no and hurried away. He needed to find the fish rack. Most of the regulars would be able to point him in the right direction, but he couldn't ask for directions. He hoped his companion and friends were waiting for him there. If they weren't, he had no idea where they would be.

The market was huge with everything one could want: fruits, vegetables, meats, jewelry, clothing, but no fish. Frustrated, Johnson began to panic. Where were the fish?

He stopped walking and stood in the middle of the market. He looked around, praying he could find the fish. Across the way was a small building, more like a tent than a building. An old man walked out of the building carrying several large fish wrapped in newspaper.

"Finally," Johnson said out loud, and made his way to the tent. "This has to be it."

Johnson walked inside. The tent was large and cold. A cooler on the side blew cold air into the tent, keeping the meat and fish fresher. Lots of exotic meats and fish hung for display throughout the tent.

Johnson carefully eyed all those inside hoping to find the driver, or even better his friends, but there was no one he knew. He retreated from the hut distraught.

Where are they? They will be here . . . they will be here.

He decided to wait and hoped they came back. He slowly perused the marketplace nearby, always keeping the door to the fish hut in sight.

* * *

"You can have the van," President Russell pleaded. "Please let me go."

"No," the young man said flatly. "I know who you are." He smiled his crooked smile. "And I know where you are from."

"I'm nobody. Please let me go."

"I went to your church once," he explained. "I went as a favor to a friend. I heard your sermon. You told a story about your childhood in America."

"Please let me go," President Russell said.

"No. I know a good thing when I see one. Normally I'm not into kidnapping, usually just burglary and car theft, but times change, and so must I."

"Why me?" President Russell asked.

"We were just stealing the car and its contents. And you happened to be in the van. And I am a man that takes what he is given." He laughed.

President Russell tried to look out the front window, but he couldn't see enough to figure out where they might be going.

"In these troubled times, an American might fetch a handsome reward," the man said under his breath. He turned away from President Russell and directed the driver where to go.

* * *

Johnson was growing impatient.

I wish they would hurry.

The longer he waited, the more nervous he got.

I need something to do, I can't just sit here.

He saw a book kiosk and decided to buy something to read. He walked over to the stand. The first thing he saw was a brand-new Book of Mormon sitting on the shelf.

"How odd."

He picked up the book. The man behind the rack immediately told him the price. It was cheap, less than what the mission paid for them. He pulled out his Kazakh money and paid the man quietly. He was careful not to speak this time. The man snatched up the money, happy to sell a book that was probably given to him for free.

Johnson took the Book of Mormon and went to a little bench to read. He opened up to Alma, his favorite book, and began reading, frequently looking up to see if his friends were near. Nothing yet.

* * *

Mila's worry grew with each passing minute. It was now well after four o'clock and still no sign of Johnson. Her fears were getting the best of her. *What if he was caught, then what? Do we try to find him, rescue him, or do we just leave him? Stop, stop, stop. Stop thinking such thoughts. Think positive. He will come. He will come.*

But he wasn't coming. There was no sign of him.

SEVENTEEN

President Russell could only see the sky and a few passing buildings from where he lay in the back of the van. It was certainly not enough to tell where he was going. He had tried to sit up, but his captors wouldn't let him; they just forced him back to the floor. They had been driving for probably fifteen or twenty minutes, so they could be almost anywhere in the city.

Oh, what a fool I am, President Russell thought. *Now I'll never be able to help the elders.* He had wanted to believe that he would somehow find them. *This massive country, and I thought I could find them.*

But foolish or not, he could not leave two missionaries behind. He was compelled to come back and help them. *And now I am in need of rescuing.* He began to pray in earnest for help.

He had no idea what his captors would do to him or what they planned for him. He truly feared for his life. He had been in scary situations before, but nothing that made him think that it could be the end.

If I do go, at least I'll go serving the Lord. The thought brought little comfort. He understood death and what happened afterward, but he was not ready to die.

Please comfort my sweet, dear wife. He closed his eyes and poured his soul to the Lord. He prayed that he would have strength to do whatever the Lord asked him to do. If it was to die, he needed the strength to suffer through. If it was live, he needed help and strength to survive what may come. Most of all, he prayed for the elders that the Lord would protect them and guide them.

* * *

Schofield paced nervously around the hotel room. He was worried about Johnson. His gut told him he was safe somewhere, but still he worried. He longed to be back with his companion. It was the longest he had been separated from a companion since he started his mission.

The longest time before this was ten minutes when his companion didn't make it on a crowded bus, and he had to get off at the next stop and wait for him.

It had been several hours since he had last seen Elder Johnson, and Elder Schofield was getting more and more nervous. He felt guilty for not sticking with him. Just days ago, Schofield had been going about his business with no real thought of the future, just finishing the mission. And now he didn't know if there would be a future. He had to get to Astana without being caught. He had to get to the embassy, where the ambassador would sort everything out.

"Where are you, Elder Johnson?" he asked, peeking through the curtains and looking out the window. He knew he wouldn't see Elder Johnson out the window, but he had to do something; he couldn't just sit and do nothing.

I can pray, he thought. *I can pray. God has helped me before, and He can help me now. If ever I needed help, it is now.*

He knelt by the bed and began to pray.

* * *

Johnson sat on the bench near the market, reading the Book of Mormon, frequently looking up, hoping he would see someone. A small boy came up and sat on the bench next to him. Johnson looked at him briefly and then went back to his book.

The little boy stared at Johnson. Johnson felt his stare, glanced at the little boy, smiled, nodded, and then went back to the Book of Mormon. The little boy smiled, continuing to gawk at him. Johnson was getting nervous. He didn't want to talk and blow his cover, but the boy was making him anxious.

Johnson stared at the Book of Mormon, too nervous to read. Several minutes of uncomfortable silence passed. The boy stared at Johnson and Johnson stared at the Book of Mormon. Finally the little boy broke the silence.

"What are you reading?" he asked.

Johnson's hands shook and his mouth filled with cotton. He didn't want to speak. He slowly turned the front of the book to the little boy so he could read it himself.

"Book of Mormon," the little boy said. "What is that about?"

Johnson pointed to the little subtitle under "Book of Mormon."

"Oh. Like the Bible."

Johnson moved his head up and down.

"So the Bible has the Old and New Testament, and this is like the new New Testament." The boy seemed genuinely interested but was confused.

Johnson quietly and softly replied, "Yes, it is another testament of Jesus Christ. It goes with the Bible to tell of Christ's teachings."

"Where can I get one of these?" he asked.

Johnson wondered why the boy would ask that.

"Here, you can have this one." Johnson handed him the Book of Mormon. "I have another one."

"Thank you." The boy hugged the Book of Mormon close to his chest. "Thank you."

"You're welcome." Johnson smiled at the boy's excitement. "Where are your parents?" he added after a moment.

"I don't have any," the boy answered.

Johnson didn't know what to say to that, so he didn't say anything.

They sat in silence for a moment.

"What are you doing?" the little boy asked.

"I'm waiting for my friends," Johnson said. "They're supposed to meet me at the market by the fish."

"At this market?"

"Yes, I was hoping they would have been here a long time ago, but I haven't seen them yet. I'm starting to get worried."

"I'm sorry you're friends haven't come yet. I'll keep you company until they do. Okay?"

"Okay." Johnson was surprised at the suggestion but accepted. "If you'd like." He was scared and alone. A little company would help, even if it was a ten-year-old boy.

"I would." The little boy smiled up at Elder Johnson.

"Maybe your friends are at the other market," he suggested.

"The other market?" Johnson asked.

"Yes, there is a market on the other side of town. Maybe they are waiting for you there."

"Is there a restaurant by the other market?" Johnson nearly tripped over his words.

"Sure. There's the Obolon and restaurant Ruslan."

"The Obolon is by the other market?"

"Yes."

"How do I get there?"

"C'mon, I'll show you." The little boy hopped off the bench and held out his hand.

Johnson followed the young boy out of the market.

"If we hurry, we can make it before the market closes," the little boy said.

"What's your name?" Johnson asked.

"Maksim."

"Is the other market far away?"

"Yes."

"Is it okay if you go that far?"

Maksim looked up at Johnson, confused.

"Won't someone worry about you?" Johnson asked.

"I live in the orphanage." Maksim replied. "They don't really care what I do as long as I am there for roll call at bedtime. They probably don't even know that I'm gone."

How sad, Johnson thought and tussled Maksim's hair affectionately.

* * *

Mila grew more worried with each passing moment. There was still no sign of Johnson. *Schofield and Papa must be frantic by now. I can't leave until I find Johnson.*

The vendors at the market were beginning to close up shop and leave. *Johnson better appear. It will be dark soon.*

Mila stood to stretch her legs for a moment.

"Where do you think you're going?" a gruff voice asked her.

She turned. Igor and his thugs stood right behind the bench. She turned to run. One thug grabbed her and threw her onto the bench.

Igor sat down next to her. The two thugs moved in close, eyeing her seriously. The one she had kicked shook his head back and forth.

"If you are still here, then I bet the two Americans are still here. You're going to tell me where they are." Igor moved his jacket to reveal a pistol tucked into the side of his pants. "If you know what is good for you."

Mila breathed a huge sigh of relief. *They don't have Johnson.*

"I don't know where they are," Mila lied. "I was hoping to meet them here. We were going to do some shopping, but now the market is closing and I'm afraid they won't be coming. And they are leaving town tomorrow, so I guess I won't see them again."

"Liar," Igor said. He reached up and grabbed a handful of her hair, pulling her closer.

Mila winced at the pain, trying to keep her composure.

"You will tell me where they are, or my comrades will drag you into the alley and I'll put a bullet between your eyes," Igor threatened.

"Even if I did know where they were, I would not tell you." She spat in his face and then braced for the inevitable hit to the face.

He pulled back to strike her but suddenly stopped.

Mila flinched, fighting to hold back the tears.

When Igor didn't strike, she looked up at him and spat in his face again. She didn't know why. He was already mad enough to kill her, but she spat again and then called him a stump.

Igor's thugs grabbed her, one by each arm, picked her up, and dragged her into the alley.

* * *

Johnson walked next to Maksim, who looked up at him and smiled. They walked slowly for a while just enjoying each other's company. They came to the bus stop, and Maksim stopped.

"You need to take the bus nine stops. You'll see the market from the bus stop."

"You're not coming?" Johnson asked. He had expected Maksim to accompany him the whole way.

"No, I need to get back to the orphanage. The gates will be locking soon. Thank you for the book." He held the book up to show Johnson.

"You're very welcome," Johnson replied. "And thank you very much for helping me find the other market. I greatly appreciate it."

"Will I see you again?" Maksim asked as the bus pulled up.

"I hope someday," Johnson said, wishing he could spend more time with Maksim. He was such a pleasant little boy.

"Good-bye!" Maksim called out as Johnson got on the bus.

Johnson waved good-bye and mouthed "Thank you" as the bus pulled away. Johnson watched Maksim until the bus rounded the corner and Maksim was out of sight.

Johnson counted the stops anxiously, hoping that Elder Schofield was waiting for him.

Stop nine came, and Elder Johnson climbed off the bus. He could see the market. Most of the people were leaving. Soon the market would be barren. He stopped at the edge of the market and looked around. Straight across from him was a man gathering all the fish from his rack and putting them away. Johnson walked slowly across the market. No one was there. *Now what do I do?*

A gunshot froze Johnson in his tracks.

* * *

President Russell was escorted out of the mission van. They were in some sort of underground parking structure. He thought about running but figured he would just be caught and decided against it. If he waited patiently, the opportunity would come to make a break for it.

He was led through a door and down a long hall. Eventually they came to an apartment. The man with a short-trimmed goatee and a shaved head went inside first. He started giving orders to the others.

"Sit down," Goatee said to President Russell. "Bogdan, get some rope and tie him up. Oleg, gag him."

Bogdan didn't go for rope; instead he used duct tape to strap President Russell firmly to a chair. Oleg used the tape to cover President Russell's mouth.

Goatee went into another room and returned with a Polaroid camera.

"I couldn't find any rope," Bogdan explained.

"It's good," Goatee said.

He took a picture of the president and shook it impatiently, waiting for it to develop.

"That's no good," he said in disgust and threw the picture on the floor. He set the camera on the counter and began punching President Russell in the face. Again and again.

President Russell tried to yell. He tugged at the tape holding his arms down, the tape digging into his flesh. All he could do was take the punches. His head shook back and forth with each crashing blow. Blood trickled down his cheek and his face felt swollen. His mind was a swirling haze. He hoped that Sergei could somehow find him.

Goatee finally stopped.

"That's better," he said, wiping the blood from his knuckles.

President Russell had cuts over both eyes and on his right cheek. Blood poured over his eyes and down his cheeks.

Goatee wiped the blood off his hands with a towel, picked up the camera, and took another picture. He washed his hands as he waited for the picture to develop.

"Much better." He smiled and handed the picture to the driver. "Clean him up," he told Bogdan and Oleg.

Goatee and the driver took the picture back into the other room.

EIGHTEEN

Michael Ivanov parked his car and got out. He had been driving for a couple hours and wanted to stretch his legs. The walk would do him good. He walked slowly toward his destination. He was in no real hurry. The police station wasn't going anywhere. The main station in downtown Balkhash would probably be a more effective place to stop, but Michael had a buddy from school who worked at this station.

Michael stopped and listened. He had heard something amid the bustle of the city. There it was again. A scream. It was a cry for help. He rounded the corner and saw two men holding a young woman up by the arms. Her legs kicked at them frantically. Several feet away stood a third man, his gun pointed at the woman's head. Michael didn't waste time. He pulled his gun and shot. The man with the gun collapsed to the ground in a heap. The other two dropped the young woman and ran.

Michael Ivanov lowered his weapon and rushed forward. The woman was sitting on the ground, crying frantically. Her long black hair framed her pretty face.

"Are you okay?" Michael asked.

"Yes, thank you." She wiped tears from her eyes. "Thank you."

"You're welcome."

Michael picked up his phone and called the local police. He had hoped to surprise his schoolmate. This would certainly surprise him, but not the surprise Michael had in mind.

The young woman tried to stand up.

"No, sit," Michael ordered.

"I have to go," she pleaded.

"You have to stay. This man was trying to kill you. I'm not from around here. You need to tell the police what was happening."

"You're not from around here?"

"No, I'm from Almaty. My name is Michael Ivanov. I'm head of the antiterrorism task force. I'm here on business. What's your name?" He offered the woman a hand, trying to calm her.

"Business?" she asked. He could see the sweat beading on her forehead. It was a cool autumn evening, but he could understand the sweat under these traumatic circumstances.

"Are you okay, miss?" he asked. She was shaking.

"Yes, I just want to go."

"Here they are." Michael Ivanov stood up and met the first police officer. He showed the officer his badge and explained the situation.

"I heard the screaming and saw him aiming a gun at the young woman." He indicated the woman, who sat next to another officer talking softly to him. "I didn't want to risk her life so I drew and fired."

The officer looked down at the corpse and gave a half smile. "Well, you won't hear us complaining about this."

Even though she was talking softly, Michael could hear the women telling the officer her side of the story. Once she was done speaking, the officer stood up and walked to Michael and the other officer. "She claims she doesn't know why they grabbed her. She says she doesn't know them."

"Miss," Michael Ivanov said, turning around, but she was gone.

* * *

Johnson stood still after hearing the gunshot. No one else acted like anything had happened though. The only person that acknowledged that he had heard the shot was an old man, who stood still for just a moment, wiped his eyes, and walked away with his fur hats.

Is there that much violence here that no one notices anymore? Johnson cautiously looked around. No one was paying attention to him. He continued his walk over to the fish rack. He noticed a bench not far away and went to sit down.

He saw Mila exit the alley.

"Mila!" Johnson called excitedly.

She held a finger to her lips, telling him to be quiet, and she quickly walked to him.

"Let's go," she whispered. She held out her hand and walked by. Johnson stood up and followed. She took his hand and tugged on it. "Quickly, the police are coming."

Johnson looked down and realized he was holding her hand. He wanted to let go, to pull away. He knew he should let go, but he wasn't about to lose his friends again, and so he held on as if his life depended on it.

Johnson followed Mila as she walked as fast as she could away from the market. As soon as they were clear of the market, Mila broke into a run, and Johnson followed her all the way to a hotel.

* * *

Michael Ivanov finished giving his statement again as to what he saw and why he shot just as his friend Anatoli arrived on the scene.

"Greetings, Michael," he called out.

"Greetings, old friend."

"What brings you to Balkhash?"

"Just following a hunch," Michael answered.

"Those two Americans who bombed the train?"

"Yes and no." He was looking for them, but he was certain they had not bombed the train.

"Your hunches are always right on, aren't they?"

"Sometimes." Michael shrugged his shoulders.

"Well, this one is dead on."

"What do you mean?" Michael asked.

"The Americans are here in Balkhash."

"Really?" Michael said. His heart raced. They were in Balkhash. He knew there was a reason he had driven out of his way to come here.

"They're traveling with an older man and a young woman."

"Are you certain it was them?"

"Absolutely. Igor, one of Balkhash's lowlifes, met them this afternoon, but they got away. He put out a call to his buddies and gave descriptions of the two traveling with the Americans."

"I need to speak with this Igor."

"You should have thought of that before you shot him."

Michael cursed. "What did the girl look like?"

"Smaller build, long black hair, pretty face."

Michael closed his eyes and rubbed his forehead. He'd had her. She could have led him to the elders, and he let her go.

"What is it?" Anatoli asked.

"The girl was here. Igor had caught her. I let her go."

"Oh, well, maybe next time," Anatoli stated. He never took anything too seriously. He patted Michael on the back. "Maybe next time."

* * *

Schofield woke to hear pounding on the door and screaming for them to open it. At first he worried it was the police.

"Open up! Open up!" It was Mila.

Yuri rushed to the door and threw it open. Schofield stood

behind him. Mila rushed in with Johnson following close behind. He slammed the door as he entered.

"Johnson!" Schofield threw his arms around him and hugged him. "Where have you been?"

"All over," Johnson said, gasping for breath.

"We have to go," Mila said. "The police are looking for us." She shook uncontrollably.

"What's wrong?" Yuri grabbed her by the shoulders.

"The thug from this afternoon found me in the market," she said, beginning to cry. "They took me in an alley, and he pointed a gun at my head. He said he was going to kill me. Some policeman shot him. Killed him right in front of me. I got away as soon as I could. I found Johnson, but we have to go. He's here for you." She looked from Schofield to Johnson before she broke down and cried uncontrollably.

"It's okay." Yuri hugged his daughter tight. "It's okay."

Schofield felt his heart race. *They're closing in on us. We have to get out of here. Before it's too late.*

* * *

President Russell sat in the chair as Bogdan took a dry towel and wiped most of the blood off President Russell's face. He and Oleg carried President Russell into a back room and left him there, still duct taped to the chair. His face still bled. Blood slowly dripped down into his eyes.

His head throbbed, and he could feel the blood collecting on his chin and slowly dripping onto his lap. President Russell breathed deeply, trying to calm himself. His heart raced like he had been sprinting. He had thought Goatee was going to kill him. The pain was so intense he almost wished he had. Slowly, he regained his composure. His breathing slowed, and the blood began to dry on his cheeks and eyebrows. It pulled on his skin as it dried.

The others had been quiet for some time. The phone rang. President Russell listened intently as the speaker spoke. He couldn't tell who it was, but he was certain it was not their leader, Goatee, or Pavel as the other two had called him. There was too much noise from neighboring apartments and the street to hear every word, but he caught several: *American, photo, Internet, cabbage*—which was slang for money—and *death.*

Suddenly he heard a door bang open, and Pavel yelling at Gennady to get off the phone and shut his mouth. There was a loud smack and something fell onto the floor. President Russell assumed it was the driver.

"Keep your mouth shut!" Pavel yelled.

President Russell did not like what he heard. He assumed they were going to post his picture on the Internet as part of their plot to get a lot of cabbage. He hoped it would not end in his death.

"You talk too much, Gennady," Pavel stated. "Let's go. We have a meeting. Bogdan, you watch the prisoner."

"Okay," Bogdan replied.

President Russell heard the TV turn on and Bogdan yelling at the TV.

President Russell looked around the dimly lit room. There was a shaded window, a small desk, a bed, and a chair. Nothing he thought he could use. But a plan began to form in his mind.

Now or never, President Russell thought. He scooted his chair over to the door and began banging on it with his feet.

* * *

"This is madness," Johnson stated. The elders sat alone in the motel room. Mila and Yuri had stepped out to get food.

"I know," Schofield agreed.

"Why are we running?"

"Because we want to live. That's why."

"What would happen if we turned ourselves in?" Johnson contemplated.

"That all depends on the person we turned ourselves in to. If they were honest, I think we'd be fine, but if they were dishonest, they would turn us over to someone else and they would probably kill us. That's a chance I'm not going to take."

"You're right. Let's not take that chance." Johnson paused for a minute. "What's the plan now?"

"We have to be at the train station at 2:00 a.m. We'll sneak onto a train and hide in a secret compartment. Hopefully by tomorrow afternoon, we'll be in Karaganda. Only one hundred miles from the embassy."

"This running is nerve wracking. I don't know how much more I can take."

"Endure to the end, my friend," Schofield encouraged. "We'll make it to the embassy, and they will straighten everything out."

"I sure hope so." Johnson lay down on the bed to take a little nap. Tomorrow was going to be another rough day.

* * *

"Stop it!" Bogdan yelled at President Russell.

President Russell kept on kicking.

"Stop it!"

President Russell kicked harder.

"Stop it!" Bogdan yelled as he jerked the door open. He pulled his arm back to hit him.

President Russell screamed through the duct tape.

"What?" Bogdan gave up and pulled the tape off his mouth.

"I have to use the restroom."

"No." Bogdan started to put the tape back on.

"Wait, I really have to go." He tried to show pain in his eyes.

"Fine." Bogdan grabbed a knife and cut the duct tape from

his arms and legs. "No funny business," he said, pointing with the knife to the bathroom. "You have one minute."

"Thank you." President Russell went into the bathroom. There was no window. He looked around for something he could use to escape. Bogdan had a knife and he didn't want to get stabbed. He saw a plunger. *Better than nothing, but not much.* The shower rod. *That will work.* President Russell set the plunger by the door, quietly pulled the shower curtain down, and removed the rod. It was a little large, but it should work. He waited for Bogdan to come and knock.

Bogdan banged on the door. "Let's go."

President Russell threw open the door, held the shower rod tight, and charged Bogdan like a knight on a horse with a lance. The shower rod caught Bogdan in the chest. He dropped his knife and grabbed the rod with both hands. President Russell kept pushing until Bogdan stumbled and fell over backward. President Russell ran to the door and dropped the rod. He unlocked the door and ran.

He was in a hall. *Left or right? Right.* He turned and ran down the hall. An exit sign. He went through a door into the stairwell. He took two steps at a time. He burst out the door, running into Pavel and knocking him over backward. He sped past Gennady and Oleg and ran down the street.

Free at last. He had a good lead on Pavel. *How much of a lead?* He turned back to look. Gennady, Oleg, and Pavel—all three were chasing him and seemed to be getting closer.

All of a sudden, President Russell slammed into the side of a car at a full sprint. His arm shattered the window, and his ribs crushed against the car frame. He fell to the ground onto his back. He gasped for breath, his lungs burning. Nothing. He couldn't breathe. He tried to move and found he couldn't. He had to get up to escape. Nothing. He gasped again. A strange man stood over him, looking at him.

Air. I need air. He tried to roll over, to sit up. But he was stuck on his back. *The sky, this man . . . He ruined my escape. I was free. Air. I need air.* He gasped.

Cold air rushed into his lungs vanquishing the fire.

Air, precious air. The man is talking. What is he saying?

He couldn't hear anything, just his gasping. His lungs filled with air each time—cool, wonderful air. He looked up at the man. Then the man flew away, backward over the car. In his place stood Oleg, then Pavel, then Gennady.

He was no longer free. He was a prisoner again. He reached up to wipe the sweat from his brow and saw his blood-covered hand.

* * *

Michael Ivanov met with his friend at the restaurant Obolon.

"I actually met the Americans the day before the bombing," Michael explained. "They were teaching about their religion. I really don't think they had anything to do with the bombing, but I must follow all the leads," he added, trying to maintain his professional appearance.

"I don't know what they did, but the underworld reward is now three times what the police are offering."

"What?"

"The man you killed was after the reward. I don't know who exactly, but someone very powerful in the Kazakh underworld wants those two Americans. Preferably alive, but dead is okay too."

"Why would they want them?" Michael asked.

"That I don't know, but I do know that every lowlife in the city is looking for them and you are going to need a lot of luck to get them first. Especially after the stunt they pulled this morning."

"What happened this morning?"

"Technically, it was this afternoon. They were having lunch here and the waitress recognized them. She called her cousin

Igor, the man you shot. Igor was a small-time racketeer and general thug but still pretty tough. He came in with two buddies and got thumped by the two Americans and a young woman, probably the one from the alley, and an older man. They thumped Igor and then vanished into the city. The girl was the only one seen again and now she is gone too."

"They thumped Igor?" Michael asked for clarification.

"Yeah, a quick attack and then they ran. I'm sure they're hiding somewhere here in the city. I'm sure they will be found. It's just a matter of when and by whom." He took a long drink and smiled at Michael.

"Do we know who these two are that are with them?"

"Nothing yet, unless the information the girl gave us is true. Then we know her name and address, but I wouldn't count on it. I've got guys checking it out. I'll let you know if I find anything."

"Thank you," Michael said. "Let me know if you find anything at all."

"Certainly."

"Excuse me," Michael said and stood up to leave. "I need to make a couple of phone calls."

"Please." Anatoli motioned to the phone booth.

Michael walked to the phone booth. He wanted to call Sasha and find out why the underworld was after the Americans, but he didn't want to tip them off as to where he was. He wanted to catch them himself.

He called on his cell phone.

"Hello," Sasha answered.

"Sasha, it's Michael. Any word on the two Americans?"

"Nothing yet. There have been rumored sightings all over the country, but nothing confirmed."

"I am getting indications the Mafia is offering a reward for their capture. What have you heard?"

"Nothing of that sort," Sasha said.

"Will you check into that? I'll get back to you."

"Sure," Sasha said. "Where are you?"

"Just following some leads," Michael answered.

"Do you need my help?"

"No, I'm good. Thank you. Just find out why the Mafia wants them."

"Okay."

Michael hung up and walked back to the table.

* * *

Sasha turned to his buddy.

"We need to get some people in Balkhash. I think Michael is on to them. Get them there quickly."

"I can have a team there in two hours."

"Good." Sasha was feeling pressure from those he regretted doing business with to find the Americans, and he did not want to fail. He could not fail.

* * *

Michael Ivanov spent several hours looking for signs of the Americans, talking to people, wanting to know if they had seen them, but no one seemed to know anything. He wasn't sure they would tell him if they did know. They wanted to find them for themselves.

It was getting dark, and the curfew would soon be in effect. He could get around the curfew if he wanted to, but he decided he could use the rest since he would be driving to Astana tomorrow if he couldn't find them. He was certain they would be heading there. It was the only move that made sense. Their government would ensure a safe and fair trial. If they were caught anywhere else, there was no such guarantee.

He found a small hotel. The Hotel Boris was not far from where they had been seen. He got a room on the eighth floor in the northwest corner and was sound asleep as soon as he lay down.

NINETEEN

Elder Schofield awoke to Yuri shaking his shoulder just before midnight.

"We have two hours to get to the train station. It's not far, but we must be cautious. There is a curfew and it's straight to jail if we are caught," Yuri said.

The elders wolfed down their sandwiches that Yuri and Mila had brought earlier and went out the fire escape. Yuri had gotten a ground floor room in the southeast corner. He had paid in advance. They didn't want anyone to know they were leaving in the middle of the night.

Yuri pulled out a map to show them where they were going. It was two miles away, but they would need to go slow and carefully in order to avoid detection.

* * *

Sasha was working round the clock. He needed those two Americans taken care of and soon. A phone started ringing.

"Hello," Sasha answered.

"I think I have something," said Detective Kuznetzov, one of the detectives he'd sent to Balkhash.

"What is it?"

"The house where the Americans were seen. The one on the shores of Lake Balkhash. The one that was destroyed."

"Yes?" Sasha said, growing impatient.

"It was owned by a Yuri Shevchenko. A Yuri Shevchenko from Balkhash Oblast registered at the Hotel Boris in Balkhash this afternoon."

"Are you going somewhere with this?"

"Yes. The Americans were reported to be traveling with an older man and a young woman. I think they are traveling with this Yuri Shevchenko and they are all at the Hotel Boris."

"Good. Very good. Check it out, but make sure it is them before you move in. I don't want anything embarrassing. Keep me posted."

"Yes, sir."

Sasha hung up, excused himself from work, and left to make a phone call to someone very eager to know the whereabouts of the Americans.

* * *

Johnson watched as Yuri slipped out the door to the fire escape. He and Elder Schofield followed close behind. Mila exited last, slowly pulling the door closed behind her. Their balcony fire escape stood just a few feet off the ground. They quietly climbed down the steps to the ground. They were in a back alley not far from the main street. Yuri crept to the corner and peered around. The streets were entirely empty. Not one single car. The only cars they should see at this point would be police cars. Yuri signaled for the others to follow him, and they came up behind him. All wore dark clothing so they could blend into the shadows better. Johnson had played games of hide-and-seek before, but never with the stakes this high.

A cool fall breeze swept through the streets. Yuri led the way, walking quickly, sticking to the shadows of the buildings whenever possible. Johnson crept along behind, occasionally looking back to make sure Schofield and Mila were still behind him. The eerie silence of the night unnerved him.

Lights flashed up ahead. They ran into an alley and ducked behind a dumpster. The police car stopped and shined its light down the alley. Shadows danced across the walls as the light moved back and forth. The police car moved on to the next alley.

They waited until the sound of the car had faded and then quickly moved back to the street. It was only 1:30 a.m. when they got to the walkway that went over the train tracks. This would be the tricky part. Going across an elevated walkway without being seen.

They needed to wait. At 2:00, the guards would begin changing and they would have their chance to find out if this driver was an honest smuggler. They hid in some bushes next to the stairs that led to the walkway and waited.

"Wait!" Schofield burst in a frenzied whisper. "The driver said we needed to enter through a gap in the fence on the north side of the train yard."

"This is the east," Yuri said.

"We need to go to the north. I totally forgot."

"I'm glad you remembered now," Yuri stated calmly. "We only have a few minutes to get there. Let's go."

Yuri walked quickly toward the north fence. The walkway would have been a treacherous path to take. They would have have gotten caught.

They found the hole in the fence just as Yuri's watch read 2:00 a.m. It was small, and they would have to squeeze through.

Mila ducked and crawled through the fence on her belly. Once through she scrambled to the shadows of the bushes nearby.

Johnson looked around nervously before ducking and crawling through the hole. He waited in the shadows by Mila for Elder Schofield and Yuri to join them.

"Where to now?" whispered Yuri as he joined the others.

"We need to find train 497."

"How are we supposed to do that?" Yuri asked. "They aren't exactly numbered."

"They're not?" Johnson asked.

"They are. Each car has a number on it, but the train numbers aren't on the train. They are only numbered for communication purposes, like on the reader board, or whatever," Schofield said.

"How are we supposed to find it then?" Johnson asked.

"We'll have to sneak into the terminal and check the board to see what it says," Yuri said.

"There can't be that many trains leaving," Johnson said.

"Probably not, but there are a lot of trains parked here," Schofield said.

"Let's go." Yuri headed off in a hundred yard run toward the terminal around the back end of several trains.

The others followed close behind.

Johnson stopped in his tracks. The others kept running on without him. He turned and looked at the train he had just passed.

There was a piece of paper taped to the back of the train with big black numbers "497."

"Wait!" Johnson called in a whisper. They couldn't hear him.

Voices—loud voices. He glanced along the train. Three guards were walking toward him, talking jovially. He looked at Schofield. Schofield, who stood next to the terminal, turned and looked back at him.

Schofield waved to Johnson. Johnson shook his head no. The guards were close.

Again Schofield waved. Johnson shook his head and waved his arms. He ducked under the train and quietly crawled along the tracks.

The shadows of the guards slowly passed by him. He breathed a sigh of relief.

* * *

Schofield saw Johnson drop to the ground and crawl under the train. Someone was coming. He ran to the nearest train and ducked under. *Guards!* Mila and Yuri climbed under the train behind.

They watched the shadows of the guards slowly move toward the terminal and inside.

"Let's find Johnson," Schofield whispered.

They crept back to where Johnson was waiting under the rear of the train. He pointed to the paper that said "497" taped to the back of the train.

"I think this is our train."

"Nice," Schofield said and walked along the train to the third car from the rear.

The door on the third car was slightly ajar. Schofield pushed it open far enough to squeeze through. It was dark inside. Some light shone in through the door, enough to light up a large wooden box and several smaller crates next to it on the far side of the cart.

He climbed on the smaller boxes until he stood on top of the large one. There was a small hatch door on the top. He opened it up to look inside. It was black.

Yuri climbed onto the train and pulled a flashlight out of his backpack. He tossed it up to Schofield.

Schofield shined the light into the crate. Several blankets, pillows, and four small bottles of water sat in the corner of the crate. Schofield motioned for the others to come up, and he jumped into the box.

Johnson pushed the door to the train car closed behind him. Mila and Yuri joined Schofield in the large box. Johnson stood on top, hesitant to climb inside.

"What?" Schofield whispered.

"I'm claustrophobic."

"It's plenty big in here. You'll be fine."

"I'll be trapped. I hate being trapped."

"You'll be fine. Come on in."

"I can't."

"Johnson," Mila called up, "we are not trapped. We can get out anytime we want. There is a door. Come on in. It is fine."

"No, I can't." Johnson began to panic.

"Come and tell me about your church," Mila called. "I have so many questions I need you to answer."

"You do?" Johnson asked.

"Yes, come tell me, please."

Johnson hesitated and then decided if Mila had questions that needed answers, he had to answer them. He took several large, deep breaths and whispered a prayer before he climbed in, pulling the lid closed behind him.

The flashlight cast an eerie light around the box. Johnson looked around nervously. The box was an eight-foot cube. Not a lot of room but enough.

Schofield handed out the blankets and pillows, and then he lay down and curled up under his blanket.

Johnson sat in the corner so he had as much space in front of him as he could and began to answer Mila's questions about the gospel.

"Back at Dima's house," Mila began. "Schofield told me that I could be with my mom again."

"Yes." Johnson smiled. "Even though she has passed on from this life, the Savior has prepared a way that you can be together again as a family." Johnson talked for an hour to Mila and Yuri about eternal families and the plan of salvation. If felt good to share the gospel again. He missed it and the Spirit that came with it.

Yuri decided they should all get some sleep while they could. They didn't know what the rest of the day would bring, so they all lay down to get some sleep.

Johnson wasn't so lucky though. His stomach churned nervously as the quiet minutes rolled along. He slowly drifted off to sleep only to dream of thugs chopping through the boxes with axes. He awoke, sweating profusely. He turned on the flashlight and examined the wood for ax marks. Eventually he fell asleep again, but this time he dreamed that the hatch door opened and a man with a gun jumped in. Again he awoke in a sweat. His stomach twisted in an ever-tightening knot. Eventually Johnson joined the others in a slightly cramped but restful sleep.

* * *

President Russell awoke with a start. The room was still dark. The first traces of sunlight crept in through the window. It was deathly silent. Something was wrong—he could feel it. Terror ran through his veins, chilling him to the bone. He was about to die a horrible death. Pavel was going to kill him. He heard a car on the street, the brakes squeaking as the car rolled to a stop. Several doors opened and closed. Another car pulled up and stopped. Doors slammed, and voices shouted orders. Then banging doors, shattering glass. Screaming. Someone was storming the apartment complex. Searching for something. More screaming, doors shattering, shouting, screaming.

He could hear Pavel shouting from the other room. The apartment complex erupted into a noisy chaos in the early morning. President Russell wished he could see what was going on from his dark room, but all he could hear were loud voices yelling and muffled screams.

"Get on the floor," a deep voice stiffly ordered. It seemed it came from just outside the apartment. President Russell wanted to scream, to call for help.

A deafening shattering crash echoed in the apartment, and President Russell flinched in his chair.

"Get on the floor!" the voice said again with alarming firmness. President Russell rocked his chair forward and fell onto his face. He rolled onto his side, still strapped to the chair.

Another crash echoed, and President Russell recognized it as a door being torn from its hinges. Screaming erupted and then there was a loud pop. A gunshot. *Please no*, President Russell thought as he realized what was about to happen. The single gunshot was followed by a string of gunfire.

Silence settled for a brief moment. *Could that be it?* President Russell thought. President Russell lay in the dark with duct tape over his mouth, wishing he could call out.

Another shot rang out. And then the silence erupted in a cacophony of gunfire, screaming, and wailing. The walls of the apartment shook and then silence again. President Russell opened his eyes, not realizing he had closed them. Several holes dotted the walls, and small bits of light shone through from the room beyond.

President Russell struggled to cover his ears with his hands tied. He wanted to silence the screaming, the shouting, and the gunfire, but he couldn't.

The gunfire slowly faded. The survivors talked quietly with each other.

The door to his room shattered open. A man in black body armor with a smoking assault rifle had kicked it. President Russell looked up at the man and saw smoke pouring from the tip of his rifle.

* * *

Schofield woke to Yuri shaking his shoulder and whispering, "Shhh."

"What is it?" Schofield whispered as he sat up.

Schofield listened and heard footsteps in the car. And then voices. They woke Johnson and Mila, signaling them to be quiet.

Several people talked happily, and they began moving crates around the car.

The four of them sat nervously in the dark, listening quietly. They were all wondering if they had been betrayed.

"Thank you," one voice called out.

"You're welcome!" They heard scuffling as people got off the train and shut the door behind them.

* * *

Detective Volodya Kuznetzov walked up to the front desk of the Hotel Boris just before 6:00 a.m. There was no one there. He looked around nervously and then rang the bell. He wasn't sure why he was so nervous. Sasha wanted him to be extra careful for some reason. In a case like this, he would have thought a lot of collateral damage would be acceptable. Who cared if they woke someone up in the middle of the night? Something wasn't right, but he needed to follow the lead. Yuri Shevchenko was the owner of the house that the Americans blew up and he was registered here at the hotel. He felt there was a connection.

The hotel manager came out of the back room.

"Good morning. Can I help you?"

"Yes," the detective stated, showing the manager his badge. "You have a man registered here by the name of Yuri Shevchenko."

"Yes," the manager said.

"Is this him?" The detective held up a picture they had of his bus driver's license.

"He's a little bit older, but I think that is him."

"Is he traveling alone?"

"I don't believe so."

"Did you see the others?"

"No, sir. I only saw Mr. Shevchenko when he checked in, but I heard multiple voices yesterday when I walked by. I'm not one to eavesdrop, sir, but I did hear mention of a train and the city Astana. Their voices were quiet, so I couldn't hear much."

"Thank you. You've been very helpful." Volodya was turning to leave when a large explosion rocked the building, blowing debris throughout the lobby. The manager screamed as the ceiling collapsed on him. Volodya rushed to pull him out, but the ceiling came crashing down, smashing the detective to the ground as well.

TWENTY

Michael Ivanov awoke to an explosion and the building shaking. It felt like it was going to collapse, but it held. Michael looked around to gain his bearings. He was in a hotel. Hotel Boris on the eighth floor. He had to get out. The fire escape.

He grabbed his things and rushed to the balcony. There was screaming—a lot of screaming. He rushed down the metal stairs to the ground and away from the building. He got dressed and rushed around to the front.

A huge chunk of the building was missing and nearly half of what was left was consumed in flames. Michael rushed forward. He could hear screaming in the building. Without a second thought, he rushed into the lobby. He couldn't let people die if he had a reasonable chance to save them. The fire and explosion seemed to have come from a room on the southeast corner. It was gone; several rooms were gone. The floors above them hung precariously by the ever-weakening steel-reinforced concrete. That part of the building could collapse at any moment and take the rest of the building with it.

Michael stopped as he entered the lobby. It was dark. His eyes needed time to adjust. The ceiling over half the room had fallen in. The lobby desk was covered in debris. Several beams had fallen, but still managed to hold up the roof above.

"Help!" a voice called out from the rubble behind the front desk.

Michael climbed over a small pile of rubble to reach the front desk, the debris crumbling with each step.

"Help!" a voice called out again. "Please."

"I'm here," Michael Ivanov said and jumped over the front desk, landing inches from a man lying on the ground with a beam on his leg.

"Help me," the hotel manager pleaded as he tried to lift the beam off his leg.

Michael squatted low, wrapped both arms around the beam, and heaved with all his might. His forearms burned with the pressure. The manager swung his leg out, and Michael dropped the beam to the floor, collapsing on top of it.

"Thank you," the manager said as he tried to stand. His broken leg wouldn't support the weight.

Michael helped him to his feet. The man wrapped one arm around Michael's neck for support, and they hobbled through the wreckage to the door. The emergency lights flicked off and on.

Moaning came from under some rubble as Michael passed. He looked and saw a hand sticking out from under broken pieces of the ceiling. It was barely visible in the flickering light.

A man met them at the entrance to the lobby and took the manager by the other side.

"Can you take him?" Michael asked.

"Yes."

Michael let go of the manager and turned back into the burning hotel.

* * *

The train jerked to a start minutes after the men had rearranged the crates. The locomotive grunted and groaned as it crawled down the tracks away from the station. It smoothed out as it picked up speed.

"Here we go," Schofield whispered calmly as they rolled down the tracks.

The group sat in silence for several minutes. All of them had expected the police at any time to open the hatch and arrest them, but now that they were on their way, they all breathed a sigh of relief.

The train continued to pick up speed and would soon be going full speed to Karaganda. They would be that much closer to Astana and the safety of the embassy.

A loud boom echoed over the thunder of the train rolling down the tracks. The noise was tremendous.

"What was that?" Johnson asked, startled.

"Thunder?"

"Whoa!" Schofield said. "I'm glad we're in here then and not out in that mess."

The noise faded away and left the four of them sitting in the crate on train 497 to Karaganda.

They had no idea how long the train ride was or what they were going to do when they got there, but Johnson decided that for the next few hours until they got to Karaganda, he was going to be a missionary and not a fugitive on the run.

Schofield suggested they have a lesson on prayer. It was something they could all use a little more of. Johnson agreed, and at the end of the lesson he shared a personal story about the power of prayer.

"Prayer," Johnson said, "is a powerful tool, a tool that can and should be used often. I was once lost in the wilderness. I was a Boy Scout and we were camping. We had been hiking for hours and I got separated from my group and got lost. I couldn't find my way out. So I climbed up to the top of a hill to look around, but then I fell down and my leg became wedged between two big rocks. I was in a deep ravine and could not be seen unless you were standing right on the edge of it. I couldn't move my legs. I screamed until I was hoarse and couldn't yell anymore. Finally I decided that I needed to pray and ask my Heavenly Father for help. And so I did. I closed my eyes and prayed that God would protect me and help me get out. As I said 'amen,' there was a rockslide above me. I covered my head. A large rock fell and knocked the rock holding me in place aside so I could get out. Immediately the rockslide stopped, and I climbed to the top of the hill again. I could see my group walking away in the valley on the other side. They were going to look somewhere else. I yelled to them, my voice louder than ever. They heard me and came and rescued me. The power of prayer saved my life. It won't always be as dramatic as that, but prayer can help you in dire situations and everyday activities. I promise you that someday, when you need it, you can say a prayer and the Lord will answer it. It might not be the answer you expect, but it will be the right answer."

* * *

Smoke billowed into the lobby from the halls, the fire spreading rapidly through the old hotel. The hotel patrons were exiting as quickly as they could. The streets filled with curious onlookers.

Michael held his hand over his mouth to filter out the smoke collecting in what was left of the Hotel Boris lobby. He ran to the pile of rubble where he had seen the hand. The hand moved slowly back and forth.

Michael knelt beside the rubble and gently grabbed the hand with both of his to let the person know he was there.

"Help!" came a muffled cry.

"I'm here," Michael replied. He quickly began removing the rubble, board by board and brick by brick.

The man looked up from the rubble and smiled. Michael recognized Detective Kuznetzov despite all the dirt on his face but didn't take the time to wonder why he was here in Balkhash. He just wanted to get him out.

"Are you okay?"

"Yes, I'm okay. Thank you."

Michael finished moving the rubble and helped him to his feet.

"Can you walk?"

"Yes." Detective Kuznetzov gripped Michael tightly by the shoulder.

Michael led him to the door as flames consumed the lobby.

* * *

President Russell looked up at the shattered doorway. The tall figure standing in the doorway rushed toward him.

"Are you okay, Mr. President?" The man knelt next to President Russell, taking the tape off President Russell's mouth.

"I am President Russell," he responded softly.

"My name is Kirill Karyov. I'm with the Kazakh Special Forces and have orders to escort you to the United States Embassy." He sat President Russell upright and cut the duct tape that held him bound.

"Thank you." President Russell moaned softly.

"Can you walk?" Kirill asked.

"I think so." President Russell forced himself to his feet. His legs ached from being strapped to the chair for several hours, but he could walk.

"This way." Kirill put his hand on President Russell's back and guided him out of the room.

President Russell saw several bodies on the ground.

"Don't look," Kirill ordered and covered President Russell's eyes. "You don't need to see that."

President Russell walked blindly toward the door, not wanting to see what he knew was there. His captors were dead and he was free, but free at what cost? His stomach tightened and turned.

"This way." Kirill led him down the stairs to a large van waiting on the street below. He climbed into the van and was surprised to see Sergei waiting for him.

"Oh my!" Sergei gasped as he looked at President Russell's beaten face covered in dried blood.

Kirill climbed in the van behind President Russell and shut the door. The van sped off into the early morning.

* * *

Detective Kuznetzov gasped for breath as they exited the Hotel Boris. They stumbled away from the building. Several fire trucks had surrounded the hotel and begun to spray massive amounts of water, trying to contain the blaze.

Michael led the detective to an ambulance a short distance away. The paramedic took the detective to assess him. A second paramedic came up to Michael to check on him.

"I'm fine," Michael said, looking back at the building. The southeast corner collapsed into a pile of brick, concrete, and flames. The firefighters rushed the onlookers away from the building. It was coming down. The explosion had caused too much structural damage for the building to hold for long.

"Just let me look at you," the paramedic insisted.

"Fine," Michael said, turning to her.

What had caused the explosion? It reminded him of the other explosion on Lake Balkhash, the one that had destroyed several homes and damaged several others.

Destruction seemed to follow these Americans everywhere they went, yet Michael felt compelled to find them. He knew in his heart they were not the direct cause of the explosions and wreckage they left behind. He needed to know more from them. He had so many questions.

"Thank you," the detective called out to Michael.

Michael turned and looked. The man was bruised and badly hurt, but he would be fine.

"You're welcome."

"I would be dead if not for you."

"Again, you're welcome."

"Were you coming for the Americans, Mr. Ivanov?"

"Yes. How do you know that?"

"My name is Volodya Kuznetzov. I'm a detective for the Kazakh Central Agency. I was following a lead and then boom. Those Americans are very crafty."

"It wasn't the Americans."

"What?" Volodya asked.

"Never mind. Are you sure the Americans were here?" He looked at the remains of the hotel.

"I did not see them, but, yes, they were here."

"Thank you." Michael stood to leave and stopped. He turned back to Detective Kuznetzov. "Do you have any idea where they were headed?"

"No. I was hoping to catch them here, or at least talk to this Yuri Shevchenko and see what he knows."

"Who is Yuri Shevchenko?"

"You don't know?"

"No, I've never heard of him."

"It was his house, the one they blew up across the lake. It was registered to Yuri Shevchenko, and he registered here yesterday afternoon."

"Yuri Shevchenko?" Michael asked.

"Yes, he is a bus driver. He drives cross-country. They found his bus burned up ten miles outside of Zhezkaglian. It was hijacked."

"Thank you for your help." Michael handed Detective Kuznetzov a card. "If you hear anything, let me know right away. Call my cell phone."

"Thank you!" the detective called out as Michael turned and walked away.

Michael Ivanov was still certain that Elders Schofield and Johnson were not responsible for the bombing, even though they were at the scene of three separate bombings now. He was confident they were heading for Astana. Balkhash was not that far out of the direct path, especially if they came here by boat. But how were they going to get from here to Astana? It was still hundreds of miles away and the military was quickly tightening its grip over the country.

Massive fighting had broken out in Astana between smaller factions. The military leader, General Shevchenko, had ordered martial law in Astana, and his order would soon be in the rest of the country. He was quickly seizing power. Michael knew General Shevchenko and wondered if he would give back control once he had it. He was a controlling man, a brilliant military strategist, and very ruthless. Everyone knew that you did not cross General Shevchenko.

Michael did not know how the Americans would get to Astana, but he was certain they would get there. They seemed to be crafty and would figure it out. He wanted to be there to meet them.

Michael returned to his car for his long drive to Astana. He hoped it would be uneventful, but he was certain there would be trouble between here and there.

* * *

Yuri insisted on silence until they knew the train was well out of the city. He didn't want to take any chances of someone hearing them, even though he knew it was not likely.

"I think it's time to relax a little and enjoy the train ride," Yuri said, after picking up bottled water and taking a long drink.

Everyone relaxed. Finally some peace. Their world had been

turned upside down. And they hadn't really had time to relax and think about what had happened to them, how they got here, and what they were doing. Smiles sneaked onto their faces as they drank water and ate the snacks that had been left for them. Among the snacks was a note.

"Please wait in the crate until I come for you. I will make sure we are clear, and then I'll come get you and lead you out of the train station. I cannot guarantee your safety if you do not follow my instructions. My brother asked that I take care of you and lead you safely into the city. I will knock four times on the side of the crate when I have come for you." It was signed "Anton."

"God is with us," Yuri said as he finished reading the note. "He is guiding us safely there."

* * *

"Hello, Sister Russell," Elder Jackson said as he exited the train. "How is President Russell?"

"What do you mean?"

"How is President Russell? Has he found the elders yet?"

"What?" Sister Russell asked again.

"Haven't you talked to President Russell?"

"Not since I got on the train in Astana."

"Oh." A look of concern crept across his face. "I thought he was going to call you. He went back to Astana. Yevgenie told him the elders were alive and so he got back on a train to Astana so he could find them."

"Oh my!" Sister Russell gasped.

"I thought he would have called you by now," Elder Jackson said softly. "I guess he's just busy." Elder Jackson feared the worst. He had been getting updates on the situation in Kazakhstan on the train. It was getting more and more grim. Escalating violence, particularly against Westerners.

"I haven't heard from him," Sister Russell said softly. "I hope he is okay." Tears welled up in her eyes.

"I'm sure he's fine," Elder Jackson tried to assure her. But he knew if President Russell hadn't called, something was definitely wrong. And now he had gone and made her feel horrible about it. *Way to go, Elder!* Elder Jackson knew what was going through her mind. Her husband was trapped in a different country, a country that was on the brink of civil war. The military had been mobilized and were now securing the country. The borders were closed. No one came in and no one went out without the knowledge of the government. People were blowing things up for the sake of blowing things up. People were dying. The violence was getting worse and worse. Everyone who could get out of the country was getting out. And President Russell was in the middle of it all.

Tears poured down her cheeks. She turned and walked back to the Moscow mission van, wiping the tears from her cheeks.

Elder Jackson felt a large knot form in his stomach as he watched her walk away. *That could not have gone any worse.*

* * *

"How did you find me?" President Russell asked Sergei. They were in the back of the van on the way to the embassy.

Sergei didn't immediately answer, his cheeks growing red. "I had to call in a favor from an old acquaintance. A favor I hoped to never have to use. The van had a tracking device on it. They used it to find you. I didn't want to, but I had no choice. I couldn't let them kill you." Tears welled in the corners of his eyes.

The van pulled to a stop just outside the gates to the US Embassy in Astana, Kazakhstan. The door opened from the outside. A man dressed in a Kazakh military uniform held out his hand to President Russell.

"Mr. Russell."

"Yes," President Russell replied, taking the man's hand.

The man gently guided President Russell out of the van. Each move hurt President Russell's tired and sore body.

"That is the United States Embassy." He motioned to a large building surrounded by a large chain link fence. "Proceed quickly to the gate."

"Thank you," President Russell said, looking at the man.

"Just doing my job, sir."

President Russell turned and walked quickly to the embassy's gate. He pulled his passport out of his pocket, showed it to the guard at the gate, and was escorted inside.

* * *

The mood in the crate was jovial. It was cramped and hot, but they were glad to be resting and moving quickly on their way toward Astana and safety. The flashlight cast an eerie glow in the crate.

"My sister mentioned your prophet Joseph Smith," Yuri said out of the blue. "Tell me about him."

Johnson brimmed with excitement. He had longed to share the gospel. All this running was tiring him out. He needed to share the gospel and remind himself he was still a missionary, a messenger from God, bringing a message of peace. Johnson looked to Schofield, who nodded in agreement.

"As a young man," Johnson started, "Joseph was searching for answers. It was a time of great religious fervor. Each group was saying, 'Come here unto the Lord,' yet their teachings were all so different. Joseph didn't know what to believe or whom to turn to.

"So many churches all taught similar teachings, but differed on so many other points. One evening, Joseph was reading in the Bible in the book of James and read 'If any of you lack wisdom, let him ask of God, that giveth to all men liberally.' That's what he decided to do. He was going to ask God if any of the churches were true.

"So he set out to the forest and found a secluded place to pour his soul to the Lord and ask His direction.

"A pillar of light appeared over his head, and in the pillar were two personages, God the Father and His Son, Jesus Christ."

"God is a man?" Yuri asked.

"God looks like a man, yes," Schofield answered.

"I always pictured God like . . ." Yuri paused. "You know I never gave much thought to what God looked like, but I never imagined Him looking like a man. I guess that makes sense. God created man in His own image, like it says in the Bible."

Johnson made sure Yuri was finished and content with the answer.

"Joseph Smith asked God which of all the churches was true. God told him none of them were true. Jesus told him that he would reestablish God's church on the earth.

"Joseph did just that. He was given plates upon which were the writings of ancient prophets that lived in the Americas. He translated them. That is the Book of Mormon." Johnson showed him the copy of the Book of Mormon.

"The Book of Mormon is the word of God and through it we can learn the gospel and learn what we must do to return to our Father in Heaven."

Johnson looked at Mila and Yuri and saw in their eyes that they wanted more. He could feel they understood what he was telling them.

"In the Book of Mormon, one of the prophets issues a challenge. He challenges you to read the Book of Mormon and then to ask God if it is true and that God will confirm it is true. I want to issue you the same challenge. Read the Book of Mormon and then ask God if it is true."

"Okay," Yuri said simply. He reached out, accepted the Book of Mormon from Johnson, and quickly opened it.

* * *

Schofield spent most of the ride to Karaganda in quiet thought while Johnson enthusiastically read from the Book of Mormon with Yuri and Mila. He had participated throughout the discussion only to add his testimony here and there.

He was concerned for his family. They had no doubt heard of the rising violence in Kazakhstan. The train he was on had blown up. They might even think he was dead. He hadn't been able to contact anyone since this craziness began.

Fear crept into his thoughts. *What if the embassy is already abandoned? They won't stick around while the country is at war with itself. They'll take their people and leave.*

What if we're stuck in this country? We'd be stuck in this war. I could probably fit in okay, but not Johnson. He is way too obvious. He sticks out like a sore thumb. He'd be forced to live in seclusion, restricted in a house somewhere.

A loud explosion shook the train.

"What was that?" Schofield asked, scrambling to his feet as if he could do something inside the box.

"I don't know." Yuri shook his head and shrugged his shoulders.

Another explosion shook the train, and the train accelerated.

"What's going on?" asked Johnson. They all tried to stand as the train accelerated.

"What do we do?" asked Mila. They held onto the walls of the crate as if it would cave in.

Panic set in and Mila screamed, throwing her hands over her head.

Yuri grabbed her to comfort her. Johnson and Schofield just watched in nervous horror.

The train accelerated again. They heard more explosions and the train shook again.

A series of explosions in short succession shook the train.

They thought it was going to wreck. It held strong and accelerated faster.

The explosions stopped, and the train stopped shaking.

No one had any real idea what had happened. They could speculate and guess, but the truth was that they would probably never know. They were just thankful that the train was still going and hadn't been wrecked by all the explosions. They were still on their way to Karaganda and hopefully Astana soon after that.

* * *

Sasha sat bleary-eyed at his computer. He had hardly slept since the train explosion. He needed to catch the Americans. If he caught them and disposed of them, then he could be done with this mess. He couldn't risk them getting away and him getting connected to the bombing. He knew the Americans didn't do it, but they would make a good scapegoat if he could catch them and kill them and then blame them for the bombing. The investigation would stop and the risk of him getting caught would be less, a more acceptable risk. There was always a risk when working for the Mafia, but if he was found out, he would lose his job and probably his life. He knew too much. General Shevchenko would never let him live.

The blip on his screen was moving north.

"Where are you going, Michael?"

Michael was always good at reading the clues. He could always guess where the terrorists were going. That's why he was the best. *He is following a lead. He knows where they're going.*

Sasha followed the blip on his screen from Balkhash to where it was now, and watched as it slowly went north. *He's going to Astana.*

How are they getting to Astana? He stared at the screen for a moment. *I don't know how, but they are going to Astana. What is in Astana?* He scratched his chin as he thought. His chin always developed an itch when he was deep in thought.

The American embassy. They are going to the embassy.

He picked up his phone.

"Yes," the woman answered.

"This is Sasha Kazachenko. I need to get to Astana right away."

"Okay," the woman replied. "Give me twenty minutes. I'll see what I can do." She was always receiving such requests, detectives going here and there. She always came through for them. It was her job, and she was good at it.

* * *

Michael saw smoke rising in the distance and slowed his car nervously. Dozens of little pillars of smoke rose against the horizon to the north. The road led right into the midst of it.

Michael slowly continued forward. He glanced about nervously looking for any sign of trouble. The smoke was getting thicker with each passing minute. Soon he would be in the midst of it. He couldn't see the road, but he hoped it turned before getting near the fires. He knew that a battlefield of some sort was coming up, and he did not want to see it. He hoped it wasn't as ugly as some he had seen.

The road continued right through the middle of the battlefield. Craters from explosions pocked the road and surrounding area. Train tracks that ran parallel to the road here were covered in debris, but the tracks seemed to be intact. Smoldering ash rose from the craters. Their pungent odor fouled the air. Michael slowly weaved his way between craters, being careful not to drive into a hole and strand himself. The thick smoke poured from the vehicles that dotted the roadway, enveloping the road. The wind whipped the smoke about. It grabbed at his throat, choking him. He gasped and held his breath. He continued to wind through the battlefield. The craters abruptly stopped, and Michael sped away, leaving the smoke and the smell of burning tires behind him.

He found it odd that throughout the wreckage and destruction he didn't see a single person. Not one body was among the wreckage.

* * *

President Russell tapped his foot on the floor as he waited to see the US ambassador. The embassy medic had looked at President Russell, bandaging up his cuts and scratches. He probably needed stitches and his ribs were likely broken, but the doctor was gone. All that was left was a medic who usually just kept people alive until they could receive proper medical attention. President Russell was sore from head to toe, but he wasn't going to die from his wounds, though he would probably have at least one good scar from the cuts.

The embassy was in chaos. Everyone was trying to wrap up their last-moment affairs and get out of the country before things got any worse. The ambassador was busy making sure everything was in order for their departure.

All nonessential personnel, mostly the families of the workers, interns, and the low-level personnel, had been immediately evacuated.

All that was left was the ambassador, a handful of administration, and security personnel.

"How can I help you?" Ambassador Jones asked as he burst into the room.

"Hello, Mr. Ambassador," President Russell said. He stood and extended his hand.

Ambassador Jones shook his hand. "We're glad you're safe. How can I help you, Mr. Russell?"

"I am president of the Kazakhstan Astana Mission and

have—" President Russell paused, emotions washing over him. "... Or *had* dozens of missionaries here. Most of them are from the United States. Two days ago, we all evacuated to Russia, except two."

"And where are they?"

"They were supposed to be on that train that blew up in Almaty."

"Those were yours?"

"Yes. You know of them?"

"Yes," the ambassador answered. "I have heard of them. They are wanted for questioning by the police. Even worse, they are wanted dead by the underworld. There's actually quite a prize on their head."

"Can you help them?"

"How do you propose I help them?" the ambassador asked. "Mr. Russell, we don't know where they are. In case you missed the memo, the State Department has ordered all Americans out of the country. It's not safe here. By noon tomorrow, we'll be flying out of here. If they come here by then, we'll protect them. So long as they are not criminals. If they were responsible for the explosion, the only help I can offer is recommending a good defense attorney."

"I assure you they are not responsible."

"I hope you're right, Mr. Russell. The Kazakh government does not deal lightly with terrorists." He gave a grim smile.

"The last helicopter leaves tomorrow at noon. You and I will be on it. If your missionaries are here by then, we'll take them with us. If not, they're on their own. You had better pray they get here by then. The country is being locked down. General Shevchenko has declared martial law and is now seizing control of the country. We're lucky to have permission to fly our helicopters out of here. I honestly wish there was more we could do, Mr. Russell, but we're under orders to evacuate. If the situation were different, I'm sure we could help them more, but under the circumstances, I don't know what we could do.

"You may stay here tonight for your protection. We'll leave here tomorrow. Private Nielson will show you to your quarters. Have a good day."

President Russell collapsed into a chair. His one hope was that the embassy could help get the elders out, but now that hope was fading.

TWENTY-ONE

Johnson was startled as the brakes on the train screeched. The train slowed and pulled to a stop. Johnson, Schofield, Yuri, and Mila all sat quietly waiting for the train to stop. They had been told Anton would come for them. Until then, they would wait.

The car jerked as the brakes ground to a halt. The squealing brakes echoed through the car. Then the train jerked to a stop.

"So we just sit here and wait?" Johnson asked, mostly to himself.

"Yes," Schofield whispered.

They turned off their flashlight and sat quietly in the dark, waiting to be freed from the crate. They still had a long ways to go to Astana and had no idea how they were going to get there. At least they were closer now. Johnson could hear their labored breathing as they all tried to remain quiet. He tried to pick out whose breath was whose to help him keep calm.

The minutes crawled as they waited to be let out. The doors ground open and several men climbed in, their voices echoing loudly in the car.

The crate passengers sat waiting, their hearts grabbing at their throats. They expected the hatch to open and the police to come in and arrest them.

"These two here and that one," a man called to the others.

The crates groaned and scraped along the floor as the men dragged them across the floor to the door. Johnson recognized the sound of a forklift reaching in and lifting up the other crates in the car and hauling them away. For twenty agonizing minutes they sat huddled in their own crate waiting, expecting at any moment to be discovered.

The forklift drove away, the rumble of its engine fading in the distance, and the massive doors slammed shut, leaving the hideaways in silence.

* * *

Michael slowed to a stop at the checkpoint just outside of Karaganda. This was the third such checkpoint he had passed since he left Balkhash. It was now pretty routine: they asked for his identification and reason for travel. He showed them his badge identifying who he was. He never offered a reason. They always saw his badge and let him pass. This time was no different. The guards looked at his badge and promptly allowed him through the checkpoint.

He drove quickly toward Karaganda. The lack of traffic on the road allowed him to drive unusually fast.

A sign on the side of the road read "Train Station 2 KM."

"I wonder," he said out loud as he followed the signs to the train station. *Is it possible they hitched a ride on a train?*

He drove past rows of apartment buildings. People here just went on living their lives despite what was going on in the rest of the country. Kids played in the park. So far they seemed to have escaped the chaos that was enveloping the rest of Kazakhstan.

Michael pulled into the parking lot of the train station. Only seven of the hundreds of parking spots were used. He walked slowly up to the station.

He opened the door to the train station and entered. The massive lobby normally packed with travelers stood empty, not a soul in sight. He walked slowly through it, his footsteps echoing in the eerie silence of the barren station.

He approached the ticket counter and rapped on the counter, hoping to fetch someone's attention from the back. There was no reply.

He walked over to the door that allowed employees into the ticket booth and knocked. Again, no reply.

He tried the handle. It was unlocked. He slowly pushed the door open and looked inside.

"Hello?" he called out. "Is anybody here?" Silence.

He began to walk in and stopped. Footsteps. Someone was coming. He quietly pulled the door shut and rushed to the ticket counter. The footsteps drew close. A man rounded the corner and stopped when he saw Michael.

"Hello," Michael called, recognizing the man's uniform as one worn by the train workers.

"Hello," the man replied. "Can I help you?"

"Yes. My name is Michael Ivanov." He pulled out his badge and displayed it for the man. "What is your name?"

"My name is Anton." They shook hands.

"I am with the antiterrorist task force. I need to find out what trains you had coming in today. And any that might be leaving today for Astana."

"You know, that is not my responsibility," Anton said. "I don't know who is coming and who is going, but I can take you to Volodya. He knows all the comings and goings of the train station."

"Thank you. That would be most helpful."

Anton walked slowly forward.

"Just take those doors," Anton said, pointing across the lobby to a set of doors. "And go down that hall. Volodya is in there and he will help you with whatever you need."

"Thank you." Michael shook Anton's hand. It felt sweaty.

"You are welcome. Good luck to you."

* * *

"Is there a phone I can use to make a call to Moscow?" President Russell asked Private Nielson as they walked along the empty corridor of the embassy.

"Yes," Private Nielson replied. "Your room has a phone. Pick up and the embassy operator will help connect you."

"Thank you."

President Russell hurried into his room, thanked Private Nielson for guiding him, and grabbed the phone. In all the excitement he had forgotten to call his wife. She was probably worried sick by now.

"Operator. May I help you?"

"Yes, I need to call Moscow."

"Okay. What is the number?"

President Russell relayed the number. He had called the Moscow mission enough times that he remembered the number. He paced as he waited for the operator to connect him.

"Russia Moscow Mission." He recognized Sister Vashenko's voice.

"Sister Vashenko, this is President Russell. Is Sister Russell there?"

"Yes, yes. Just one minute."

"Hello?" Sister Russell said as she came on.

"Hi—" President Russell started.

"Why didn't you call me?" she interrupted.

"I'm sorry," was all President Russell could say.

After a moment he continued. "I found out the elders were alive and I had to go back for them. I've been a little busy since then."

"Well, the next time you decide to head off into a war zone, at least have the decency to call me first."

"I . . . I . . . ," he stuttered, not knowing what to say.

"I'm just happy you're okay," she said softly.

He breathed a sigh of relief. He was just happy to hear her voice. She didn't need to know all he had been through. Not now anyway.

* * *

The door to the train car crashed open with a roar. Schofield hopped to his feet. He couldn't see anything in the dark, but something felt wrong.

Someone climbed on the boxes outside. The door flung open and a man stuck his head in and his arm.

"Quickly," he called, extending his hand. "They're coming for you!"

Schofield jumped up and took his hand. Anton pulled him out of the crate. Schofield reached back in.

"Hand me our stuff," he ordered.

"Who's coming for us?" Mila asked, handing Schofield their backpacks.

"The police," Anton answered. "I saw him in the terminal. He was asking what train came in today."

Schofield pulled Mila up and she climbed out of the crate. They pulled Johnson and Yuri out. Anton rushed to the door of the car. He peered around the corner both ways.

"Let's go," Anton said and jumped off the car onto the gravel. The rocks grating together echoed throughout the train yard. He stopped. Footsteps echoed on the gravel from across the train yard. He turned back into the car and held his finger to his mouth. Schofield's heart raced. After so much time sitting and now they would have to run. Anton paused for a second and then motioned for them to follow him.

They slowly climbed from the car and headed quickly to the back of the train. The crunch of the gravel seemed like the roar of a lion.

Anton held up his hand for them to stop as he reached the

back. He crept around the back to peer along the train. The path was empty between the two trains. They crept to the next train. Anton checked to see if it was clear and they moved to the next one.

* * *

"Would you like to see the departing trains or arriving trains first?" the station manager asked.

"Arriving," Michael answered quickly.

"Train 497 arrived from Balkhash just thirty minutes ago."

"Good." If they were here, that would be the train they came in on.

They walked slowly past several trains. "Train 497 is on the far track."

"Thank you," Michael replied, looking carefully at the parked trains.

He hoped to find the elders in the train yard. They rounded the second to last set of cars.

"This is train 497 from Balkesh. What is it you would like?"

"Have you unloaded anything from the train?"

"I believe they unloaded a handful of crates, but most of the train is just as it was when it arrived."

"Very good. Let's start here at the front." Michael climbed onto the locomotive and began snooping around. He knew that some engineers would stow goods and sometimes people in compartments under their beds. He found no such compartment here. He moved on to the next car and the next, searching for a place where people could hide.

* * *

Elder Schofield gasped for breath as he tried to keep up with Anton.

"Follow me!" Anton ordered

They quickly and quietly crept toward the terminal. As they rounded the backside of the building, he heard massive wheels begin to roll. An engine roared to life, but there was no horn blowing.

"Quickly! Run!" Anton shouted and sprinted away. They followed close behind him.

"You must get on this train. It's going to Moscow but will pass very close to Astana." They ran across the tracks, sprinting toward a train that was slowly creeping away from the station. It was gaining speed with each passing moment. The front of the train was now turning away from the station.

Breathing hard, Anton ordered them on the last car. "Hurry! Climb the steps."

"Get off the train before you reach the border," Anton said. "They will search the train at the border."

Schofield jumped onto the steps and grabbed the rail. He held out his hand. Mila grabbed it and he pulled her on. She scrambled up the steps and into the last car of the train. Johnson quickly followed her and finally Schofield pulled Yuri onto the train.

"Good luck!" Anton called out as he slowed to a walk.

"Thank you!" Schofield waved and entered the car.

The caboose was just a small room with a couple of benches and a telephone. It was mostly used for people to sit and watch the scenery go by. In World War II, it had been used as a lookout to prevent enemies from sneaking up on the back of the trains. It was still used as a lookout on occasions when the train was carrying valuable supplies. Fortunately, on this particular trip, the car was empty.

"Should we stay here or find somewhere else to ride?" Schofield asked as he surveyed the room.

"Somewhere else," Johnson replied, waving his hand in front of his nose. The car reeked of smoke.

"Good call," Schofield said and slowly opened the door to the next car. He cracked it just enough to peek through. It was a passenger car with two rows of wooden benches lining the walls. The stench of sweat and smoke permeated the room. They crept through, hoping to find some cabins to hide in because these open passenger cars would not provide much cover. Schofield cracked the door to the next car and peeked through. It was a cabin car, or at least it looked like it. A hallway ran down the middle, the wooden floors worn from years of foot traffic. Three doors lined each side of the hall. Schofield motioned for the others to wait while he checked out the rooms.

"I should go," Yuri suggested.

Schofield paused and then agreed.

Yuri crept quietly into the car and stopped at the first door. He stuck his ear to the door. It was quiet. He tried the door. Locked.

* * *

Yuri checked the door across the hall. Locked.

He walked to the next door and stuck his ear to the door. Silence. He tried the door. Locked. He walked across the hall and stopped. A door was opening—the last door. He grabbed the fourth door. Unlocked. The end door swung wide, blocking Yuri from sight. He pulled open the door and ducked inside. Schofield watched as a large man closed his door and exited out the front of the car. His heart raced. The man could have easily come this way and they would have been caught.

* * *

Michael searched one car after another, no sign of any stowaways. Either the missionaries were very good at hiding their tracks, or they weren't here. Still, he continued on to the next car. Only three more cars and his hunch would be a dud. This car showed some promise. A huge crate sat in the corner next to several smaller crates. He climbed in the car and then onto the smallest crate. He took a step to the next one. It was almost like stairs leading to the top. He looked on top of the crate and saw an open hatch on the top of it. He looked inside. It was dark, but he could see well enough. There were pillows, blankets, and wrappers. Someone had been here.

"When is the train leaving for Astana?" Michael asked

The station manager checked his watch. "In thirty minutes."

"Not anymore. Stop that train."

* * *

Detective Sasha Kazachenko boarded a military plane headed for Astana. The transportation that had been arranged for him was most fortunate. There was no baggage check on the military planes because there was no need for it. Most of the passengers were military and some politicians, and they usually traveled with their own security forces that preferred to take their weapons with them. The lack of concern for weapons on the plane was a benefit for Sasha. He had his standard police issue sidearm, but he also had several assault weapons in his suitcase. He needed to eliminate the Americans before someone determined they were not responsible. He could not have General Shevchenko implicated in this mess; there was too much at stake. He never should have hired those fools to blow up the train. The explosion had been spectacular, but they were sloppy and left too much evidence. They had been eliminated. Sasha made sure of that, but the evidence could still link him and the general to the bombing, and that would be disastrous. He needed to kill the Americans and blame the bombing on them. If they were dead and people thought they did it, the pressure on him and the general would lessen. He wasn't sure how he was going to take care of the Americans, but he was sure that he would think of something.

In two hours he would be in Astana, hopefully long before the Americans arrived.

* * *

Michael and the station manager proceeded quickly to the train scheduled to leave for Astana. He ordered the station manager to place guards at both ends of the train, one on each side so no one could escape undetected, while he searched the train. He noticed another train pulling out of the station.

"Where is that train going?"

"That one is going to Moscow."

"What is it carrying?"

"It's mostly empty cars. It will be searched at the border, sir."

Michael watched it for a moment, wondering if he should stop it, before turning back to the train scheduled for Astana.

He followed the same pattern as he had on the previous train, starting at the front and searching each car thoroughly. He tediously began searching each of the train's 129 cars. There were numerous places where people could hide, but the train was empty of life. There was no indication that anyone had or would be stowing away on this train.

In car 74, he found something that he was certainly not looking for. It looked almost like a handful of giant scuba tanks strapped together with wires, but Michael recognized it immediately: a massive bomb.

He slowly backed out of the car and away from the train.

"What exactly is this train transporting?" he asked the station manager.

"I'm not sure. It arrived from Baikonur yesterday, and I was to add four cars of produce to the back and send it on its way."

Michael knew Baikonur was where they launched the Russian space fleet. Anything coming from there had the possibility of being highly incendiary.

"Get everyone away from the train!" Michael yelled. He ran away and the others followed.

"What is it?" the manager asked as he caught up to Michael.

"A bomb, a very big bomb." In that moment, Michael doubted his belief in the missionaries. It seemed everywhere they went, explosions followed them. The train station in Almaty, the beach house on Lake Balkhash, the Hotel Boris, and now a train headed to Astana. He had read the Book of Mormon and he felt it was true, but how could men preaching something so good be connected with atrocities?

Michael continued running until they reached the other side of the train station several hundred feet away and protected by the station itself.

"Get everyone out of the area," he ordered the manager. "Now!"

The manager got on his radio and announced that all station workers needed to evacuate the station immediately.

Michael called the local police and informed them of the bomb. The bomb squad would be arriving soon. They needed to get farther away. He described the bomb to the dispatcher, who patched him through to the bomb squad.

"Run far and fast," the man said.

"Let's go!" Michael ordered and led everyone completely out of the train yard, making sure to keep the building between them and the bomb. If it did go off, he wanted as much protection as he could get.

"What time was that train scheduled to leave?" he asked the station manager.

"Five minutes ago."

"I don't think there is enough time."

"What?"

The roar of the explosion cut him off. A massive ball of fire rose into the sky on the other side of the train station, and a screech pierced the air. Fiery balls of shrapnel flew through the sky.

Michael tried to yell, "Take cover!" But the noise was too loud, and no one could hear him. A second explosion shook the ground they stood on and then a third. He covered his ears, but the sound was deafening. Heat from the flames singed his eyebrows, and the building was consumed in flames. Michael turned and ran. Massive chunks of twisted, burning steel hit the ground next to him and rolled into a parked car, demolishing it.

Michael ran for his life. The flames were growing stronger, and Michael felt like they were chasing him down the streets, swallowing everything in its path. He could feel the heat on his neck as he ran. *Just a little farther and I can hide behind a building.* An apartment building loomed ahead of him. Michael hoped it would protect him from the flames. He ducked behind the building and kept running, and the roar of flames and wind rushed past him. He tripped and collapsed to the ground, gasping for breath. The flames had consumed all of the oxygen; there was nothing left for him to breathe. He rolled onto his hands and knees, facing the fire, and gasped for air. He looked at the flames rushing past. *What of the others?* he thought. *Where are they? Surely I wasn't the only one who escaped the wrath.* Seven people were standing with him when the bomb went off, and this was the first safe place. He hoped that his worst fears were wrong.

The flames from the initial explosions died down, leaving the buildings caught in its wake to burn of their own accord. Michael wasn't out of danger yet. He stood between two large apartment buildings that were covered in flames. He covered his mouth with his shirt. The air was thin, and he needed to move or die of suffocation. More explosions shook the ground, and the buildings swayed from the shock waves. If he didn't suffocate first, he would be crushed.

Michael looked both ways and ran back the way he came. He remembered seeing a park not far from here. That would be the safest place. There would be no burning buildings and hopefully lots of fresh air. His back ached. Michael rubbed his neck and found that all the hair was gone. He pulled his shirt up over his mouth again and ran into the street. He glanced back at the train station, or where the train station used to stand. It was now just a burning pile of rubble. He turned and ran for the park. His lungs burned as they struggled for air, the smell of the smoke permeating. Michael didn't look back again; he just ran.

* * *

Yuri ducked into the cabin and quickly and softly closed the door behind him.

"Hello," a voice said loudly.

Yuri turned to see an older man dressed in a train engineer outfit sitting at the table. He was holding a bottle of vodka.

"Hello," Yuri answered

"Come, let us drink." The man held up his bottle and then waved it, signaling for Yuri to come. He patted the table. "Come, sit."

Yuri walked forward and extended his hand. The man took it, and they shook.

"Yuri," Yuri stated.

"Vladimir."

"Are you the engineer?"

"Not today my friend. Today I am just another drunken passenger." He reached under the table, pulled up another bottle, and offered it to Yuri.

"Perhaps later," Yuri answered. "I need to find my room first."

"There are no passengers today. It's just me and my brother.

He is across the hall, but he is the engineer today. Not really, but there's no one on the tracks until we get to Russia, and he wanted to drive and I didn't, so he bought the vodka, and he and my assistant are driving, and I am relaxing. So please join me." He patted the table again.

"After I get settled, I will join you for company, but first I must get settled." Yuri was nervous talking to him, but the bottle was almost empty, and the man was acting like he was well on his way to an alcohol-induced nap. Yuri wanted to get what information he could from the man. "What room can I have?"

"They are all empty, except number four in this car. I am staying in the back so I can drink till my heart is content. So help yourself to the end room. Hey, why not take the last two? If any one gives you trouble, tell them you are with Vladimir, and no one will bother you." He handed Yuri a ring of keys.

"Thank you, Vladimir. That is very kind of you."

"Anything for a drinking buddy. Please come join me as soon as you get settled."

"Thank you," Yuri said. He opened the door and slipped out.

* * *

Schofield opened the car door and walked into the hallway. He walked cautiously toward the door that Yuri slipped into. He put his ear to the door to listen. He could hear voices, but couldn't make out what they were saying. It didn't not seem like hostile talking, though. The door handle turned. He ducked back against the wall, his heart pounding. The door opened wide and Yuri stepped out, closing the door behind him. He turned and saw Schofield with his back against the wall. Holding his finger to his lips, Yuri motioned for Schofield to go. Schofield walked back toward Johnson and Mila. Yuri stopped him at the last door and indicated that he should go in.

Schofield quietly opened the door and slipped into the room.

Johnson and Mila soon joined Schofield. Yuri followed shortly after, closed the door behind him, and locked it.

"We are in luck, maybe," Yuri explained. "The engineer is across the hall and will soon be asleep, thanks to his vodka. His brother will be driving the train. That could be a good or bad thing. They should stay up at the front of the train."

"Finally some decent rest!" Johnson exclaimed.

"Maybe. The conductor so far is a happy drunk. He invited me to drink with him, not caring that I shouldn't be on the train. Let's hope he doesn't become a hostile drunk after he drinks some more. You never can tell how vodka will affect people. We still need to be cautious."

"So what do we do now?" Johnson asked Schofield.

"I guess we wait. It should only be a couple hours to Astana from here, so we just hang tight and hope the train isn't going too fast when we get to Astana."

"What do you mean by that?"

"By what?"

"The train going too fast," Johnson said.

"Anton said this train is going to Moscow, but will go by Astana. It probably won't stop in Astana," Schofield explained.

"So . . . we have to jump?" Johnson asked.

"Unless you have a better idea of how to get off a moving train," Schofield said.

"Nothing comes to mind, but there has to be a better way of getting off a moving train than jumping."

"Who knows," Schofield joked, "maybe we'll find a nice soft place to land,"

"Maybe there will be a big pile of leaves piled up next to the tracks that we could jump into."

"There is a river," Mila interjected.

"A river?" Johnson asked.

"Yeah. I lived with my friend one summer in Astana when I

was young. The tracks used to go over a large river. We used to jump off the bridge into the river. It's a long drop, but it is definitely doable."

"Good then." Schofield smiled. "We'll jump off a moving train into a river that may or may not have water in it. Great plan."

The sound of an explosion raced through the train.

"What was that?" Johnson asked.

"I don't know," Schofield said.

They rushed out of their cabin toward the back of the train. In the distance, they saw a massive ball of fire slowly rising into the sky above the city. The flames crept slowly into the sky chased quickly by billowing black clouds that poured up from the ground, enveloping the flames.

"Whoa," Johnson said as he walked onto the platform at the back of the train.

"What happened there?" Mila asked.

"Some sort of explosion."

"Not just some sort of explosion," Schofield said. "That's a massive explosion. It's as big or maybe bigger than the one in Almaty. What is going on?"

"It is war," Mila said. "Each group is trying to seize power. It will get worse before it gets better. You two really need to get out of here."

"We should get back inside," Yuri said from the doorway. "We don't want people to see us here."

"Who's going to be looking at the train when there's that?" Johnson pointed to the smoke billowing up from the city.

"Let's go," Yuri ordered and guided them all back to their room.

Johnson realized that if they weren't at the embassy by tomorrow, they wouldn't be leaving the country—the country that was quickly falling into chaos.

TWENTY-TWO

Michael lay on his back in the middle of a soccer field staring up at the black smoke billowing across the sky. A warm breeze blew across his body. He still fought for oxygen with every breath, but it was getting easier to breathe. Sirens blared from all directions, converging on the chaos that used to be the train station. Michael sat up and put his arms around his knees. All that was left of the train station was bricks and flames. This bomb was much larger than the first in Almaty. Either that, or there was highly explosive material on the train. That was certainly possible, considering the train's cargo originated in Baikonur. Michael wondered what he should do. In his heart he felt the missionaries were not responsible for the bombings. He believed their book. He had prayed about it and God told him it was true. His mind told a different story. Everywhere the missionaries went, destruction followed. Not just casual mayhem, but full-fledged destruction: the two largest explosions he had ever seen. The missionaries eluded him at every turn. Could it be just chance that they had avoided him? Were they trying to get anyone off their trail? He knew it couldn't be a coincidence these explosions happened at every location the missionaries were tied to. He had to get some help. He wasn't going to catch them by himself.

He picked up his phone and called his office.

"Hello."

"Lyuba, give me Sasha,"

"Sasha left earlier and hasn't been back. No one has seen him in hours. I've been trying to reach him, but no one can find him. How are you, Michael?"

"I'm fine, thank you. I was almost blown to little pieces, but I am fine."

"What happened?" Lyuba asked.

"I'll give you the short version. I've been following the Americans. They're heading to Astana, probably to the US embassy, but every time I get close, something blows up. This time it was the train station in Karaganda, and it was worse than the explosion in Almaty."

"Are you okay?" Lyuba asked.

"Yes, but I don't know if I can make it to Astana before the Americans do. My car was just destroyed. Get the police there looking for them. We need to catch them; I want them alive. I need to find out where they're getting their supplies."

"Okay. Do you need anything else?"

"I'll be okay. Make sure the police know the Americans are coming and to keep a look out for them. I'll call you if I hear anything."

"You want me to have Sasha call you if I hear from him?"

"Yes. Thank you, Lyuba *dorogaya*."

"It's nothing."

Michael hung up and looked around. "I need a car," he said to himself.

"You need a taxi?" a voice from behind him asked.

Michael jumped. He hadn't heard anyone approach, but his ears were ringing. He'd had a hard time hearing Lyuba. He turned and looked. A young man with a thin mustache and a sweat suit stood over him.

"Yes," Michael answered. "I need to get to Astana,"

"Sorry. The military has all the roads closed going into Astana. Anywhere else I can take you?"

"They will let me in." He took out his badge and showed the young man.

"Very well then. Let's go." He turned and headed toward a BMW parked next to the field.

"You drive a BMW for a taxi?" Michael asked.

"I'm not a taxi driver," the young man answered.

"Okay," Michael said. It was a common, if frowned upon, practice for regular people to double as taxi drivers if they were going somewhere. Michael had his ride into Astana and wasn't going to complain about the young man's lack of taxi license.

* * *

"We should be in Astana in less than two hours," Yuri stated. "Let's stay here out of sight. We should be able to see Astana from this window. I'm not sure how we're going to get off the train, but I guess we'll worry about that when we get there."

"I can't handle this anymore. Everywhere we go things are blowing up. We have to get out of here," Schofield said.

"We're almost there," assured Johnson. He wanted to maintain a positive attitude, but it was getting harder. It had been a very tiring few days and he hoped the madness would end soon. They just needed to get to Astana and to the embassy. Johnson realized he wasn't sure where the embassy was. *One thing after another*, he thought.

* * *

Sasha sat comfortably in his seat on the military transport plane. The plane was nearly ready to depart for Astana. He was planning how he would eliminate the Americans. He hoped he could do it without being caught. He would be okay. After all, they were criminals. At least that was what the media had been led to believe. He might get some sort of punishment, but it certainly wouldn't be severe. He might just have to shoot them first and ask questions later.

His phone rang. It was the office again. He was tempted to ignore it but decided this time he should answer it. Otherwise, they would just keep calling.

"Hello."

"Sasha," Lyuba started, "I've been trying to reach you all day. Where have you been?"

Sasha knew she didn't need an answer, and he didn't need to answer.

"I've been here and there. What's up?"

"Michael called. He said the Americans are headed for Astana, and he thinks they're trying to get to the US embassy. We need to call the police there and capture them."

"Have you already contacted the police in Astana?"

"No. I wanted to contact you first."

"I'm actually on my way to Astana now. I'll take care of all the arrangements there. Don't you worry about a thing."

"Why are you going to Astana?"

"I'm just following a lead. I should be there in two hours. I'll take care of them."

"Really," Lyuba said. "It's no bother for me to call them."

"No," Sasha said. "I think it will come better from me if I talk to them personally. I am going there anyway. I'll be there soon and I'll talk to them personally. That way they know how serious we really are."

"Okay, I'll let you take care of it then. Thank you."

"No problem. Hey, where is Michael anyway?"

"He's in Karaganda. There was another bomb there. The Americans had been there. They sure are causing a lot of grief. I hope you catch them."

"Sounds to me like I may have to kill them. They probably won't let me capture them, but I'll try."

He was happy that Michael had confirmed his suspicions that they were heading to Astana. He just had to get to the embassy and find a good sniper location. He would shoot them from a distance and escape. No one would be the wiser. They couldn't trace the gun to him because he had taken it from a lowlife he had killed years ago. No one knew the gun existed, let alone in his possession. Sasha smiled and leaned back in his seat as the captain announced that the plane would be leaving momentarily.

* * *

Michael followed the young man toward his BMW. It seemed odd to him that the young man was offering him a ride. *How does a young kid afford a car like that? And why was he asking if I needed a taxi?* Something was not right.

"What was your name?" Michael asked as he caught up to the young man.

"Dennis." The young man held out his hand to shake. "And your name is?"

"Michael Ivanov." He shook hands. "Where are you from?"

"Los Angeles," Dennis answered.

"Los Angeles, America?"

"Yes. I moved here years ago when I got married. She was from here and was going to school in America but didn't like it, so we moved back here."

"You speak very good Russian."

"Thank you."

"You're not afraid of all the violence and the war that is breaking out?"

"Not really." Dennis opened the door and let Michael enter the car.

Dennis got into the car and quickly drove away from the chaos that was quickly enveloping Karaganda.

"All this chaos and you aren't going to leave?"

"Why would I? My wife and daughter are here. Where would I go? They can't leave."

"Where are your wife and daughter now?"

"Actually, in Astana. I was on a business trip when the violence broke out, and now I can't get in."

"With me you can. What a coincidence."

"It's not a coincidence."

"What do you mean?"

"I didn't know how to get back to Astana, so I prayed. I asked God how to get to my family, so I could protect and comfort them. I was given the impression that I should come to this park in Karaganda and I would find a way into the city."

"Really?"

"It's true. I've never been to Karaganda before. I didn't know this park even existed. But I do know that God answers prayers, so I followed that still, small voice and it guided me here. And then I found you, and you can get us into Astana, and I'll be able to be with my family again."

Dennis left the city and headed on the empty highway toward Astana.

"What religion are you?" Michael asked.

Dennis just looked at him.

"I don't mean to be so bold, but you seem like a religious man. I've only recently discovered religion and thought maybe I could ask you some questions."

"I'm a member of The Church of Jesus Christ of Latter-day Saints," Dennis answered

"I think I may have heard of that church before. Do you know much about other religions?

"I know a little bit."

"What about scriptures? Do you know the scriptures?"

"I do know the scriptures. Did you have a specific question?"

"What do you know of the Book of Mormon?"

"The Book of Mormon is a translation of writings written by prophets thousands of years ago in the Americas."

"So you've heard of it then."

"Yes, I've heard of it." Dennis smiled. "Could you reach under your seat and grab that for me?"

"Of course." Michael reached under his seat, grabbed a book, and pulled it up. It was the Book of Mormon.

"You have one of these?"

"Yes. That's one of the scriptures members of The Church of Jesus Christ of Latter-day Saints read."

"So you're a member of this church?

"Yes. Did you read the Book of Mormon?" Dennis asked.

"Yes, I did. It was fantastic, and I did what I was told. I prayed about it and I was told by the Holy Ghost that it is true," Michael said.

"It sounds to me like you need to meet with missionaries some more."

"Yes, I have lots of questions, but I don't know . . . There are so many questions and so much confusion."

"Can I answer some questions for you?"

"Yes, maybe. I'll start at the beginning." Michael took a deep breath.

"Three days ago I was focused on my job. I am the head of the antiterrorist task force. We were investigating all foreigners in Almaty. There was a lot of chatter that something big was going to happen, and we didn't know what, so we were following leads. A friend of mine is a member of your church and he invited me to come hear the American missionaries. I went—not to hear the missionaries, but to find out more about these two Americans. Americans aren't on the top of our list of potential terrorists, but we have to investigate everyone. Something about them interested me after I met them. Then one of them, Elder

Johnson, gave me a Book of Mormon and challenged me to read it, which I did. At first it was work related. I just wanted to find out what they were preaching, but the book touched me and I couldn't put it down. I had to finish it."

Michael paused, taking a big breath before continuing.

"The next morning a big bomb at the train station in Almaty went off, and these two missionaries were seen leaving the train right before the explosion. So immediately they were suspects."

"Wait," Dennis said. "These two missionaries who are on the news are the same two who met with you?"

"Yes," Michael said. "But I didn't believe they had anything to do with it, so I followed some leads on my own. I wanted to catch them and clear them as suspects. I've been following them for days and everywhere I go there are more explosions. I don't know what to believe. My heart tells me that this is all true and important, but my mind says that they're involved in the bombings. I don't know what to do. I want to catch them, but my people may not be as careful as I would. They don't mind eliminating a potential threat, whether or not the threat is real."

"I don't know much about your missionaries, but I can tell you that you received inspiration from the Holy Ghost once. He told you the Book of Mormon was true. And it is. Maybe you should ask God if these guys are a real threat or if it is just a case of being in the wrong place at the wrong time, twice."

"Four times actually—the train in Almaty, a house by Lake Balkhash, a hotel in Balkhash, and the train station in Karaganda."

"Sounds to me like someone is trying to blow *them* up. And almost succeeding four times."

"There have been thousands of explosions across the country in the last couple days, but in the back of my mind I still wonder if they are somehow involved."

"Think about it and then ask God," Dennis suggested. "Like you did with the Book of Mormon. He will give you an answer to any question you have."

Michael sat and wondered if God would answer him again. He had answered him about the Book of Mormon. Would He answer him about the elders?

* * *

"There she is!" Schofield called.

It had been months since Mila had been in Astana, and she was glad to see it. It meant an end to the madness of the last few days. At least she hoped it did. If all went well, Schofield and Johnson would be safely evacuated, but she and Yuri would be in another city, with no way to get home. They had some acquaintances they hoped would help them, but they just didn't know.

Schofield came and sat back down. They were discussing the Restoration of the gospel and how important it was to the salvation of man. Yuri had a lot of questions, and Johnson was always ecstatic to answer them. In the midst of all the chaos, Johnson had called down the Holy Ghost to testify to Yuri and Mila of the truth of the Restoration, that Joseph Smith was indeed a prophet and had seen God the Father and Jesus Christ, and that the Book of Mormon was true. The train was quiet and calm despite everything else. Mila sat and enjoyed the feeling that swept over her as Johnson described how Joseph Smith received the priesthood and established the Church.

She looked over at Schofield. He watched as Johnson taught the lesson. Occasionally he would add in a thought or two of support, but usually he just let Johnson teach. He seemed to enjoy watching Johnson teach. Mila still didn't know a lot about the Church, but she wanted to know more. She wanted this feeling to stay with her forever. For a while she could forget about the madness of the world, her dying lake, and her mom. She missed her mom, but when the missionaries talked to Mila, the pain was bearable. Life seemed to have meaning again. She wished she could just listen to them forever, but she knew that wasn't possible. In just a short while, the elders would be leaving, and she would be stuck here with nothing but memories, memories of a crazy flight from Lake Balkhash to Astana, and memories of the feeling that these two young men brought with them. The feelings were what she hoped most to keep.

She hoped that her dad felt it too. She looked over at him and saw a twinkle in his eye that she hadn't seen in a long time. She knew he had tried to move on after Mom died, but he still struggled. Some days the sadness would eat at him until he broke down and cried. And then he would struggle on some more, bearing the burden of his wife's death. He needed something more in his life besides hardship and sorrow. And now two young boys from halfway around the world had brought him joy—true joy—in the midst of a civil war. He looked happier than he had in a long time.

* * *

Sasha gathered his things after the military transport landed at an airfield just outside of Astana. He carried his case that had three assault rifles and loads of ammunition off the plane. He'd brought three different guns because he wasn't sure how the final encounter would play out, and he wanted to be prepared for any and all possibilities. Now it seemed to him all he would need would be his sniper rifle.

He had fond memories of his time in the military. Sasha signed up early so he could train with Special Forces and spent two years in sniper training, a job at which he excelled. He ranked highest among all the snipers in his division. He had to eliminate the Americans and make it look like they were involved with the bombings. He had already planted evidence that he could use to incriminate them as long as they weren't around to discredit it. Sasha wasn't sure how exactly he was going to kill them. He had to find the embassy and find a good place from which to shoot them, a place where he could shoot, escape quickly, and not get caught. If he did get caught, he could rationalize the shooting, but he hoped it wouldn't come to that.

He walked off the plane with his luggage and headed for the terminal. There was no baggage check and no security checkpoint. He just took his luggage into the terminal and found a bus that was heading from the base to Astana. The driver was more than happy to help him. Sasha was not very familiar with Astana, so he asked the driver for directions.

"Do you know where the United States Embassy is?" Sasha asked the driver. "I'm supposed to meet some associates there."

"I'm not sure of the exact location of the embassy, but I know the general area. We'll be passing by there, so I'll get you close and you can ask for exact directions when we get there."

"Thank you."

TWENTY-THREE

"There it is!" Mila called out.

Johnson peered out and looked past her until he could see the ravine ahead. They were standing on the balcony at the back of the train. She had told them about how when she was younger they used to jump from this bridge into the river. Of course, they weren't jumping from a moving train then. The train had slowed significantly as it came into a large bend that cut just to the west of Astana. She climbed carefully onto the railing and held on. Schofield climbed up next to her. They were going to jump and then Johnson and Yuri would follow immediately after. They had drawn straws to decide the order.

Johnson stood behind Mila, getting ready to climb onto the railing. Mila had remembered the river used to be huge, forty or fifty meters across, but that was when she was young and she wasn't confident how wide the river was now. Mila and Schofield had to jump as soon as they were over the ravine in order to allow Yuri and Johnson time to get up and jump before the train crossed the ravine. Yuri threw all of their gear off the train before the ravine so it wouldn't get wet. They would just climb up and get it. Schofield stood on the railing of the balcony, his legs shaking, the wind blowing his hair.

"I see the water," Mila called.

The train sped along. The distance to the ravine drew closer. Schofield crouched precariously on the edge of the train car as the train approached the ravine. Mila crouched, and they jumped early, hoping their momentum would carry them into the water fifty feet below.

* * *

Yuri scrambled up onto the ledge. He looked at Johnson, who stood on the ledge. Yuri jumped. The water was narrow, not near as wide as they had hoped. Johnson crouched and jumped as the train raced onward, but he slipped and his pants caught on the railing. He crashed into the side of the train and hung briefly upside down, his head bashing against the side of the train. His pants ripped and he fell off the train, narrowly missing the tracks, into the deep ravine. For what seemed like an eternity, Johnson watched the train race away. He struggled to roll over to see where he was going to land. When he did, he saw the ground just feet away, and he crashed into the shallow water on the edge of the bank. He gasped as he hit the bottom of the river. He had landed in just two feet of water. The impact forced the air from his lungs. He gasped, inhaling mud and water, and choked before all went black.

* * *

Sasha found the embassy with little difficulty. The driver dropped him off just two blocks away, and it was easy to find from there. It didn't look like a good place for a sniper. It was on a large street and surrounded by a large fence. The entrance to the compound was a massive steel gate set next to a small building that served both as a protection and a lookout. There was a bulletproof window on the building that the guards used to check people in. They could slide their passports under a little gap. The guard would verify the ID, and a second guard would let them in the gate. The gate was actually two gates. Only one door could be open at a time, so the person entering the embassy would pass through the first gate and it would close, and then the second gate would open, allowing them onto the embassy grounds. They then had thirty feet to go to the main building, which was also protected by bulletproof glass.

Sasha slowly walked by the embassy, examining it to determine where might be the best location to shoot the Americans. Thirty minutes later he walked by again, finding a number of locations that could work. Now he needed to find a place to take the shot from, preferably one that would give him ample cover and a large potential target area. A small park was up the street that could be an ideal place for sniping. It provided adequate coverage and an easy escape route by foot to the subway station on the other side of the park. He found a bench to sit on and rest. This wouldn't work for the shooting, but it was a good place from which to watch. He just needed to make sure they hadn't already arrived at the embassy. Unfortunately, the embassy wouldn't give out that sort of information. He suspected they weren't here, but he wanted to be certain.

Sasha figured that when he saw the Americans, he would go to a tree at the top of a hill in the park where he could rest his gun and shoot them. It wasn't a long shot, only a couple hundred yards. Nice and easy for an experienced sniper like him.

* * *

Schofield touched the bottom of the river and pushed off with his legs, forcing him back to the surface. He burst out of the water gasping for air. The impact of the water had winded him, and he paddled madly, gasping for air and looking around for the others. Mila surfaced next to him. Yuri a few seconds later resurfaced near the middle of the river. Where was Johnson? Schofield frantically searched for him.

"Where's Johnson?" he asked, swimming quickly to the opposite shore. Mila, gasping for breath, swam after him.

Yuri pointed to Johnson's still form floating near the shore among the tall grass.

"Here!" he called and raced toward him. Johnson lay face down, and Yuri flipped him over, mud pouring out of Johnson's mouth. Yuri grabbed Johnson under the arms and dragged him to the shore. The shore was a steep ravine, and there was nowhere good to put him, so he laid Johnson on his side and knelt beside him using his knees to keep Johnson from rolling back into the river. He reached in and fished more dirt out of his mouth. He wasn't breathing, he wasn't moving, and it looked as if he was dead.

Yuri immediately tried to revive Johnson. He rolled Johnson onto his back and beat on his chest, trying to start Johnson's heart. Yuri had no medical training, and he didn't know what to do. Schofield and Mila swam ashore and scrambled up to where Yuri had Johnson.

"He's dead," Yuri announced.

"No!" Schofield gasped in disbelief.

He checked Johnson's pulse. Nothing. He wasn't breathing.

"What do I do?" he muttered softly to himself.

He was an Eagle Scout and had been trained in lifesaving techniques, but being able to tell someone how to do it and being able to do it yourself are two very different things.

"God, please help me," Schofield said softly as he began chest compressions. Schofield rhythmically pushed on Johnson's chest, but he knew that wouldn't be enough,

I need to breathe for him.

Schofield plugged Johnson's nose, put his mouth over his, and blew air into his lungs.

He took a deep breath and did it again.

He continued the chest compressions and then breathed for Johnson.

And he did it again.

Schofield stopped his chest compressions. He needed to see if the chest was moving. He blew again and Johnson's chest rose. He was getting air. Schofield started pumping and breathed air into him again.

He followed that pattern until Johnson coughed and gagged. He rolled onto his side, and Schofield patted his back. Johnson coughed up a mouth full of dirt and vomit and spit it on the ground. He lay on his side, gasping for breath. Blood trickled from the cut on his forehead into his hair.

Tears poured down everyone's cheeks. Schofield threw his arms around Johnson and squeezed him.

Thank you, Father. Thank you!

"We need to get you warmed up," Schofield said as Johnson shivered.

"It's so cold," Johnson moaned, holding his arm. His wrist was bent at an odd angle. It was broken. "What happened?" he asked as Schofield bandaged the cut on his forehead.

"You kind of missed the river."

"What?" How? Johnson looked around in a daze.

"Can you walk?" Schofield asked.

"I think so."

Schofield stood and helped Johnson to his feet.

He yelped in pain and grabbed his side with his good arm.

"Are you okay?"

"I'm hurt." Johnson shivered again. His lips were turning blue. It wasn't cold, but Johnson was freezing.

"We need to get him somewhere warm," Yuri said. "Out of this water."

"Yes," Schofield agreed.

They struggled up the steep ravine. Johnson grabbed his side as Schofield and Yuri held him by the arms and helped him up the hill. He struggled to breathe, his sides ached, and his left wrist hung limply. He shivered as they reached the top of the ravine. They were on the wrong side. All of their equipment was on the other side. Someone would have to cross the train bridge and fetch their stuff. They didn't have any clothes, and they needed to get Johnson warmed up. He was in shock. Johnson lay on a patch of soft grass. Mila sat with him and kept him talking to keep him awake while Yuri and Schofield crossed the river to get their stuff.

* * *

Dennis and Michael were stopped at a military checkpoint ten miles from Astana. They waited in line for twenty minutes as the cars in front of them argued with guards at the checkpoint, trying to convince them to allow them through. After a lot of arguing, all of them eventually turned around.

"There is no access to the city," the guard said as he approached the vehicle. Dennis leaned back in his seat so Michael Ivanov could speak.

"My name is Michael Ivanov. I'm chief detective of the anti-terror task force, and we need to get into the city. It's a matter of national security." He showed the man his badge.

"Michael Ivanov?" the security guard confirmed.

"Yes."

"Just a minute." The guard walked back to the booth and picked up the phone.

Michael and Dennis sat in silence as the guard talked on the phone. Several minutes passed as the guard waited on the phone. Dennis fidgeted. Michael noticed that he had been calm the whole trip until now. To have come so far to get back with his family only to be turned away would be horrible. The guard came back out.

"You need to check at the next gate." The guard pointed up the road. In the distance was a small building.

"Thank you," Michael said.

The gate opened, and Dennis and Michael drove through. Michael watched as Dennis broke into a huge smile. Michael was looking forward to having a long private talk with the Lord. He had so many questions.

They stopped at the second gate, and another guard came to the passenger side of the car. Michael rolled down the window.

"I need to see your identification."

"Certainly." Michael pulled out his badge and police identification and handed it to the guard.

"Just a moment."

The guard took the ID and went back into the building. They couldn't see what he was doing, but he was gone for some time before he came back to the car and handed it to Michael.

"You need to be careful in the city. It's not the same safe place that it once was. Get your business done and get out of the city."

"Thank you."

The guard leaned in and looked into the car at Dennis. He stared at him for a moment and then said, "Have a nice day, gentlemen." He stood up and opened the second gate, and Dennis smiled as he pulled the car forward.

* * *

Michael looked cautiously about as Dennis drove down the empty streets of Astana; there were not a lot of people out. It was strange to see the city so desolate. The closer to the center of town they got, the fewer people they saw. Every few blocks they would see a burning car or a car that had been burned. They passed several buildings that had been damaged in an explosion. The streets were filled with smoke from the wreckage. It reminded him of a movie he had seen about a post-apocalyptic world. It was surreal, almost like a dream. As they climbed the hill into what was considered the nice part of town, most of the fires were gone. The upper class neighborhoods and the financial business district were relatively untouched.

Dennis drove slowly through the streets toward the embassy. He said he had been there several times, but he seemed nervous now, as if he expected violence near the embassy, but there was nothing. Somehow Dennis had taken a wrong turn and ended up on the back side of the embassy.

"Thank you," Michael said and held out his hand.

"You're welcome," Dennis said, shaking it.

"You should come to the embassy too. They would protect you."

"I know," Dennis answered, "but I must get to my family. I could not leave without my family."

"Well, I wish you the best of luck then," Michael said.

Michael stepped out of the car and Dennis drove away. He turned and looked at the embassy. It was the back side of the complex; a large chain link fence surrounded the building with electrical wire and barbs running along the top. He could see several military personnel standing guard inside the compound. He walked toward the front. He had no idea how the Americans would have gotten here so fast, but he needed to know if they were. He walked to the side of the compound and along the fence toward the front.

As Michael walked up to the gate, the guard came out to meet him.

"Do you speak Russian?" Michael asked.

"No," the guard, an American Marine, responded.

"Is there someone here that does speak Russian?" Michael held up his badge. "It is really important."

"One moment." The guard held up one finger, turned, and got on the phone. Oftentimes there would be a translator on duty at the embassy, but not today. The guard called to see if there was someone who could help this man.

Sasha sat at a little bistro, three blocks from the embassy. There weren't a lot of places still working with all the chaos that was going on. Most people were holed up in their apartments or had fled the city to the countryside where there was less violence, but there were always people who needed food and those that could put it on the table, no matter the cost.

Sasha ordered and paid. He should be watching the embassy, but he was starving and could not ignore his stomach. So he took his food from the poor man in the bistro, sat at a small table, ate his deep fried hot dog, and drank his *kvas*.

Sasha wondered how and why he had gotten so involved in this mess. He once had great aspirations. When he started as a detective, he planned to be one of the best detectives in the country, and he was. Michael Ivanov picked him for that exact reason. He was good at what he did. But now he wasn't even a real detective anymore. He was always worried about making sure he covered his tracks so he wouldn't get caught. If he was caught, plenty of other people working for General Shevchenko would not let him live long enough to talk. He needed to get out and soon. He would finish this job and take care of the Americans. Then General Shevchenko could finish his coup, and if he took charge of the country, then maybe Sasha could retire at a nice resort in Crimea. That would be nice. He should have enough money to retire there comfortably. That is, after General Shevchenko paid him for completing this mission.

"That will be nice," Sasha said softly to himself. He stood up from the table, picked up his case, and began walking back to the park. A light rain began to fall, and he looked up at the sky. Dark clouds rolled in from the north. A storm was coming. He needed to find better shelter. He quickened his pace back to the park by the embassy.

* * *

Johnson lay on his back in the grass struggling to understand what was going on around him. Mila kept rubbing his head. He knew it was important. She would gently shake him every couple minutes. She struggled to keep him talking.

"Tell me about your home," she pleaded.

"It's nice," Johnson started. "The grass is green, the cows are cold; it's so cold." His hurt arm was large and swollen. Johnson squeezed himself with his other arm, trying to create warmth. His lips were turning purple, and he shivered constantly. He mumbled something incoherent and closed his eyes. Mila shook him and his eyes opened again.

"I'm so tired."

"Please hurry," Mila pleaded, looking across the ravine, but Johnson didn't know what she wanted to hurry. Johnson closed his eyes again.

He could hear her soft voice as she began to whisper. "Please, God. Help Elder Johnson."

* * *

Schofield walked carefully along the train tracks across the old wooden bridge. He was amazed it even held the train. The bridge creaked and moaned in the breeze blowing in from the north.

Schofield scoured the tall grass near the tracks looking for their backpacks. They quickly located one, so they knew they were looking in the right place. It took some time to find the other three. Two of them had lodged themselves under a bush as they tumbled to a stop. Yuri found them, pulled them out, and then stopped.

"Did you get them?" Schofield called as he jogged over. Yuri's face was white as he stared at the ground where the backpacks had been.

* * *

Mila shook Johnson to wake him. Still he slept. She shook him again.

"Stay with me," she cried softly. Johnson rolled onto his side and moaned, his lips now blue. His wrist was swollen and his face was white, all color draining from his rosy cheeks.

She shook him again. "Wake up."

She gently laid him in the grass, stood up, and yelled.

"Papa! Schofield! Hurry!" No response.

"Papa, hurry!" she yelled again. Again no response. She looked back at Johnson. She didn't know what to do. He was dying, and there was nothing she could do. Tears poured down her cheeks.

"Help!" she yelled.

* * *

Yuri stared at a snake in the hole where the backpacks had been. It was at least eight feet long, coiled and ready to strike. Yuri didn't know much about snakes, but he knew enough to be worried about this one. A lot of snakes could kill a man in less than a minute; he hoped this was not one of them. He stood perfectly still. Any move could set the snake off and it would strike.

"What is it?" Schofield called as he approached.

"Don't move," Yuri said softly.

"What?" Schofield walked closer.

"Stop moving," Yuri mumbled, barely moving his lips as he spoke.

Schofield didn't understand him. "What?"

"Stop!" Yuri screamed, still eyeing the snake. It hadn't moved yet. It stayed coiled, its head looking at Yuri, its forked tongue flicking in and out. Schofield put his hand on Yuri's shoulder and stepped next to him. The snake hissed up at them, threatening them.

"Papa! Schofield! Hurry!" Mila called out in the distance. They didn't dare move. The snake was too close. They stood still hoping the snake would give up and slither back into its hole.

"Papa, hurry!" Mila called again.

They stood still, staring at the snake staring back at them. Neither one dared to move.

"Help!" Mila screamed frantically.

* * *

"Where are you, Papa?" Mila cried frantically, looking down at Johnson. His face looked like the pale moon. His breathing was labored. She couldn't wake him. She grabbed his hand in hers and squeezed it tight. "Hold on, Johnson." She remembered their ride from Balkhash to Karaganda. Johnson had told a story about prayer.

If prayer can help Johnson, then prayer can help me.

Still holding Johnson's hand in hers, she knelt, bowed her head, and prayed her first prayer. "Please, God. Help Elder Johnson. He is a good man and he deserves to live. I know I'm not perfect, but I'm trying. Thank you for bringing the missionaries to me. They have changed my life. I need them. I need Johnson. Please help him. Amen."

Tears poured down Mila's cheeks. They fell onto her hands and rolled down her interlocked fingers onto Johnson's cold hands.

* * *

Yuri and Schofield silently stared at the menacing snake. It bobbed its head, looking and hissing at them all the while. Mila had stopped screaming, but there was something definitely wrong on the other side of the ravine.

"What do we do?" Schofield whispered to Yuri, his head nearly resting on Yuri's shoulder.

"I don't know." Yuri slowly shook his head back and forth. They could try and wait it out. The snake probably had more patience than they did. It would sit and wait as long as it thought there was danger. Schofield couldn't stay still much longer. His legs ached. He was in an awkward position but didn't dare move. Schofield could see the sweat on Yuri's neck despite the cool northerly breeze.

The snake stopped hissing, turned, and slithered into its hole.

* * *

Mila brushed the tears from her cheeks. She looked down at Johnson; his skin was still pale and he labored to breathe. She was scared. She hadn't been this scared since her mom died.

After her mom's death, Mila had cut herself off from everyone. If she wasn't close to anyone, she couldn't get hurt. But she had allowed herself to get close to this American and he was being taken away. Why did they have to die? Every time she got close to someone, they would leave her. Why?

Raindrops landed softly on Johnson's cheek. He turned slowly and moaned. There were more drops. The wind blew stronger from the north, sending a shiver through Mila's body. She looked up at the black sky rumbling her way, and the rain fell all around her.

* * *

Yuri looked over to where Mila and Johnson were. A wall of rain passed over them and rushed toward him. Yuri grabbed their bags and ran back to the train tracks. Schofield followed right behind him.

"What was that?" Schofield asked, looking at where the snake had disappeared into the ground.

"I don't know. Maybe the snake felt the rain coming."

"We need to get Johnson out of the rain. He's already in bad shape. We have to move!" Schofield ran across the bridge, the cold rain crashing all around him. The bridge was slick, and Yuri slowed to a walk. He held onto the guardrail with one hand and held two backpacks in the other. Schofield continued to run, a backpack in each hand.

"Slow down!" Yuri yelled at him.

The driving rain buried the sound.

A bolt of lightning destroyed a tree on the bank. The thunder shook the bridge and Schofield slipped, dropping a backpack off the edge. He watched as the backpack slowly fell toward the river. He reached out for it, but it was gone. It landed with a splash and slowly drifted away.

Yuri caught up to Schofield and helped him to his feet.

"Are you okay?"

"Yes, but I lost the backpack."

"It's okay."

The thunder again shook the bridge.

"Let's go!" Yuri shouted over the roar of the rain. They cautiously went the rest of the way and rushed toward Mila and Johnson.

Mila sat next to Johnson, trying to protect him from the rain. They were both drenched and shivering.

"We need to get out of the rain!" Schofield yelled as he reached them.

"He's dying," Mila said, looking up, her eyes red with tears.

"What?" Schofield asked, not understanding what he heard.

"He's dying." She looked down at Johnson. His chest moved sporadically as he struggled to breathe.

"We need to help him," Mila pleaded.

"Okay. We need to get out of the rain."

There were several trees around, but none that would provide them adequate protection from the elements. There was mostly tall grass from here to the city.

"The bridge," Yuri suggested.

Schofield looked back at the bridge. Perhaps there was a spot under the bridge they could take him. They had no other options.

"Okay!" Schofield shouted over the howling wind and driving rain. "Let's go."

He bent over and picked Johnson up over his shoulder. Johnson moaned in pain. Schofield started through the tall, wet grass to the bridge where he hoped to find shelter.

TWENTY-FOUR

Excuse me, Mr. Russell?" a voice called at the door.

"Yes," President Russell said. He stood up and answered the door.

"Do you speak Russian?" the marine asked.

"Yes."

"Could you help us, please? There's a man at the front gate that needs some assistance, and of all the personnel left here, only the ambassador speaks Russian. Would you be willing to translate for us?"

"Sure." President Russell had been growing bored in his room. He had nothing to do, and the longer it went, the more worried he was about his missionaries. Perhaps lending some service would help get his mind off his troubles.

President Russell followed the private to the guard booth. President Russell entered it and approached a glass window. On the other side of the window stood a man in a suit. He was covered in dust, and it looked like he and his suit had been singed.

"We need you to translate for us if you will," the guard said. "I don't speak much Russian and this police officer has a question, I guess, but I can't understand him."

"Okay." President Russell looked at the man and asked in Russian, "Can I help you?"

"Yes, my name is Michael Ivanov. I am head of the

antiterrorist task force. I'm looking for two Americans who I believe are headed here to the embassy."

President Russell turned and translated for the marines.

"Who are these Americans? What are their names?" the guard asked.

President Russell translated back to Michael.

Michael pulled a picture out of his front pocket and held it up to the window. "Elder Johnson and Elder Schofield."

President Russell gasped when he saw the picture. It was the elders at the train station in Almaty.

"What do you need them for?" President Russell asked, gasping for breath.

"They are wanted for questioning in relation to the bombing of the train in Almaty and several other explosions."

A look of horror spread across President Russell's face. He had heard that they were wanted. Only now did it really sink in. He stood there in stunned silence.

Michael Ivanov looked at him curiously. "Do you know them?"

President Russell didn't answer.

"What is going on?" the guard asked, obviously not understanding the conversation.

"You do know them?" Michael asked again.

"Yes, I know them," stammered President Russell, "but I can assure you that they had nothing to do with that bombing."

"How do you know them?" asked Michael Ivanov.

"What is going on?" insisted the guard.

"One moment." President Russell held up a hand to the guard.

"I am their mission president, and I know they would not blow up a train, killing innocent people."

"You are with their church?" Michael asked.

"Yes. I'm the president of the Kazakhstan Astana Mission."

"You are certain they had nothing to do with the bombing?"

"Yes, they are good men. They wouldn't do such a thing," President Russell pleaded.

"I want to believe you, but evidence suggests that they were involved in that bombing, plus a house on Lake Balkhash, a hotel in Balkhash, and another train in Karaganda." He brushed some dust from his tattered coat.

"There must be some mistake." President Russell knew that the elders would never blow up a train, but he didn't know how to convince this detective of that.

"I hope so, but I can't be certain. Tell me why you think they are innocent."

"Just a minute. I'm coming out."

President Russell turned to the guard. "I need to go help this man. I'll be back shortly."

"Okay," the guard replied and led President Russell to the gate to let him out.

President Russell walked up and shook Michael Ivanov's hand. "I'm President Russell."

"Michael Ivanov."

President Russell led Michael Ivanov away from the front gate to a bus stop bench across the street.

"Tell me, Mr. Russell, how you are so certain that these two are not responsible?"

"They are my missionaries. I speak with each of them regularly. I interview them. They are here to spread the gospel, not to spread destruction."

"I read your book. There is a lot of violence in the book."

"Yes, but the message is peace. The violence comes when people fail to follow the commandments of God."

"Are you saying that we do not follow the commandments of God?"

"Not at all, but in the Book of Mormon the Lord protected

His people when they would hearken unto His words. When they wouldn't listen, He offered them no protection. This situation we are in now is also spoken of."

Michael looked at him curiously.

"The prophets prophesied that there would be wars and rumors of wars, great violence, and terror in the last days."

"I remember that, but I never realized that those prophecies were referring to the present."

"The elders are not setting off bombs to get people's attention. They're teaching people of Jesus Christ and helping bring people to Him."

Michael rubbed his head and sighed.

"What is it?" President Russell asked.

"All my experience as a detective tells me that they have something to do with the bombings. I can place them at four of the largest bombings in Kazakh history. If they are not involved, that is a huge coincidence. As a detective I would take them in and convict them, but my heart tells me that they are not involved. My heart tells me that the Book of Mormon is true and they are messengers of God and as such could not be messengers of destruction. They couldn't be involved in such atrocities. I am so confused." He shook his head and then rested it in his hands.

"So tell me, Mr. Ivanov—" President Russell started.

"Please, call me Michael."

"Okay, Michael, what first drew you to the missionaries?"

"Honestly, it was just work. At first it was. I took your book and read it. I even prayed about it. I believe the Book of Mormon is true, but now I am confused. I've been following the missionaries and every time I get close, something blows up. It is as if they don't want me to catch them. They know I'm following them and they don't want to be caught, so they blow up something to get me off their trail."

"Is it possible that these explosions are coincidence?"

"I suppose it is possible, but I don't know how. Four massive explosions and they are at the scene of each of them."

"I don't believe the elders had anything to do with any of those explosions, but we won't know that until we ask them."

"Are they here?" Michael asked excitedly.

"Not yet, but I'm hoping they will be soon," President Russell said. "Tomorrow at noon the last helicopter is leaving from here, and I hope they are here, because if not, they'll be stuck in Astana until the conflict is resolved, and that could be a long time."

* * *

"Would you like to learn more of the Church?" President Russell asked.

"Yes, I would. I need to know more," Michael said.

"Please give me your number and I will have missionaries contact you and teach you more about the Church."

"Haven't you evacuated all the missionaries?"

"Yes, all of the missionaries have been evacuated, but there are many more Kazakh citizens that will continue the missionary work. The work of the Lord will continue. There is nothing that can stand in the way of the Lord's work."

"Yes, please have them call me." Michael Ivanov pulled a business card out of his pocket and handed it to President Russell.

A raindrop fell onto the card, followed by several more all around them.

"It looks as if I must go," President Russell stated, looking up at the sky. "I'll have missionaries call you as soon as they are able."

"Thank you. Thank you very much." Michael Ivanov shook his hand. He was happy. He had found a leader of the Church and now he could learn more. "Is there a number I can reach you at if I don't hear from your missionaries?"

"I'll give you the number for the mission office here in Astana. I hope it will be up and running soon, but I can't be certain. I'll make sure that missionaries call you."

President Russell gave him the number for the mission office before he stood and walked back toward the embassy.

Michael watched as President Russell walked away. The rain was soaking him, yet he continued to watch President Russell. He longed to stay with him. He carried with him the same feeling he got when he read the Book of Mormon and that was a feeling he wanted to keep with him forever.

* * *

Schofield struggled to the bridge as he carried Johnson over his shoulder. Johnson moaned constantly, which Schofield took as a good sign. At least he still felt pain, which meant he wasn't too far gone.

Yuri walked in front, leading the way and making sure there wasn't anything in their path. The rain beat down around them. The tall grass now leaned slightly under the weight of the water. It was slick, and Schofield struggled to keep his footing. Mila reached out and steadied him several times.

Yuri crawled under the bridge. It was dry. There was a small area that had been dug out, and they couldn't tell if it was made by man or animal, but it was large enough for all four of them to fit comfortably. Schofield laid Johnson on the ground, and Yuri pulled him in under the bridge. Schofield dried him off and wrapped him in a blanket they had taken from the train and held him tight. The blanket wasn't completely dry, but it was better than nothing. Johnson didn't move. He just moaned and struggled to breathe.

"Isn't there something you can do?" Mila asked Schofield.

"We need to keep him warm," Schofield replied.

"No, you are a man of God. Can't you heal him?" Mila said.

"Yes," Yuri added. "Johnson told me of the priesthood you and he have. He said it was the power of God and you could work miracles with it."

Schofield didn't answer. He had given his fair share of blessings, but never one that would determine life and death. Most of the blessings he ever gave were blessings for comfort or minor illnesses. He had never given a blessing where someone's life depended on his faith. Now he was faced with such a responsibility. He had the authority. Did he have the faith?

* * *

Sasha arrived back at the park by the embassy. The tree would have provided adequate protection for a light rain, but it was no match for this downpour. The rain had already found its way through the thick leaves and was dripping onto the ground. He needed better cover. He needed to complete his task. The Americans would not travel in such a rain; the streets were deserted. It would soon be night. He hoped they would stop somewhere and spend the night. He shook the rain from his hair and headed to a hotel he had seen just up the street. He would get some rest and come back as soon as the rain let up. A thunderclap emphasized his decision to leave, and he headed quickly toward the hotel, the cold rain pounding him as he went.

* * *

President Russell returned to his room at the embassy smiling widely. He was glad to have met Michael Ivanov. It gave him hope. There were still good people here, people still searching for the truth. That gave him hope that this civil war would end soon and the spreading of the gospel would continue. Michael Ivanov gave him hope for his missionaries. He thought they were alive and on their way to the embassy. President Russell knelt at his bed and prayed for his missionaries, and he prayed for Michael Ivanov. He was exhausted when he climbed into bed and quickly fell asleep.

* * *

Michael sat quietly in the pouring rain on the bench by the bus stop. He didn't notice the rain. He sat and enjoyed the incredible feeling of peace and warmth that came when he had talked to President Russell. It was the same feeling he felt when he read the Book of Mormon. It was a feeling he believed came from God, confirming to him that the Book of Mormon was true and President Russell was a leader in that church. He wanted to join that church. He didn't really know what that meant, but if there was a chance he could always have this feeling of peace and warmth, it was a chance he was willing to take.

A clap of thunder shook him out of his bliss, and he realized he was soaked to the bone. He slowly stood up and made his way up the street. He had seen a hotel there. He needed to get out of the rain.

When he arrived at the hotel, it seemed deserted. He rang the bell for service and waited patiently. It was a nice hotel. He couldn't imagine it being abandoned; the outside doors were open. Someone had to be here. He rang the bell again, but there was still no response. He was about to leave when he heard the elevator down the hall open and footsteps walking toward him.

"Oh, hello," the man said. "I hope you haven't been waiting long."

"No, sir," Michael replied.

"Would you like a room?" the man asked as he made his way behind the counter.

"Yes, please."

"I'm very sorry to keep you waiting, but you're the first person today to come in. Almost everyone has fled the city. Most of my staff is gone as well, so I was attending to another guest. Please forgive my absence."

"It's really not a problem."

"The hotel is mostly vacant, so I will put you up in a suite for a regular price."

"That's not really necessary," Michael said.

"Please, I insist. I kept you waiting. It is the least I can do. Here you go." He handed Michael the key card. "You are on the top floor, Room 1. Please enjoy your stay. If there is anything I can do for you, please let me know."

Michael started to walk away and stopped. He turned back to the man and asked, "Do you have any reading material, books and such?"

"Yes, each room has a Bible, and on the top floor at the end of the hall there is a small library. I don't maintain it, one of my associates does, but your key card will let you in and allow you to check out any of the books two at a time. Just follow the instructions on the door."

"Thank you." Michael headed for the elevator. He climbed in and pushed "25" for the top floor. The doors closed quickly, and Michael was on his way.

* * *

Sasha walked into the hotel, and the man at the desk smiled at him. "Good evening."

"Evening," Sasha replied. He looked at the elevator where he had just seen Michael enter and watched as it went to the twenty-fifth floor.

"Would you like a room?"

"Yes, please."

The man laughed heartily. "All day not one guest, and now two in two minutes."

"Interesting," Sasha said, handing him his identification.

Sasha took his key card and walked happily to the elevator. If Michael was here, then the Americans had not made it to the embassy yet. Sasha drummed a happy tune on the wall as he waited for the elevator to come.

* * *

Schofield knelt at Johnson's head. Johnson was lying on his back in the dirt of the small cave under the train bridge. Johnson still struggled to breathe. His arm was now large and swollen, and the shades of blue and purple were growing rapidly. He coughed and hacked violently. Blood and saliva dripped slowly from the side of his mouth.

Mila gasped and wiped it away. Tears poured down her cheeks.

Schofield's heart raced. He didn't know what to do. He knew what to do, but he wasn't sure he could do it. Sweat beaded up on his forehead and began to trickle down his nose. He breathed deeply.

Johnson coughed up more blood. Mila wiped it away and cried to Schofield, "Please help him!"

Schofield anointed Johnson's head with oil. He closed his eyes and put his hands on Johnson's head. "Elder Robert Johnson," he began.

What followed was the most intense two minutes of any of their lives. Schofield blessed Johnson and gave him more than just a blessing of health. He blessed him that he would heal, and that he would continue to be a powerful servant of God in bringing others to the truth. The Spirit descended upon them all and filled the cave with warmth. Schofield could feel the words come to him unbidden. They weren't his words he was speaking, but words that were given to him. The doubts about his faith faded. He knew in that moment he could do whatever the Lord asked him to. He knew whatever words the Lord put in his mind, he would say and they would come true.

Schofield's eyes reddened and his voice quavered as he continued to follow the Spirit in blessing Elder Johnson. Schofield finished the blessing and collapsed to the ground next to Johnson, exhausted. The color in Elder Johnson's face quickly returned, and his breathing eased. He didn't cough anymore, and Mila no longer had to wipe the blood from his lips. The cave filled with warmth that lasted long into the night.

* * *

Michael didn't go straight to his room; instead, he went to the library the manager spoke of. He knew it was a long shot, but he really wanted to read the Book of Mormon again and his book had been in his car when it was destroyed. He swiped his key card through the reader and the lock clicked open. Michael opened the door and walked in. It looked as if one of the rooms had been converted into a library. It was substantial in size. He had to walk through a glass turnstile and then entered the main library. There were rows and rows of books lining the walls. All the greats were here: Tolstoy, Dostoevsky, Bulgakov. He browsed the walls until he found a small little nook with nearly a hundred religious books in it. His heart raced. Maybe it was here. He quickly glanced through the books. *Please be here, please be here.*

There it was, the Book of Mormon. Right next to it sat another book by the same church. He grabbed them both and headed to the door. He swiped his key card at the door and then had the bar code read on both the books. The door lock clicked, and he quickly went through and walked to his room.

He opened the door to his suite and entered. It was a massive room with a big screen television, high speed Internet, and all the other amenities one could want, but all he was after was a chair. He quickly found one and sat down. He was exhausted but too excited to sleep. He had again found the Church and now in a library on the top floor of a hotel, he found the book he had been longing to read and another book from the same church. Excitedly he picked it up and read the cover of the Doctrine and Covenants and the Pearl of Great Price. *It seems to be two books in one.* He opened the book, giddy in anticipation, and began reading. He wanted to know more about this church and the feeling he got every time he read the Book of Mormon and when he had talked to the president of the mission. He repositioned himself to make himself comfortable and began reading.

* * *

Sasha got to his room. He was tired. He was a little concerned that Michael was at the same hotel, but it shouldn't be a problem. They were both after the same two people; Sasha just wanted them dead. He was sure that Michael would not be here if he had already apprehended them. He would be interrogating them somewhere, finding out that they had nothing to do with the bomb. That couldn't be allowed. He couldn't risk missing the Americans and allowing them to enter the embassy. He called the front desk and asked to be woken up when the rain stopped or at first light, whichever came first. He climbed into bed and went to sleep.

* * *

Michael stayed up long into the night reading the Doctrine and Covenants. He was fascinated at the thought that there were modern day prophets. Someone on the earth today was receiving revelation from God. What an incredible blessing, to speak with God. He had that feeling, the feeling he had come to love. He knew this book was true, that Joseph Smith was a prophet. A man led by God. *What would it be like?* Late into the night, Michael decided he should get some rest. He longed to learn more of the gospel, and he wanted the feeling to stay, but he had things to do. He had to find the real bombers. Now that the elders were no longer suspects in his mind, he needed to find those responsible, and for that he would need rest. He sat the book down and knelt at the side of his bed to offer up a prayer.

He prayed for guidance. He confessed that he knew the Church was true and needed to know what to do from here. He talked to God long into the night, like he never had before. He told of his trials and struggles and asked God for help. As he prayed, the feeling of peace and comfort, the warmth he had come to love, overwhelmed him and he began to weep. He knew that he would be guided in his actions. He would join the Church and join God. He knew he would be asked to do a great many things. He prayed for the strength to do those things. He knelt at his bedside long after he finished praying. The Lord would soon ask him to do something, and he needed to follow the guidance of the Lord. He climbed into his bed and fell asleep, rejoicing in the Spirit of the Lord.

TWENTY-FIVE

Johnson felt like he had been run over by a train. Muscles he didn't know he had ached, and his throat burned. He looked around. He was lying on his back. Some sort of cement ceiling was above his head. He turned to his side. Schofield, Yuri, and Mila were all there lying in the dirt.

"Where am I?" he asked. The world began to shake. He looked around. Everything was shaking, and dirt fell from the ceiling. The ceiling seemed like it was going to collapse. A blaring deafening scream echoed through the cave. Johnson tried to cover his ears, but one arm wouldn't move.

Johnson looked at Mila and she at him. He could see she had no fear of the shaking. She smiled at him. "You're awake!" she shouted, but he could not hear over the rumbling moving overhead.

Schofield saw Johnson, who was now sitting up. He threw his arms around him and hugged him.

"You're alive!"

The noise ceased.

"Why wouldn't I be alive?"

"You jumped off a bridge and landed in two feet of water. You're lucky to be alive."

"I don't feel alive." Johnson struggled to move. "Where are we?"

"We're under the bridge."

"The bridge? So that noise was a train?"

The others nodded.

"My leg got caught on the railing of the train," Johnson explained, "and then I fell into the river."

Mila came over and sat next to Johnson.

"Schofield blessed you and now you are alive. It is a miracle."

"You did?" Johnson asked.

"You gave me no choice. You were dying," Schofield said.

"You didn't heal me very good. I ache all over," Johnson joked, smiling.

"At least you're alive." Schofield smiled back.

"That's a good point." Johnson smiled, even though it hurt. He was alive. He was grateful for that.

"How do you feel?" Yuri asked.

"I hurt," was all Johnson could say.

"Can you move?"

"I don't know," Johnson said, sighing. "There's only one way to find out."

He leaned forward and helped himself up with his good arm. The other arm was still black and blue and swollen nearly twice the size it should have been. His ribs crushed his lungs, and he gasped for breath. He bent over and forced air in his lungs. That eased the pain. He could move but not very well.

"Where are we?"

"We're under the train tracks. It was pouring rain and we had nowhere else to go."

"How far are we from Astana?" Johnson asked between deep breaths.

"Five or six kilometers," Yuri answered.

"We should get going then."

The rain had stopped and the sun was now coming over the horizon. They crawled from under the bridge and stretched in the early morning sun.

Johnson looked down at his arm and shook his head. He knew his arm hurt, but he had no idea that it was swollen that bad. It throbbed with every pump of his heart.

* * *

The sunlight shining in the window awoke Sasha from a deep sleep. He jumped from his bed and began cursing the inept management of the hotel for not waking him as he requested. He quickly threw his things together and headed out the door. He only hoped it wasn't too late. He needed to stop the Americans from reaching the embassy. His plans were quickly unraveling and the only hope of salvaging them was blaming the first bombing on those two Americans. He cursed at the slow moving elevator as it counted off the floors.

As the elevator doors opened to the lobby, he stormed out to the front desk and lit into the manager for not waking him.

"We've been trying your room for hours, sir, but have gotten no response. We do apologize for any inconvenience this may have caused you."

A thought crept into Sasha's head. "Is Michael Ivanov still here or has he checked out?"

"One moment and I will check. Do you know what room he was staying in?"

"Yes, somewhere on floor twenty-five."

"He has not checked out yet."

"Good." Sasha breathed a sigh of relief. If Michael was still in his room, then he wasn't expecting them this morning. *There's still time.* Sasha grabbed a bagel on his way out of the hotel and headed to the park across from the embassy. He needed to get to his spot and make sure he was ready. It was important that he finish the Americans off quickly. One shot each and then a run through the park and into the city where no one would find him.

* * *

"How do we get to the city from here?" Schofield asked as they stepped onto the bridge.

Johnson stopped and looked into the deep ravine that had nearly taken his life.

"It's okay," Schofield said quietly, patting him on the back. Johnson slowly made his way onto the bridge.

"There should be a dirt road over there that we can follow to the highway." Mila pointed across the river downstream. "That's the road we used when we would come swimming in the summer."

"Let's go then." Johnson seemed overly eager to get to the city. Perhaps it was all the pain he was in. Schofield wished he had something to ease Johnson's pain, but he didn't have anything to give him.

Schofield, Mila, and Yuri all donned a backpack. The fourth backpack had been swept away in the river. Schofield led the way across the wet and slippery bridge. They held tightly to the guardrail, not wanting to lose anything else or anyone into the river. Johnson walked slowly, grabbing tightly to the rail. He had no intention of going over again. He slipped on the wet wood and fell into the guardrail, smashing his sore ribs. He gasped loudly and grabbed the rail. He fell to the walkway, still holding the rail, and gasped for breath. His broken arm hung loosely at his side.

Schofield helped Johnson to his feet, and they continued along the bridge. He could see that Johnson ached with every breath. Johnson touched his broken arm constantly. Schofield began to wonder if Johnson could handle the pain. They made it safely across the bridge and began trudging through the chest high grass now covered in rain. Schofield led the way, trying to trample the grass as much as possible to let Elder Johnson walk unobstructed. The grass cleared and they walked onto the dirt road. Soaked through from the wet grass, they were glad to be out of it and onto a dryer path, except the path wasn't dry. It was muddy and looked treacherous. Large puddles spotted the road.

"Which way?" Schofield asked as he walked onto the road. The road went north and south, but Astana was to the east.

"I don't know," Mila said. "I don't remember this road."

An engine roared in the distance, growing louder as it came toward them.

* * *

Sasha found the tree from the day before. He stopped and examined the spot. It was still a good spot. It provided him excellent cover, yet still left a great view of the gate to the embassy. Most of the people at the embassy were already gone. Security there should be light. Sasha walked the short distance to the park bench and sat down. He bit into his bagel and wished he had brought a drink and a newspaper to read. He looked at the front gate of the embassy. He could be wasting his time. They might already be inside waiting to be whisked away to safety by one of the helicopters that sat on the roof. Sasha thought briefly about shooting the helicopter down as it took off, but quickly dismissed that idea as a very last resort. That would probably result in his death; he did not want the American military personnel that guarded the embassy to come after him or the inevitable international incident that the general would rightfully blame him for. All he needed were the two Americans who happened to be in the wrong place at the wrong time to come walking up to the gate.

Sasha examined every car that passed in front of the embassy. He didn't want to miss them.

* * *

Mila watched as a truck raced down the dirt road toward them, mud flying behind it. The driver saw them standing in the road and slammed on his brakes, sliding to a halt just feet from them. The wipers on the windshield cleaned away the mud and the driver, a young man, looked out at them. A young lady sat in the passenger seat.

She rolled down her window to get a better look at them.

They stood there wet and covered in mud. Johnson's swollen arm hung limply at his side, his face growing paler with each passing moment.

"Are you okay?" she asked

"No," Mila answered. "We need to get into Astana as soon as possible. He is hurt and needs a doctor."

"Do you have any money?" the driver asked.

The girl in the passenger seat smacked the driver in the shoulder and waved them over.

"You'll have to ride in the back, but we can take you there," she said.

"Thank you." Mila grabbed Johnson's good arm and walked him toward the truck.

"What happened to him?" the driver asked.

"He fell off the bridge," Yuri answered quickly.

"And he lived?"

"Yes, just barely," Yuri replied.

The girl scooted to the middle of the seat in the small truck. "Please sit here," she invited, indicating for Johnson to climb into the truck's cab. Mila and Yuri helped Johnson into the truck. Mila worried he was not as sharp as he had been earlier. The pain was getting to him.

Yuri closed the door and climbed into the back of the truck with Mila and Schofield. The bed was covered in mud, but it would be a lot faster than walking into Astana. As soon as they were seated in the bed, the driver turned around and sped off down the muddy road, mud flying behind the truck.

* * *

Michael woke as the sun peeked in on him through the partially drawn curtains. He was refreshed. He felt better than he had in a long time. He sat momentarily in bed, contemplating things. He decided he would read some more before he would make his next move; he didn't yet know what his next move would be. He knew the elders were innocent, but he still had to find them so he could protect them, and he also had to find the real bombers. He wanted to read more of the word of God, so he called the front desk and asked them to bring up breakfast. He wanted to eat in peace rather than in the restaurant or lobby. He opened the Doctrine and Covenants to his bookmark and began reading.

* * *

Johnson looked up to see Schofield tapping on the back window of the truck. He mouthed, "How are you doing?"

Johnson gave a weak thumbs-up.

"My name is Katya, and this is my brother, Kostya. What is your name?"

Johnson wanted to answer, but instead he just looked at her and moaned.

The truck went over a large bump and jostled all those on board. Johnson winced in pain.

"Are you okay?" Katya asked.

"I don't know," Johnson said, breathing deeply.

"Do you need something?"

"I'm fine."

"Are you sure?"

"Yes, thank you."

* * *

"He doesn't look so good," Mila said, looking in at Johnson. "We should take him to the hospital."

"I don't know," Schofield said.

"What do you mean? He needs medical attention."

"I think they have medical personnel at the embassy that can take care of him."

"Really?"

"Yes, they have most everything at the embassy. I had to go there when my visa expired. We needed help in getting it renewed."

"I guess we go to the embassy then," Mila said, sighing. "I'm still worried about him."

"He'll be fine," Yuri interjected. "You blessed him that he would be okay and so he will be okay."

"You believe in his blessing?" Mila asked.

"Yes. I saw the light in his eyes return while Schofield prayed over him. He was near death and now he is fine, or will be soon. I watched him as Schofield blessed him and saw the life return to him. He will not die from these wounds. I don't believe in much, but that I believe."

* * *

President Russell was eating breakfast in the embassy cafeteria when the ambassador came in.

"Good morning," President Russell called to the ambassador.

"It is indeed morning, although I would not call it good."

President Russell didn't know what to say to that. He just looked down at his cereal.

The ambassador got a bowl of cereal and sat down by President Russell.

"Forgive me for being so blunt, but we are evacuating the embassy today. I would hardly call that a good day."

"I see," President Russell responded.

"I was hoping to avoid the evacuation. I've been here for four years and have grown quite attached to the place. I always do, but I have never been forced to leave like this. I feel as if all I have worked for will be lost."

"I know what you mean."

"Do you?" the ambassador asked cynically.

"I do. I've been here for two and a half years and have done a lot in establishing our church here. I don't know how well it will continue without close supervision. I'm afraid it will all collapse if we're not allowed to nurture it."

"I know you have a lot invested here, as do I. It will be hard to leave, but it's no longer safe here. The country is at war with itself. General Shevchenko is trying to assume power, saying that martial law is the only way to restore order. If he gains control of the country, I fear for all of us. He's a power hungry madman. Lots of people are blaming the whole war on us, the United States, thanks in part to your missionaries."

"They didn't do it," President Russell insisted.

"I know they didn't do it, but the Kazakh people think they did. And that is what matters. General Shevchenko is playing on their fears and making them hate us so he can set himself in charge of one of the largest countries in the world, one that still has a fair number of nuclear weapons kicking around. A frightening thought indeed."

"How do we stop him?"

"We don't stop him. We're leaving in an hour. The helicopters are getting ready now and our air support will be here soon."

"Air support?"

"Yes. We have two apache helicopters coming to escort us out of the country. There will also be two F-16s flying overhead as support."

"Whoa. Is that really necessary?"

"Unfortunately, yes, it is. The embassy has become a target, as have we all. We need to leave now. Get your things and meet me at the helicopter pad."

The ambassador finished his cereal, stood, and walked out the door.

"Wait! What about my missionaries? You said we were leaving at noon. It's not noon yet."

The ambassador turned and looked at President Russell.

"You had better hope that they get here soon." He gave a forced smile as if to say "sorry for your loss" and walked out of the room.

* * *

Schofield leaned up and looked at Johnson.

Katya opened the back window to talk to Schofield.

"Your friend is not doing well." Johnson was leaning against the window, his face pale, his arm still swelling. His eyes drooped. And he mumbled incoherently.

"How soon can we be at the US embassy?" Schofield asked Kostya.

"I don't know where the embassy is."

"How long until we reach Astana?" Schofield asked

"Maybe five minutes," Kostya said.

"I know where the embassy is," Katya interjected.

"How do you know where the embassy is?" Kostya demanded.

"There is a park across the street from it where I used to meet my boyfriend."

"Oh."

"You know where the embassy is?" Schofield said.

"Yes, I can get us there." Katya smiled.

"Good." Schofield breathed a sigh of relief. "Hang in there, Johnson."

* * *

Michael was absorbing the Doctrine and Covenants. Never had

he ever enjoyed reading something as he had reading the Book of Mormon and the Doctrine of Covenants. He had read the Bible when he was younger in college, but it wasn't the same. He learned a lot, but it didn't have the same feeling the Book of Mormon did. He determined that a lot of that might have been the time in his life, and he wasn't really interested in religion then. But now his life was at a turning point. He had been working a hundred hours a week for weeks on end tracking and capturing suspected terrorists. He was doing something that was important, but he had begun to feel that something was missing in life, and he didn't know what. He couldn't take time off from work to reflect on life. There was just too much to do. Then the Book of Mormon had fallen into his lap and now all he wanted to do was learn more about this church and Jesus Christ. It consumed him, and he loved it.

He continued to eat breakfast and read the Doctrine and Covenants, basking in the Spirit of the Lord, and then he abruptly stopped.

* * *

President Russell walked slowly to his room. He didn't want to leave without the elders, but he couldn't stay any longer. The embassy personnel were evacuating, and all hope of the elders' survival was leaving with them. They were hated in a country at war with itself. If they weren't here within minutes, they would be stuck here in Kazakhstan, an ordeal they would probably not survive. President Russell had done all he could.

They are in God's hands now. I hope He still has need of them here.

A loud alarm blared throughout the empty hall. *What's going on?*

President Russell ran into his room, grabbed his few items, and rushed out into the hall. A marine rushed to meet him.

"We are evacuating now. You need to get to the roof," the marine ordered. "Follow me."

President Russell followed the marine down the hall and up several flights of stairs to a door that led out onto the roof, where there were two large helicopters, their propellers spinning wildly through the air. President Russell fell back into the door in surprise. The marine grabbed him.

"Stay close to the ground!" the marine yelled over the roaring wind. "The wind is less near the ground." President Russell looked up. He could see two Apache helicopters hovering a hundred feet above the embassy roof. The roar of jet engines raced across the sky as two F-16s flew far overhead.

"That one!" the marine yelled, pointing to the helicopter on the far side of the roof. "Stay low and run."

President Russell ran low across the large roof toward the helicopter ready to fly him out of the war zone. A loud explosion roared in the distance. President Russell stopped to look and saw a huge cloud of dust and smoke rising on the horizon. He raced to his helicopter and stopped at the door. He turned to look back at the city he loved, the city he had called home for two and a half years. This was possibly the last time he would ever see the country, the city, and the park across the street from the embassy where he had met a man who had quickly become a good friend and a leader of the Church in Kazakhstan. He looked to find the park. There it was, just as it was two and a half years ago. President Russell stared at the park across the street. A man sat on the very bench where he had taught his first lesson in Kazakhstan. Then the man on the bench got up and started climbing a large tree in the park.

* * *

Michael looked around. He had heard something. It was familiar, but he couldn't tell what it was. He listened; there it was again. This time he recognized it. It was a voice, but he couldn't quite make out what it was saying.

"Run!" the voice said powerfully.

He jumped out of his seat and ran. He didn't know where he was running, but the voice carried with it the same feeling he had grown to love, and he knew he had to follow it. He ran down the hall to the lobby elevators and took the elevator to the bottom floor. He exited the elevator and raced through the lobby. He didn't know where he was going, but he knew he had to get there fast. He burst through the hotel doors into the street and ran as fast as he could away from the hotel.

* * *

"How far to the embassy?" Schofield asked through the window. They were driving through the streets of Astana, and Schofield didn't recognize anything. He had only been to the embassy once and that was months ago. Although he had served a year in Astana, he apparently never made it to this part of town.

"We're almost there," Katya replied with a smile.

Johnson coughed violently, hacking and wheezing. He grabbed his throat with his good hand and coughed again. He collapsed against the window of the truck.

His chest heaved as he gasped for breath. He turned and looked at Schofield, a terrified look. Blood slowly trickled down from the corner of his mouth. Johnson forced a smile, a small painful smile. He closed his eyes and slumped again against the window.

"He's dying!" cried Katya.

Schofield reached in, wiped the blood from Johnson's lips, and then felt his forehead. He was cold and clammy. He wasn't doing well.

"How far?" Schofield asked Katya.

"Just a few blocks." She forced her tears back.

"Almost there." Schofield looked at Mila and Yuri. Tears welled up in his eyes.

"Thank you so much for your help. We couldn't have done it without you."

"It was nothing," Yuri responded with a smile.

Mila pulled out a pen and a paper from the backpack, wrote a number on it, and handed it to him.

"This is the number of my apartment. Please call and let us know you're safe."

He paused because it was against the mission rules to get her number—but no. This was different.

"Thank you. I will." He tucked the paper in his pocket.

"There it is," Katya called back and pointed ahead.

Schofield stood up and looked forward over the back of the cab. He could see the embassy compound several blocks ahead. There were two transport helicopters on the roof landing pads. Two more helicopters circled high overhead. The roar of jet engines preceded two jet fighters as they raced across the sky.

They were finally here. Mila and Yuri stood up on each side of him and looked at the embassy.

"There it is," Schofield said softly.

TWENTY-SIX

Sasha stood patiently leaning on one of the lower branches of the tree. It had provided a surprisingly good view of the front of the embassy and an excellent rest for his rifle. He had seen the helicopters on the roof preparing for takeoff and got excited. The embassy was making its final evacuation. If the Americans weren't in the embassy now, they only had a few minutes to get here. If they were in the embassy, perhaps he could shoot at them on the roof. A pickup truck raced around the corner and down the street. A man stood up in the back of the truck. It was one of the Americans. Now was the time.

* * *

The truck pulled to a stop in the street right next to the front gate of the embassy. Kostya parked with the passenger side facing the embassy so they could get Johnson out easier. Schofield hopped out of the truck and opened the door to help get Johnson. Katya pulled Johnson away from the door, and he collapsed on her lap. Schofield turned and ran to the gate.

The guard looked at Schofield, eyeing the mud and dirt he was covered in.

"Can I help you?"

Schofield pulled his passport out of his pocket and showed it to the guard.

"My companion is hurt and needs help."

The guard signaled a second guard to go check it out. He left the guardhouse and came out toward the truck. He was dressed in full military gear, including an M-16 strapped to his back and a sidearm. His hand rested comfortably on the grip. Schofield and the guard returned to the truck. Mila and Yuri helped Johnson as he struggled to extricate himself from the truck. Schofield stood back to give them room to get Johnson out.

Johnson was conscious but just barely. He groggily looked up at the marine and smiled.

"We made it!" he cried.

* * *

Sasha laid his rifle on a branch for support and looked through the scope. The marine was in the way.

"Stupid American soldier," Sasha cursed and almost shot him out of spite, but that might eliminate his chances of getting both of the Americans, so he held steady, waiting for the perfect moment. He abandoned the plan of taking Schofield first. Now he would take whatever he could get.

* * *

Michael Ivanov raced toward the embassy. He saw the truck parked in front of the embassy. People were getting out of the back of the truck. And was that Elder Schofield? He raced on, still not knowing what it was he was going to do.

* * *

President Russell ducked and ran to the edge of the building to get a better look. A truck stopped at the gate to the embassy. Three people stood in the back of the truck. There, in the middle, was Elder Schofield, but where was Elder Johnson? His heart leaped with joy. He yelled to Elder Schofield.

* * *

Sasha watched through his scope, cautiously waiting for the right moment. Schofield stepped back. Sasha put his finger on the trigger and pulled.

* * *

Elder Schofield heard his name and turned to look. Then he heard a crack and a bullet ripped through his forearm between the bones. Blood splattered on the marine as the bullet impacted his Kevlar vest, knocking the marine backward onto the ground.

Schofield screamed in pain, grabbing his arm.

* * *

"Get down!" Michael Ivanov raced past them. He pulled his gun from his holster. The marine in the booth scrambled out of the booth to see what was going on. He called on his radio that they were under fire. Michael raced toward the park. He saw Sasha in a tree. He couldn't believe Sasha was shooting at them. This was not how it was supposed to happen. He should be arresting them, not sniping them.

* * *

Sasha took aim at Johnson. Schofield was now completely blocked by the truck. The girl, that stupid girl, was blocking his view, holding him up.

Oh well. Maybe I'll take a two for one.

Johnson squirmed. The girl struggled to hold him up.

Sasha aimed at the girl's back, knowing the bullet would go right through her and into Johnson.

Sasha fired. The girl lost her grip on Johnson and bent to grab him. The bullet ripped through her shoulder, knocking her forward.

The truck driver panicked, put the truck into gear, and raced away, exposing them all as he left. Sasha took aim again.

* * *

Michael raced up the hill toward Sasha. He aimed his gun and fired, hitting Sasha in the leg. Sasha dropped his rifle and collapsed to the ground next to the tree. Sasha saw him coming, pulled out his pistol, and fired, narrowly missing Michael.

Michael aimed and fired again, hitting Sasha in the arm, forcing him to drop his gun.

* * *

A wave of marines raced out of the embassy and surrounded the small group. President Russell followed right behind.

Schofield lay on the ground, screaming in agony. The young woman lay on top of an unconscious Johnson, blood pouring from her shoulder.

An older man bent to help the young girl, but an incoming marine pushed him aside to check the wounds.

"Help us!" Schofield cried.

"Are they American?" one marine asked.

"Yes!" yelled President Russell.

"Who are they?" the marine asked.

"Missionaries!"

Several marines began examining the wounds.

"We need to get these guys medical attention immediately. They look pretty bad."

One of the marines pulled bandages out of a bag he had brought with him and began bandaging Schofield's arm.

Another marine checked on the young girl.

"What's your name, miss?"

She didn't answer. She rolled off of Johnson onto her back.

The bullet had gone all the way through and out her front just to the side of the collarbone.

"Miss, what is your name?"

"Her name is Mila," Schofield said through the pain.

"Mila? Is she a local?"

"Yes."

"Private, get us an ambulance for her."

He bent over and examined the wound. It was nasty. He padded gobs of gauze on it to stop the bleeding.

Johnson's broken arm had been cut when he fell and now gushed blood, the swelling decreasing as the blood and fluid rushed out onto the street.

The marine examining him gagged at the stench.

"This one is rotten," he called out. Two marines rushed out of the embassy with stretchers.

"We've got to go, boys!" one of the marines yelled.

"We've got company."

One of the Apaches overhead fired a missile. It raced into its target with a massive explosion.

"Get them on the choppers," a voice called out over the radio. The marines loaded the elders onto stretchers and rushed them off to the waiting helicopters, leaving the older man crouched over his daughter. They had bandaged her up, but she was still bleeding. An ambulance siren wailed in the distance.

"Thank you!" President Russell said to Yuri. He then followed the marines up the stairs to the helicopters. Johnson just moaned, while Schofield tried to talk. The medic told him to be quiet. They loaded all three of them on the same helicopter.

The Apaches fired several more missiles and a hundred rounds of machine gun fire. Then the transport choppers were in the air with all the embassy personnel on board, including President Russell and two severely wounded missionaries.

* * *

Michael handcuffed Sasha.

"What are you doing here, Sasha?"

"I'm eliminating the terrorists." Sasha grimaced in pain.

"By shooting them with a sniper rifle?" Michael nodded to the rifle on the ground.

"By any means necessary," Sasha said.

"That's not how we work," Michael said. Yet he knew that sometimes it had been done that way, but this shouldn't have been one of those cases.

A local policeman came up and Michael directed him to watch Sasha and make sure he was properly cared for. He ran down to the scene of the shooting to see if he could sort out what had happened. An ambulance and several police cars pulled up next to the embassy. The young woman he had met in Balkhash was loaded into the ambulance and hauled away. A second ambulance arrived for Sasha.

Michael ordered them to keep him locked up at all times while they were treating his wounds. The local police officer climbed into the ambulance with Sasha.

"Why am I being treating like a criminal?" Sasha screamed at Michael as the doors to the ambulance closed. "I was here to stop them and you let them get away. You let them get away."

Michael stood next to Yuri, and they watched the ambulances drive away. As they drove off, Michael turned to the older man.

"Michael Ivanov," he said as held out his hand.

"Yuri Shevchenko." They shook hands.

"Were you with them the whole time?" Michael asked.

"With Johnson and Schofield?" Yuri asked.

"Yes."

"They were on my bus when it was hijacked and I felt something. I knew I needed to help them. I'm sure you won't understand, but I felt like I had to help them, like I was compelled to."

Michael understood what he meant. A week ago he wouldn't have believed someone could be compelled like that, but now things were different.

"I do know what you mean. They had the same influence on me." Michael smiled widely. He had saved the Americans. Sasha would surely have killed them, but the Lord had other plans.

"Come, I will accompany you to the hospital to see your daughter, and you can tell me about your journey with the missionaries."

Side by side they walked to the hospital. Yuri told Michael of their journey from Balkhash to Astana and of their journey from darkness to light.

EPILOGUE

Elder Schofield lay on his back in the helicopter. The medic had given him a shot for the pain. He couldn't really feel anything right now. He looked at his arm. He was bandaged up quite nicely.

"How did you make it from Almaty to Astana?" President Russell asked.

"How long is our flight?" Elder Schofield asked, smiling.

President Russell laughed, and they both looked over at Elder Johnson, who was now sleeping comfortably. The medic worked on him, looking at his numerous wounds.

"How is he?" Schofield asked the medic over the roar of the helicopter.

"He'll live." The medic smiled. "I'm going out on a limb and guessing six or eight broken ribs. This arm is completely messed up. His jaw is definitely broken. He probably has a concussion. That's just what I can see without any sort of proper equipment."

Schofield was relieved Johnson would live, but he knew that already.

"He is an amazing missionary." Elder Schofield nodded toward Elder Johnson.

President Russell smiled, happy to hear that come from Elder Schofield. When he had first put them together, Elder Schofield had had some concerns about working with Elder Johnson.

"Please tell me about him," President Russell said, hoping to keep Schofield talking. Johnson still slept.

"The whole country is collapsing into war, and Elder Johnson is sharing the gospel." Schofield wiped a tear from his eye with his good arm as he began the story of their flight from Almaty. "Everywhere we turned, Johnson never forgot who he was. He always remembered he was a missionary. He helped me to be a better missionary. He reminded me why I was there. I had forgotten for a time."

President Russell looked down at Elder Schofield and smiled. He knew that he had made the right choice putting them together; or rather he had followed the correct prompting. It felt good to know that sometimes he got things right. Schofield paused in his story and cried for a moment, and President Russell wondered what was wrong. He decided not to press him, but just let him take his time.

* * *

In that moment Schofield realized that he wouldn't ever come back to Kazakhstan as a missionary. An overwhelming sadness enveloped him as he knew his mission to Kazakhstan was done. He had spent nearly two years as a missionary and it was cut short. He worried that he wouldn't have that same guidance he had had as a missionary. Perhaps he could come back as a tourist and visit the Tian Shan Mountains, but it wouldn't be the same. He wouldn't be a missionary.

He lay there for a moment and let the tears flow in silence, not explaining to President Russell the reason. Finally the tears stopped. He wiped his eyes and began the story again.

* * *

"Thank you for your time," Michael said as he put away his notebook. He had just finished interviewing Mila and Yuri, and had definitely cleared the elders from all but the initial bomb. They had strong alibis for the other three.

"You're welcome," Yuri said.

Mila just smiled up from the bed. Her wound had been merely superficial. That would help when he went to deal with Sasha later. Had she died, there would be nothing he could do for Sasha, but now he had some room to move.

"Can I ask you some personal questions?" Michael asked.

"Of course," Yuri asked.

"What are your plans now?" Michael asked. "You spent several days with the missionaries. Do you plan to join their church?"

"Yes," Mila said from the bed.

Yuri looked at her and smiled. "Yes, we plan to join the Church, but first we have to find it. Besides my sister in Samara, the elders were our only contact with the Church."

Michael pulled out a contact card and handed it to them. "I have the contact information for the Church. The mission president gave it to me. And I know a few members of the Church in Almaty. I too plan on joining the Church. It has changed my life. And I think that's just the beginning."

"Thank you," Yuri said.

"My pleasure." Michael shook hands with both of them and turned to leave, but stopped at the door. "If either of you hear from the elders, let me know. I would like to know how they are."

With that he turned and left. He was happy for those two. They told a wonderful tale of adventure, and Johnson had taught them so much about the gospel. Michael longed to learn more. He wished he had the chance to speak more to them, but for now he had other urgent matters.

* * *

Sasha lay shackled to a hospital bed. He knew a guard waited outside. He had been caught. Against all odds, he had been caught. And now somebody was going to come kill him. He knew that he was going to die. *Any minute someone is going to walk in that door and kill me.* The door opened and he jumped.

Michael walked in and sat down in a chair next to him. He didn't say anything at first. He just sat there silently.

"What?" Sasha said finally.

"Why?" Michael asked.

Why what? Why is he always so cryptic? Sasha hated how Michael asked questions without obvious answers.

They sat in silence for a few minutes, Michael looking to Sasha with his eyes, those eyes that seem to look right into the soul. *How much does he know?*

Finally Sasha decided to take a gamble and hope Michael didn't know anything.

"I decided to shoot them because I didn't think the embassy would let me take them in for questioning."

* * *

Michael looked at Sasha. He took too long to answer that question. *He's hiding something*

"That's not what I was talking about, Sasha."

He watched Sasha's eyes and knew he had him. It was only a matter of time.

"What are you talking about?" Sasha asked.

"Sasha, I am tired. I don't want to play with you. I know you're dirty. You shot an innocent girl. I can put you away for that. Whoever you are working for will likely kill you as soon as they realize you have failed. Or you can work with me. And I can protect you."

"Can you protect me?" Beads of sweat pooled on Sasha's forehead.

"You know I can, Sasha."

"Promise me."

"Tell me what you know, and I promise to protect you," Michael Ivanov said.

And with that promise, Sasha began talking.

* * *

Elder Johnson awoke in a hospital in Germany. Elder Schofield lay in a bed nearby. President Russell was nearby on a chair. He didn't feel any pain, but he felt like he should be by how President Russell looked at him. Johnson could see that his arm was bandaged and his chest was wrapped, and he had something wrapped round his face.

"Welcome back," Elder Schofield said and sat up in his bed.

"Thanks," Elder Johnson tried to say, but it came out kind of muffled.

"You won't be doing much talking for a while. They had to do some work on your jaw," President Russell said, standing next to Elder Johnson's bed. President Russell had some bandages above his eyes and one of his arms was wrapped up. "The doctor said it was a miracle you even survived."

Elder Johnson looked over at Schofield and smiled.

Schofield just nodded.

"What now?" Johnson said.

"Well," President Russell started, "I'll be leaving tomorrow for Moscow. Elder Schofield will be going home in a few days. And whenever you are better, you'll head home too. You have a long road to recovery. They had to repair your arm. It was quite damaged."

"What about my mission?" Elder Johnson asked.

"What do you mean?" President Russell said.

"When I am healed, can I finish my mission?"

"I imagine that's a possibility. When you're fully healed you could finish your mission. Who knows? Maybe if they reopen the Kazakhstan Astana Mission, you could finish there."

Elder Johnson closed his eyes for a moment and took a deep breath. When he opened them, he smiled. He could go back.

ABOUT THE AUTHOR

Born and raised in Springville, Utah, Nathan Huffaker boarded a plane for the first time when he was leaving home to serve a mission for The Church of Jesus Christ of Latter-day Saints in Kiev, Ukraine. He spent two years in Kiev, and his experiences there later assisted him when he wrote *Stranded*. He recently graduated from Utah Valley University with a degree in English. He currently resides in Spanish Fork with his wife and five kids.